PANCAKES

Lacey Black

Rockland Falls Book 1

Lacey Black

Lacey Black

Love and Pancakes

Rockland Falls Book 1

Copyright © 2019 Lacey Black

Photograph by Sara Eirew
Cover Models: Cristina Bel & Lucas Bloms

Cover Design by Melissa Gill Designs

Editing by Kara Hildebrand

Proofreading by Joanne Thompson & Karen Hrdlicka

Format by Brenda Wright, Formatting Done Wright

Index

Also by Lacey Black

Rivers Edge series
Trust Me, Rivers Edge book 1 (Maddox and Avery) – FREE at all retailers
> ~ *#1 Bestseller in Contemporary Romance & #3 in overall free e-books*
> ~ *#2 Bestseller in overall free e-books on another retailer*

Fight Me, Rivers Edge book 2 (Jake and Erin)
Expect Me, Rivers Edge book 3 (Travis and Josselyn)
Promise Me: A Novella, Rivers Edge book 3.5 (Jase and Holly)
Protect Me, Rivers Edge book 4 (Nate and Lia)
Boss Me, Rivers Edge book 5 (Will and Carmen)
Trust Us: A Rivers Edge Christmas Novella (Maddox and Avery)
> ~ *This novella was originally part of the Christmas Miracles Anthology*

BOX SET – contains all 5 novels, 2 novellas, and a BONUS short story

Bound Together series
Submerged, Bound Together book 1 (Blake and Carly)
> ~ *An International Bestseller*

Profited, Bound Together book 2 (Reid and Dani)
> ~*A Bestseller, reaching Top 100 on 2 e-retailers*

Entwined, Bound Together book 3 (Luke and Sidney)

Summer Sisters series
My Kinda Kisses, Summer Sisters book 1 (Jaime and Ryan)
> ~*A Bestseller, reaching Top 100 on 2 e-retailers*

My Kinda Night, Summer Sisters book 2 (Payton and Dean)
My Kinda Song, Summer Sisters book 3 (Abby and Levi)
My Kinda Mess, Summer Sisters book 4 (Lexi and Linkin)
My Kinda Player, Summer Sisters book 5 (AJ and Sawyer)

My Kinda Player, Summer Sisters book 6 (Meghan and Nick)
My Kinda Wedding, A Summer Sisters Novella book 7
(Meghan and Nick)

Standalone
Music Notes, a sexy contemporary romance standalone
A Place To Call Home, a novella
Exes and Ho Ho Ho's, a sexy contemporary romance
standalone novella

*Coming Soon from Lacey Black
Book 2 in the Rockland Falls series, a new contemporary series

Lacey Black

Dedication

To Danielle Palumbo
for her knowledge and help with dealing with fire and cleanup,
but most importantly, for her friendship and love for small town
romance.

Lacey Black

Chapter One

Marissa

"I'm sorry, miss, but you won't be able to get in there for a few days. Not until after the fire marshal has completed his investigation and ruled out arson," the fire chief states, a look of pity mixed with soot smeared on his aged face.

The words strike my heart with the force of an arrow. Arson? Who? Why? What?

Sighing dramatically, I gaze up at the huge two-story, six thousand square foot Southern Colonial house that I've considered my home for the last two decades. It has everything. Ground to roof pillars, freshly repainted black shutters, large front porch, six and a half baths, seven bedrooms, and the biggest kitchen I've ever had the pleasure of working in. Now, everything is probably soaked and covered in soot as remnants of smoke filters from the back.

Ever since I was a child, I imagined what it would be like to take this beautiful house and truly make it my own. Every day was a step in the right direction. Though my mom is the official business owner, in the last few years, I've taken over many of the day-to-day duties, including all of the cooking and reservations, and when we're at capacity, I help with the cleaning and assist the guests too. Now all of those dreams have gone up in smoke thanks to old, shoddy wiring that should have been updated years ago, apparently.

"I can't believe this," I mumble for probably the tenth time in the last hour. The chief gives me a sad smile before he heads over to where a fireman strings yellow caution tape around the exterior of the house.

I gaze up, my eyes instantly filling with tears. We have everything in this house. Well, I guess it's more accurate to say my mom has everything in this house. Financially, yes, but personally as well. This house holds my memories – both good and bad, and now it looks like a giant crime scene with yellow caution tape strung from tree to tree and big muddy boot prints caking the front walk.

A vehicle door slamming pulls my attention away from the house. My brother, Jensen, is back, his entire body riddled with fatigue. "How did it go?" I ask, and take in his appearance as he approaches. His jeans look clean, but his T-shirt is wrinkled and his boots not laced. I'm also pretty sure they're on the wrong feet too.

"Fine. The Clawsons took them both in, no problem. They weren't at capacity yet either," he replies, a yawn spilling from his mouth.

The Clawsons own one of the other bed and breakfasts in Rockland Falls, and as of a half hour ago, they now house our two couples who were guests in our home. As I gaze back at the mess, I can't help but wonder if they were our final guests too.

"I'm just glad everyone was able to get out in time," Jensen adds, pulling me into his tall, lean frame for a hug. "You're still shaking."

I wrap my arms tighter around my chest and watch the smoke. It's almost nonexistent at this point, but I can still see it. And smell it. It smells like someone threw a bunch of trash in a bonfire. There's a melted plastic stench in addition to the smoldering wood that was once walls used to keep the outside, well, out. Now, there's a hole in the back of the place, right next to where my mother's bed used to sit.

"I'll be fine," I mumble, turning my head and resting it on his chest. My brother is so much taller than me, a trait he inherited from our father. Both of my brothers are on the tall side, actually.

Well, and my sister too. At five foot three inches, I'm the only one of us Grayson kids who got their height from our X-chromosome contributor.

My mind floods with details in a rapid-fire sequence. Insurance, which, thankfully, my oldest brother, Samuel, is handling as we speak. Construction, rewiring. Plus, there's the pending cancellation of reservations for the 'foreseeable future, which will mean loss of income, as we head into the busiest time of the year. All those phone calls. All those reservations. Gone.

And let's not forget that the fire marshal still has to rule out arson. Who would intentionally start this fire? When we have guests inside! Who would do something so horrific, and for what? Insurance money? I'd much rather have my childhood home and the bed and breakfast than money.

My brain starts to hurt.

"He's on his way," Samuel says, dropping his cell phone into the inside pocket of his suit. Even now, at two in the morning, he looks completely put together – in that anal retentive kinda way we all tease him about. Who arrives to the scene of a fire in a charcoal gray business suit? My brother, Samuel, that's who. As the oldest of four, he's always taken his duties as firstborn to the max. It's annoying as hell, really, but it's the way he's wired and we love him the same (even if we want to kill him half the time).

"Thank you. You guys could probably head home," I suggest. They've been here since I called them nearly four hours ago.

"We're not leaving until Mom arrives. How far away is she?" Jensen asks, suppressing another yawn. The poor guy is up before the sun every morning getting his day organized. He owns a landscaping business in town and works from sunup to sundown most days, yet still has time to co-parent his four-year-old son, Max.

"She should be here anytime," my sister, Harper, adds as she joins our little group, two steaming cups of coffee in her hands. She hands one to me and waits expectantly for me to take a drink. When I do, I don't taste the bitter coffee. I don't taste anything, actually, but the cup feels warm against my cold, numb fingers.

"Good," Samuel replies. (P.S. Don't call him Sam – or worse, Sammy – unless you want to be bored to death with the history behind his name and why he prefers to go by the formal one listed on his birth certificate.)

As if on cue, headlights illuminate the tree line that leads to Grayson Bed and Breakfast. The four of us turn and watch as Mom's car slows just outside of the yellow caution tape, the passenger door flying open before the car comes to a complete stop. Even in the dark of night, I can see the tears streaming down her face as she approaches.

"Oh my word," she whispers through a sob as she runs up and pulls me into a tight hug. "You're all right? Everyone is okay?" she asks, pushing me back and giving me a once-over, Mom-style.

"I'm fine. Everyone is fine," I choke out over my own emotion as she pulls me into another lung-crushing hug.

"I can't believe this," she mumbles, turning and giving the home her attention.

Samuel steps up beside her, wrapping our mom in his long arms. "The insurance agent will be here soon, and the adjuster first thing tomorrow morning."

"Thank you, Samuel." Mom sighs deeply, worry lines creasing her sad green eyes.

The five of us stand together, our arms wrapped around each other as we watch the firemen come out of the house we've called home. I may be the only one who still lives on the property, but there's no mistaking the look of pure sadness reflected in the eyes of my three siblings.

"Oh, Mary Ann," a woman says behind us. We all turn at the sound of an unfamiliar voice and find a petite older man and woman, their eyes both filled with unshed tears and their hands entwined together.

"Oh my goodness, where are my manners," Mom says, sniffling and taking a step toward the couple. "I'm so sorry. Kids, I'd like you to meet my brother, Orval, and his wife, Emma."

Now it makes sense. Mom left today to drive about three hours north to see her half brother that she hadn't spoken with in nearly forty years. It was a shock when we all learned about our extended family recently, a secret she kept, not out of spite, but out of distance.

They were never close, according to Mom. In fact, there's a twenty-five year age difference between them. Apparently, Grandpa was married before. He and his first wife had a son, Orval, and lived in Virginia. When his first wife passed away, Grandpa remarried quickly to a much younger woman. A woman who was almost the same age as his son.

Grandpa Samuel and Grandma Phoebe moved to North Carolina, where my mother, Mary Ann, was born. She grew up not knowing her half brother, not even when Grandpa passed away when Mom was twenty. For forty years, she moved on with her life, not really knowing the man who shared her blood.

Then, one day a few weeks back, Mom received an invitation. She didn't recognize the names printed on the beautiful document, but the handwritten note that accompanied it explained. Emma, Orval's wife, had written to Mom and invited her to come meet her family. She explained that it was far past time for the two siblings to get reacquainted. Life was too short to not know your family, and neither one of them were getting any younger.

Mom had showed us all the note, the delicate handwriting of an elderly woman, and contemplated on whether or not to go. For me, it was an easy decision. They were family, and I was intrigued. Samuel, being the sole voice of reason, and often opposition, argued that it wasn't the appropriate time for a three-hour long drive to surprise family that may, or may not, be happy to see her.

In the end, she decided to go, which is why she was gone when the fire started just a few short hours ago in the en suite bathroom of her bedroom at our family bed and breakfast.

"It's lovely to finally meet you," Aunt Emma says, taking a few steps forward. She steps up to my brother Jensen first, and as he extends his hand toward her, she pushes it aside and brings him in for a tight hug. The image is almost comical since she's half the size of my brother.

Suddenly, he jerks back a bit, his eyes as big as saucers, and turns toward me and mouths, "She just patted my ass."

The shock and fear in my brother's eyes causes laughter to bubble in my chest. My first bit of emotion that isn't sadness, and I can barely keep it contained. I actually have to cover my mouth with my hand and fake a cough, which draws a bit of attention from my other siblings.

"Emma, Orval, this is Jensen. He's my third child," Mary Ann introduces as my brother gives the petite old woman the stink eye.

"Sorry about that, Jen. Old habits die hard. Every day is like a locker room to me," Emma says sweetly, drawing everyone's attention. She also doesn't release my brother.

"You coached?" Jensen asks, a look of shock on his face.

"Of course, back in the day. Dan was such a troublemaker when he was younger, and a real charmer with all the ladies. I knew he'd make it professionally, though. Miami was a great choice for him. No Super Bowl ring, but he played with passion and intensity, just like in high school, on and *off* the field, if you know what I mean," Emma adds, everyone's eyebrows pulling together in question.

"Wait, you coached Dan Marino?" my oldest brother, Samuel, asks.

"He was definitely rough around the edges, but he shaped up to be amazing at handling his balls," she replies casually, as if she didn't just tell our family she used to coach high school football...*and* Dan Marino!

"And this lovely woman?" Emma asks, changing the subject just as quickly as she started it. She releases my soldier-still brother and makes a grab for my sister, Harper.

"This is Harper. She's the second oldest," Mary Ann boasts proudly.

"What a beauty, you are. Come give Auntie Emma some sugar," Emma says, pulling my sister into her arms and squeezing tightly. "You know, Uncle Orvie and I know some people, if you'd like to model. Your hips and boobs are fabulous," Emma croons, making my shell-shocked sister choke on air.

"Actually, Harper owns a business in town," Mom adds, trying to gloss over the weird compliment.

"What kind of business?" Orval asks, stepping forward and giving my sister a friendly hug.

"A lingerie store," Harper brags proudly.

Emma's eyes light up. "Tell me more later, dear. I have six granddaughters who I love to shop for," she says, excited in a way that I've never seen when an elderly woman talks about lingerie.

Most of the old biddies in town frown upon my sister's store. In fact, when she opened it, the mayor and aldermen gave her way more grief and trouble than anticipated. But in the end, Harper followed their rules to a T and was still able to open the store of her dreams.

No one seems to be complaining now that they're seeing a huge influx in tax dollars.

"This young lady is Marissa, my youngest," Mom says, drawing our attention away from Harper (and the awkwardness of Emma shopping for lingerie for her granddaughters), waving a hand toward me.

"Oh, from the website. I recognize you, dear. You help run the bed and breakfast," Emma says, not really asking a question.

"I do," I reply, my eyes instantly tearing up again as memories of the last few hours slam back into my chest with the force of a tire swing.

"And finally, my oldest, Samuel," Mom says, all eyes turning toward my brother.

"Samuel," Orval says quietly, almost to himself.

"Yes," Mom says, shifting her weight. "I named him after Dad."

Everyone is silent as Orval takes a step forward, then another, until he's standing directly in front of Samuel. "It's a strong name, a good name. Even if he was a stubborn jackass," Orval says boldly before a warm smile spreads across his face. We all chuckle at his comment, at the way he breaks the unspoken tension. Well, everyone but Samuel, who rarely laughs.

"I'm honored to be named after my grandfather," Samuel states, his shoulders square and his eyes on our uncle.

"Yes, well, I'm happy someone is," Orval grumbles before reaching out and shaking his oldest nephew's hand. Samuel watches with a cautious eye, but eventually puts his hand into Orval's and shakes.

"Mom, we're not going to be able to get in tonight, and probably not for a few days. They have to conduct an investigation," Jensen says, bringing our attention back to the reason for our impromptu family reunion.

"Oh. Of course," Mom says, turning and looking at the house.

"Why don't you come stay with me?" Harper says, wrapping an arm around Mom's shoulder and pulling her in for a hug.

"Umm," Mom starts, glancing over at her brother and sister-in-law.

"I have two guest rooms. You can all stay with me," Samuel offers.

"What about Marissa?" Jensen asks, all eyes turning my way.

"I'll just stay at my place," I say, my voice still a bit shaky from emotion.

"I don't think they'll let you yet, Riss. Not until the investigation is finished," Jensen says, insinuating that I might not be able to go back to my own home tonight. Not until they rule out arson.

"Do you really think so? The fire didn't touch the back cottage, did it?" Mom asks, giving her full attention to me.

"No, it didn't," I confirm.

"I'll go find out," Samuel offers, turning and walking toward the fire chief.

Conversation happens around me, but I'm unable to focus on anything other than the mess in front of me. The house is being cleared out, but the damage remains. What they'll find from their investigation is beyond me, but I know it wasn't arson. It couldn't be. Everyone loves this house, and no one would ever think to cause damage, especially when there are guests inside.

"It's as we thought. Riss, you won't be able to stay in the cottage until after the fire marshal and insurance adjustor finish their investigations. He said he could arrange for someone to accompany you inside so you could gather some of your personal belongings such as clothes, but nothing else. Mom, unfortunately, you can't go inside the house for any of yours. Not until it has been cleared," Samuel confirms.

"Since Mom, Emma, and Orval are staying with Samuel, you can stay with me," Harper offers, a sad smile crossing her beautiful face. Unable to speak, I nod my head in agreement.

About thirty minutes later, Jensen is loading my bag into the back of Harper's car. A few items of clothing and some of my toiletries was all I was allowed to take, but at least it's something. There's no way I could fit into my sister's clothes – not by a long shot. Our height difference alone would make that practically impossible, let alone her subtle curves and leaner frame. Throw in our hair colors (her red to my blonde), and we're as different as night and day.

"I'm not sure I could sleep yet, and I'm dying to find out what happened," Mom says, her attention focused on the house.

"Let's all go back to my place. We can all fill you in before trying to sleep," Samuel suggests, then turns and looks to me for confirmation.

"That's fine. I'm not sure I could sleep either," I add, my voice sounding distant and hollow.

I climb into my sister's car, and glance back at the now-empty house. Everything is in that place: my heart and soul, my passion, my financial stability. We slowly make our way down the lane, the house fading and eventually disappearing from sight. As we head toward Samuel's house, I try to close my eyes, but all I can see is the spark. All I can hear is the zap of electricity. All I can smell is the burnt plastic and molten wiring.

It's going to be a long night.

One I'll never forget.

Chapter Two

Rhenn

The drive from my hometown of Jupiter Bay, Virginia, to Rockland Falls, North Carolina is only a few hours, but it feels like I've been on this particular stretch of road for days. Maybe that has something to do with the lack of sleep I had last night, and I can't even say it was the enjoyable kind. No, there was no woman warming my bed, as preferred, but another last-minute work emergency that kept me up until about three in the morning. Someone broke into a new house across town, and the result was a rework of their security system. At midnight.

Good times.

But when money is thrown at the boss, he takes it, which is why I was called out shortly after midnight for a job that would normally have been completed during daylight hours.

I crank up the Metallica, letting the heavy metal pulse through my veins and energize me. Well, I guess I can thank the three cups of coffee I've consumed since I pulled out of town at eight this morning for that. I'm accustomed to rising early, but this morning had my system all out of whack, thanks to work.

I yawn for the thousandth fucking time as I finally spy the Welcome to Rockland Falls sign. Thank Christ. I could use a big sandwich, a hot shower, and a bed – and I'm not really particular of the order.

My GPS takes me to the heart of the city, with its big, brick storefronts and large town square. There's a strong Mayberry vibe here, not too dissimilar from my own hometown. The entire block is nothing but festive gardens, large walking paths, park benches, a few gazebos, and in the center, a band shell. It's large, covered, and shows a bit of wear – probably more so from usage than anything else.

When I reach my destination, I pull along the street, anxious to get out and stretch my legs. A large white house sits before me, with dozens of bright flowerpots and hanging baskets in all shapes and colors. An American flag is perched on one of the white pillars and a welcome mat in front of the front door. I've definitely landed right smack-dab in the heart of small-town America.

"You must be Mr. Burleski," an older woman greets me as she steps out the front door.

"I am, and call me Rhenn, please," I reply, walking up the steps.

"I'm Janice Clawson, it's a pleasure to have you stay with us," she says as she steps forward. I reach out my hand, but she quickly swats it away, resorting to pulling me in for a big hug instead. "My husband is Clyde and he ran to the store. He'll be back shortly," she adds, opening the front door and waving me inside.

Without saying a word, I follow the petite older woman into her home. I've never stayed at a bed and breakfast before, but from what I'm gathering, Rockland Falls is full of them. Not one hotel for miles. The place is definitely homey, even though I'd consider it a tad on the formal side. Wingback chairs in a floral print and a large matching sofa adorn the living room area, while the dining room is filled with a massive ceremonial table that must seat sixteen. Fresh flowers that match portraits on the walls, rich cherry woodwork, and the scent of freshly baked bread top off the ambiance of my new home away from home for the foreseeable future.

"You're lucky you came to town this week and not the next. The closer we get to the Memorial Day holiday, the fuller our reservation calendar," Janice says, approaching a small desk in the main foyer.

"I'm glad you were able to accommodate me on such short notice," I tell her, trying to recall everything my boss, Craig, said about this trip. He was able to find me a reservation for five nights, but after that, it was a bit more challenging. With the Grayson Bed and Breakfast out of commission for the time being, everything else became completely booked in a matter of hours. Adjustments to schedules had to be made, which is why finding a room for myself in a thirty-mile radius became practically impossible. No one could accommodate me for more than a night, here and there.

That's when we had to come up with Plan B.

"We're happy to have you stay with us. All of the information you need is in this pamphlet. Breakfast is served six until nine, lunch from eleven to one-thirty, and dinner is served at six o'clock. The first two meals are buffet-style, while dinner is a wonderful sit-down affair. We hope you'll be able to join us nightly," she details, handing me the pamphlet and telling me about my room's amenities.

"Do you have any questions?" she asks, her bright blue eyes sparkling warmly.

"I don't think so, Janice."

"Then I'll show you to your room. You're in the Roosevelt room at the top of the stairs, first door on the left." She chats the entire time we ascend the wide staircase, telling me about the history of their business. It's all fascinating, really, but all I want is that hot shower, big sandwich, and warm bed. Hell, I'm not even picky on the warm bed part. I could probably sleep for days in one of those stiff wingback chairs.

But a decent nap isn't on my schedule yet.

I have an appointment at one with the homeowner of the bed and breakfast I'm here to work on. The favor I'm doing for a friend and his family, even though I'm being paid for the job. It took a bit of workload juggling to make this happen, but that's okay. I would have done it again in a heartbeat for my friend, Nick, and his new wife, Meghan.

Speaking of…

My phone starts to ring in my pocket, and I smile the moment I see his name on the screen.

"I'll let you get settled," Janice says with a wave as she retreats from the room, securing the door on her way out.

"Aren't you supposed to be balls deep in the only woman you ever get to screw for the rest of your life? Why the fuck are you calling me? Can't keep it up?" I tease in way of greeting to the man who has been my closest friend since grade school.

"Actually, he has no problem whatsoever getting it up. It's up…quite a bit, actually, and I just finished taking advantage of him. He's resting." Her soft voice filters through the phone, making me bark out a laugh.

"Sorry, Meg. I thought it was my ugly friend calling."

Her laughter fills the phone line. "He's actually finishing up with a patient. We're going to lunch soon, but I thought I'd call to make sure you arrived," Meghan says.

Nick and Meghan were married almost two weeks ago, and after a week-long honeymoon in Hawaii, are just now getting back into the swing of things as husband and wife. And co-workers, actually, though they've been that for many years. My friend is a dentist and his new bride his hygienist. What started out as friends turned into much more. To be honest, I saw this day coming for quite a while. Even though they were both in denial of their feelings, I could tell that my friend was completely smitten by his employee.

Even though I love to rib on him for attaching the old ball and chain, I'm slightly envious of their relationship.

Not that I would tell him that.

Ever.

"I just made it to the bed and breakfast I'm staying at this week. I'm meeting your great aunt at her place at one," I confirm.

"All right, well, I'll let you go. I wanted to make sure you made it," she says right before I hear mumbling through the phone line, and what sounds like kissing.

"Can he not keep it in his pants for five seconds? Tell him you're on the phone with his sexy best friend," I grumble lightheartedly.

Meghan laughs. "He says eat shit."

I smile. "Go make babies on your lunch, you crazy kids. I'm going to grab a shower and get ready to head over to the house."

"We'll see you this weekend," she says.

"Bye, asshole," Nick hollers into the phone right before the line goes dead.

Dick.

Shaking my head, I drop my phone onto the bed. I'd never begrudge either of them the happiness they've found. After Meghan lost her former fiancé, Josh, it took her a while to come to terms with her budding feelings for my friend. Now, they're living one of those picture-perfect lives together, and I honestly couldn't be happier for them.

It's just not for me.

No picket fences.

No cute little wife waiting for me when I get home.

No fairy-tale ending.

Fairy tales are crap.

They're a mirage set in place to give off the appearance of happily ever after.

But I know it's shit.

And why would a man want that when he can have a bit of variety in his life?

Only, variety doesn't quite hold the appeal it once held. I blame Nick and Meghan and the tearful declarations they made two weeks ago on the beach. Hell, even their exchange caused me to fight off a few unshed tears. I'm man enough to admit it. Their love story is pretty epic, but that doesn't mean the lifestyle is for me. Even if my original plan doesn't quite hold the same appeal it once did. Again, I blame the wedding. I haven't felt the urge to go out since my best friend said "I do."

What I really need to do is get back on the fucking horse. I need to go out, find a gorgeous female who wouldn't mind a few hours of uncomplicated, mind-blowing sex, and who knows the score when we're done. Who understands that I'm walking away after with no intentions of looking back, and believe me, there are plenty of women out there who are willing to jump in bed with someone like me. They're after one thing: pleasure. And that's what I offer.

Nothing more.

Nothing less.

My plan is set for tonight. I'm sure Mayberry has a few watering holes that single ladies like to frequent. Even on a Tuesday night. If Miss Fun and Run is out there, I'll find her. It's kinda like my secret talent.

But first thing's first. A quick shower to wash off my travels, and then I'll follow my nose back downstairs to whatever was smelling so fucking good when I arrived. After a bite to eat, I'll meet the homeowner of the bed and breakfast that requires my services. This job is expected to take several weeks, considering it's a complete rewire of an old home. A home that's used as a business.

A few weeks away in this picturesque sleepy little town? Sure, I'll be working, but that's never stopped me before from having a little fun on the side. A new location, a chance to do a little sailing, and the prospect of beautiful women accompanying me…

I could get used to this.

* * *

I pull onto the long driveway, surrounded by massive, old oak trees and perfectly trimmed shrubbery. It's evident, at first glance, that someone takes great care of the property. I steer my truck up the gravel lane and am completely awestruck when I reach the clearing in the trees. There before me is the biggest house I've ever seen. With massive white pillars that extend all the way to the roof and a brightly painted front door, I can tell instantly that a lot of time goes into maintaining this place. Even if it could use a fresh coat of paint and updated windows, the owners have clearly taken care of their home to the best of their ability.

I pull off to the side and park along a row of trucks that must belong to the contractors. This place is going to need a lot of work to fix the damage that the fire caused. And not just the fire, but smoke, soot, and water damage too. The Graysons have a massive undertaking here to get this place operational again.

Stepping out of my truck, I stretch my back, grab my clipboard, and head toward the front door. It's standing open, the screen door separating me from the interior with the breeze helping mask the intensity of the mid-May afternoon heat. Before my boots even hit the front steps, the woman I remember as Mary Ann steps out, a small smile playing on her lips.

"Good afternoon, Mrs. Grayson," I say, taking the steps two at a time until I'm standing before the petite woman.

"Just Mary Ann, thank you. It's good to see you again, Rhenn. I appreciate you coming down," she says, shaking my hand with a firm grip.

"It was no problem. I'm just glad to help out," I tell her as she motions toward a small table with chairs sitting over in the corner on the front porch. I take a seat at the chair across from the piles of folders and papers, a clear indication that Mary Ann has been out here working for a while now.

"Can I get you something to drink? We don't have power, of course, but Jensen has been keeping a cooler with cold beverages stocked."

"I'm fine, thank you."

She pulls what looks like blueprints out of one of the folders and opens the large document. "He should be here soon. Jensen had to run and finish a job not too far from here, but will be back shortly. You'll also meet Marissa. She's upstairs starting to clean the guest rooms. We got lucky that they were free of water damage, but unfortunately, the soot covered about every surface in the house."

"I've worked a few electrical fire repairs. No one ever really thinks about the damage caused by smoke and soot, but it's horrible," I say, leaning back in the chair to get a good look at the property.

There's a large garage with a storage shed out back, an old tire swing hanging from a branch of one of the big oak trees, and lush green grass. Even with the addition of several extra work trucks and the load of lumber and building supplies that was dropped in the driveway off to the left and out of the way, it's still an impressive property.

"We have over ten acres here," she says, drawing my attention away from the green leaves and gently swaying branches. "Our property extends about one hundred yards from that tree line, and all the way back to the ocean. When Jensen gets here, I'll have him take you for a tour," she says politely, taking a sip of what I'm assuming is iced tea.

"It's great here. Very serene," I note, trying to ignore the deep strum of my heart and weird sense of longing that tries to settle in as I take in the almost picture-perfect location.

"That it is," she replies, digging out a folder and sliding it across the table. "Here is everything we were given from the contractor. I believe he forwarded the same to your boss."

"He did. We went over it together before I arrived."

"So you're good?" she asks, twisting her hands on the table top in a nervous gesture. Frankly, she's holding it together a lot better than other homeowners I've seen in this same predicament. Nothing brings on all of the damn emotions like the threat or reality of losing everything you own.

"I am. My supplies should be here first thing tomorrow and I'll be here to oversee the shipment, as well as start immediately."

Mary Ann takes a deep breath and seems to relax just a bit. "Thank you, Rhenn. It means so much to me to have a familiar face here to help. It has been incredibly stressful, and not just on me, but on my children." She looks over my shoulder, not really focusing on anything. "Especially Marissa."

I nod my head, understanding what she's saying, but at the same time, I'm not really as close as she may think. To tell the truth, I don't really know her at all. We have mutual connections. My best friend's wife is the granddaughter of Mary Ann's brother – the one she just recently reconnected with. So there's a family connection, and while I'm not family, I was there at Nick and Meghan's wedding when Orval introduced Mary Ann as his sister.

"And Marissa is…"

"My youngest daughter. She was here when the fire started and called 911," Mary Ann says.

I remember now. She's the one who runs this place with Mary Ann. She made the phone call to her mom when she was with all of us at Nick and Meghan's wedding.

"If you have any questions, you can find either her or me. I'll be in and out, but Marissa lives in the cottage out back, so she'll be on site most of the time," Mary Ann adds just as the screen door opens and slams behind me.

"Mom, I'm going to call Jensen and see if he can…" the sweetest voice I've ever heard says behind me. I turn toward the sound, my eyes colliding with intoxicating green eyes. Something strong stirs in my chest. It's as if a tornado has touched down, leaving my blood pumping and my breathing erratic. She is, without a doubt, the most beautiful woman I've ever seen.

And she's filthy.

"Marissa, this is Rhenn. He's going to do all of the electrical work on the house," Mary Ann says casually, standing up to greet her daughter. I follow suit, though I'm not really sure I should. Thank Christ for thick denim material. I only pray that it helps conceal the impact Marissa has on my body.

Specifically the lower half.

This angel, with her long, thick sandy blonde hair piled high on her head and smudges of dirt and soot smeared on her lightly freckled skin, gazes up at me with a look of shock. I'm not sure if she's feeling the same pull as I am, or if it's the fact that she looks like Cinderella right now after cleaning the entire castle.

But I can't ignore the way my heartbeat speeds up and my body tightens.

I'm completely intrigued.

And so very well screwed.

Chapter Three

Marissa

Holy Mother of God, he's beautiful.

Can a man be beautiful?

The answer is yes.

Yes, he most certainly can.

With his long, dark eye lashes that frame the most striking ocean blue eyes, dark blond hair that's a touch on the tussled side, and tall, solid frame, this man is definitely gorgeous. And don't get me started on the hint of a tattoo peeking out from the sleeve of his tight T-shirt. He oozes confidence and sexuality just by standing, and I can tell at first glance this man is trouble.

So. Much. Trouble.

"Marissa, this is Rhenn, the electrician," Mom says, pulling my attention from the stunning creature beside her. The electrician? I have to, like, work with this man all up in my space for the next few weeks?

My head screams, *kill me now*, while my body starts to do a little celebratory dance. This is bad. Very, very bad.

"Hello," he says, his voice as smooth as silk. He takes a step toward me, his body moving like it was made for... sex. God! Now I'm thinking about sex! With this man! This stranger!

"Hi," I reply, though it comes out an awkward squeak. I sound like a chipmunk. Awesome.

"We were just going over the plans for the electrical work. Jensen was supposed to be here to give Rhenn a quick tour," Mom says, glancing at her watch. My eyes immediately go back to the man standing in front of me. He's staring at me, his mouth slightly gaped open, and his eyes wide with wonderment.

But then I recall my appearance as I glanced in the bathroom mirror about twenty minutes ago. My hand flies up to my hair, which is piled on top of my head and sticking out in every which direction possible. There are smudges of soot and grime smeared all over my legs, arms, and cheeks. I'm filthy and gross – sweating in places I've never experienced before, thanks to the lack of air conditioning. My God, I get why he's staring at me.

It's not wonder; it's disgust.

Mom is talking, but I have no idea what she's saying – or for how long she's been speaking, for that matter. I'm stuck, staring at the sexiest man alive, while resembling a homeless person who hasn't showered in a week.

"…give him a call to see what's taking him so long," Mom says, pulling me from the lusty haze surrounding me.

"What?" I ask, turning her way and blinking.

"Are you feeling all right?" she asks, a look of concern on her face as she steps forward and presses the back of her hand on my forehead.

I shake her off. "I'm fine." I keep my eyes focused on her worried ones, knowing I shouldn't look at the man beside me, or risk turning into a stumbling idiot once more.

She gives me that Mom look and exhales deeply. "I said I was going to call Jensen to see what's keeping him," she repeats, pulling her cell phone from her pocket. I watch as she brings it to her ear and silently steps away when my brother answers the phone.

The air becomes thick and the silence deafening around me, while I wait for my mom to finish up her call. I can sense his eyes on me, feel the weight of his stare, which makes me both nervous and a tad bit giddy.

But mostly nervous.

Heavy on the nervousness.

"Sorry about that," Mom says when she hangs up the phone. "Ashley called while he was running errands and said Max wasn't feeling good. Jensen had to go pick him up and will keep him until Ashley gets home from work. He says he'll stop by later tonight and deliver the supplies he picked up."

"He can just bring them in the morning. There's no need for him to make another trip out here," I state, knowing my brother has been running ragged trying to get everything ready for the work that's about to start at the bed and breakfast. Plus, his son isn't feeling well, and he's needed elsewhere right now.

"Rhenn, I'm sorry, but the tour may have to wait. I'm sure he'll be able to do it as soon as you get here in the morning," Mom says. "Unless," she adds, turning and looking my way, "Marissa wants to go ahead and get it out of the way. She knows this place better than anyone." Mom smiles proudly at me, and I'll admit something stirs in my chest. I do know this place better than anyone, maybe even better than her. I've lived and breathed our home, our bed and breakfast, for my entire adult life, and even a good chunk of my childhood.

But alone with Rhenn? Giving him a tour when I look like I haven't slept, showered, or eaten in days?

"I'm not so–" I start, but am cut off when Rhenn speaks up for the first time since our introduction.

"I'd be honored if Marissa would give me a tour." His grin is inviting, charming even, and something tells me I have yet to discover the true powers of this man's smile.

"Great! I'll go make sure the contractor is ready to start tomorrow, and be out of your hair," Mom says, a too bright, and almost too knowing, smile on her face. I watch her walk away, feeling oddly like I've been played.

Or worse, set up.

"Shall we?" he asks, pulling my attention away from the front door my mom just exited by and back to brilliant blue eyes that do naughty things to my unmentionables.

With a quick head nod, I walk toward the door, following in the wake of my mom's subtle perfume. Rhenn is behind me, even though neither of us speaks. I can feel him there; I can feel how close his body is to mine. A shiver sweeps through my limbs, and I'm pretty sure it has nothing to do with the temperature.

As we enter the place that was once my beloved sanctuary, the musty, mildew scent permeates my senses. "I'm sorry about the smell. We're trying to keep all of the windows and doors open, but it doesn't seem to be helping much. Everything downstairs was soaked, and the contractors will work on ripping up the flooring tomorrow. We're hoping the subfloor won't be too bad, but something tells me luck won't be on our side," I ramble as I head toward the grand staircase in front of us.

Rhenn doesn't say a word, and even though I'm curious as to where his attention lies, I keep my eyes focused forward. The last thing I need is to see the disgusted look on his face at the gross mess he has to work in for the next few weeks. Besides, I'll probably trip and fall over a step if I don't keep my eyes straight ahead.

"This house was built in eighteen sixty-four by a wealthy English settler, a gift for his new bride. He purchased over two thousand acres of land along the Atlantic, but once the Depression hit in nineteen twenty-nine, his heirs eventually had to sell off large chunks of the property because of the big hit they took after the stock market crashed. This house, along with the ten acres around it, was the only asset the family was able to keep during that time.

"It changed hands several times between the fifties and nineties when my mom and dad purchased it. It was her dream to turn this old, worn down house into a bed and breakfast," I state proudly as I reach the first guest room upstairs, realizing I've been blabbering for a few minutes.

I quickly turn to see if Rhenn is still behind me, or more accurately, if he got bored with my history lesson for today and decided to make a break for it. When my eyes meet his, I find him staring at me, a look of awe and fascination written all over his gorgeous face. "I'm so sorry. Sometimes I get so wrapped up in the story of this place, I just…"

"No, I didn't mind," he says, taking a step toward me. Very close to me, actually. He's right in front of me, so near that I could reach out and touch the day-old stubble on his jaw. "I liked hearing about it. Your passion for this place comes through loud and clear when you talk about it."

I continue to stare at him. The corner of his lip turns upward, and it appears as genuine as they come. He doesn't seem to be mocking me, as Erik, my ex, used to do. He hated this place and often rolled his eyes every time someone would ask me about it, knowing I could spend hours talking about the history and day-to-day life of living here.

"Thank you," I whisper, gazing up at him. My heart starts to pound in my chest and my throat is suddenly dry. I basically turn into my fifteen-year-old self, when one of my brothers' football friends said hello to me in passing in the hall.

I'm not sure how long we stand there, staring at each other, but a barrage of inappropriate thoughts flit through my mind. Like is he a boxers or briefs kinda guy or does he prefers to be on top or bottom. I can feel the blush burn my cheeks because I can tell just by looking at Rhenn Burleski what the answers are to my wonderings.

And those answers leave me breathless.

Something falls one floor below us, breaking the spell we seem to be cast under. I jump back, anxious to get away from his powerful stare, yet so eager and curious as to why I want to stay trapped under that enticing look at the same time. His blue eyes shine like sapphires under the mid-afternoon sunlight, and I can't get over the way he's looking at me. Like I'm a puzzle he's trying to figure out or a problem he's trying to solve. It's completely disarming and turning me into someone I'm usually not. I need to get away from him.

Fast.

Clearing my throat, I take a giant step back, only to connect with the wall. "Shit," I mumble, trying to regain my balance and make it look like I meant to do that.

"Are you okay?" he asks, taking another step forward.

He's so freaking close, I'm not sure I could answer his question. Hell, I'm not even sure I'm breathing at this point. "Yep!" I squeak out in a high-pitched noise that rivals a toddler.

Suddenly, I feel his hand. It starts at the base of my neck and gently slides upward, his fingers tangling into my hair. Now I know I'm not breathing. The little black dots peppering my vision confirm it.

"Breathe, Angel," he whispers, soft as a feather, as his thumb caresses the back of my neck. "You hit your head."

"I'm fine," I gasp, sucking in big gulps of precious oxygen – in a very lady-like fashion, mind you.

He seems to stare just a few minutes longer, his fingers continuing to light a fire against my skin. I hope this man has no idea what he's doing to me, but something tells me he does. He most certainly knows how to play a woman's body as if it were a finely tuned musical instrument that he was born to play. Rhenn oozes sex appeal, and if I had to wager a guess, I'd say he's well versed in the art of seduction.

Hell, he probably majored in it.

"Okay," he finally says, taking a step back, yet leaving his fingers to linger just a few extra seconds on my skin.

I'm not liable to survive this day. Shit, probably not this series of weeks in which I have to work near this man. My body is already hypersensitive and my mind working overtime on images I should not be having. Yet, as hard as I try, I can't get the picture of a very naked Rhenn out of my mind.

The contact is finally severed, and it's followed very quickly by sight. He looks away so fast and stands so casually it makes me wonder if I just imagined our entire exchange. Looking at him now, he's calm and collected Rhenn, here to do a job.

It hits me square in the chest like a hammer. Of course that's what he's here to do. Not play around with the owner's daughter. There's no denying how gorgeous this man is. He probably has women throwing themselves at him on a regular basis, so why in the hell would he waste his time on a plain Jane like me? Especially one who is covered in grime and smells like she hasn't showered in days.

Giving myself a mental slap across the head, I turn my attention back to the tour. That's what I'm here to do – not lust after the subcontractor. My cheeks burn once more, but this time with mortification. I can't believe I ever thought someone like Rhenn would be interested in someone like me. He probably stares like that at all women. You know, the 'I want to do dirty things to your body' look that turns women into a pile of mush? Clearly Rhenn is well versed in the look, as well as the reaction it invokes.

Just wait until he meets Harper.

That thought makes my stomach drop to my shoes.

My sister is everything men want: tall, gorgeous, subtle curves, and legs for days. She's a redhead too, which is like the unicorn of sexual conquests. I've never begrudged my sister of the looks she was born with, but dammit, why couldn't just a little bit of it have rubbed off on me? I never stand a chance when you pin her next to me. They fawn over her every time, leaving me wanting to crawl back into the book-filled hole I came from.

Straightening my spine, I turn and face the first door. "We have five guest rooms upstairs, all with their own attached bath. It took a little remodeling work those first few years after Mom and Dad purchased this place, but it was worth the investment. We learned quickly that guests prefer the comfort of their own bathroom within their room," I state, stepping into the first room.

I glance around at my favorite room. It faces the east and gives the faintest hint of the ocean beyond the trees. It's decorated in a subtle beach theme, with soft blue, sheer curtains and a blue and white bedspread. Right now, though, the room is looking a little sad. Even the sunlight filtering through the large windows is no match of the nasty soot and smoke covering nearly every square inch of the room.

"I've started in this room," I say absently as I walk toward the antique dresser, running my hand along the smooth dark wood I just spent an hour cleaning. "The dry cleaner thinks he can get the bedding and curtains clean, but I'm not so sure. I've never seen something so vibrant and beautiful look so dirty and hopeless.

"When we redecorated the guest rooms two years ago, this one was my favorite. I spent hours combing through website after website, looking for the perfect blend of beach and sensuality. I wanted this room to be an oasis for couples to come and relax, or reconnect as lovers. Now, the place I purchased from has closed down, I'm not sure I could find new décor that rivals the old stuff."

The silence that fills the space causes me to turn around. Rhenn is standing there, his wide blue eyes riveted on me, and leaving me with the feeling of being completely exposed. He doesn't take his eyes off mine when he says, "Beautiful."

The crazy thing is…

I'm not so sure he's talking about the room.

Chapter Four

Rhenn

We finish the rest of the tour rather quickly after that. I could tell by the look in her eyes that she didn't know how to take my comment. Yes, the room was beautiful, but it doesn't hold a candle to the elegant beauty that she possesses. Just looking at her makes me ache in places I have no business aching – and no, I'm not talking about the throb in my pants, though that has been prominent since the moment I laid eyes on her.

Marissa is stunning, and not in the fake, collagen-filled way I'm used to. She's all sunlight and roses, while I'm more accustomed to leather and red lipstick. She couldn't be any more different from the women I'm usually attracted to, but for some reason, I feel myself drawn to her like the tide to the shore.

Which is exactly why I need to keep my distance.

The last time I felt this kinda pull (the kind that doesn't involve just my dick), I found myself in a serious relationship. It also went down faster than a barfly in a bathroom stall right before last call.

When we finally step outside, I can't help but feel thankful for the fresh air. No, it's wasn't the soot-filled, smoke-lingering scents of the house that I couldn't wait to get away from, but from her. Marissa. I could smell her everywhere we went. The cleanliness of her shampoo. The sweetness of her body lotion. It all fucked with my mind, making me want to explore every square inch of her body.

With my tongue.

Adjusting my pants as subtly as possible, I follow as she heads toward the tree line. I do everything I can to focus on our surroundings, yet my eyes still return to the gentle sway of her hips and the delicate roundness of her ass. It's an ass that would fit perfectly in my palms – an ass that is made to be squeezed right as I drive myself deep inside her.

I groan. I can't help it, nor can I stop the sound from falling from my lips. Marissa turns to face me. "Are you okay?" she asks, worrying her bottom lip between her teeth.

Fuck.

"Yeah," I reply, giving no further explanation as I watch in complete fascination as she holds that plump lip between her teeth. She probably doesn't even know she's doing it. It's not one of those fuck-me-now ploys that so many women do. She's not doing it to catch my attention. She's doing it because that's what she does when she's worried or nervous. She's what every other woman in America tries to be, even though she does it so naturally, without even realizing it.

I'm so screwed.

Marissa begins to walk again, heading toward the clearing in the trees. She glances off to her right, and even though I caught sight of the small building out back, it's the first time I really see it. It's a cute little house, probably only one bedroom. It's small and quaint, and exactly how I'd picture her place to be. Mary Ann mentioned Marissa lives on-site, but I didn't really think too much about it.

Until now.

"That's my place," she says without stopping. She obviously saw me looking and isn't offering me any further explanation.

"It's nice," I reply honestly, noticing the single rocking chair on the tiny porch. I can picture her sitting out there in the evening, watching as the sun dips behind the trees and the birds start to sing. She'd probably have a book in one hand and a hot cocoa in the other, and that's another reason why I should be running in the other direction.

The temperature drops several degrees as we follow the path, stepping into the wooded area and in the shade. I have to take large steps to keep pace. For such a short thing, she's got quite a long stride. Instantly, I think about her stamina. I bet she's a wildcat in bed.

Not that I'll ever find out.

I can hear the ocean before I see it. As soon as I reach the clearing, my feet hit sand and I stop in my tracks. The Atlantic Ocean spreads out as far as the eye can see. Even though I grew up on the Bay, it never ceases to amaze me at the tranquility and beauty of the ocean. It's the main reason I purchased my boat as soon as I could afford it. The sea calls to me, like the waves call to a surfer. It's in my blood, deep in my bones. It's part of my survival.

Stepping up to the shore, I let the waves crash over my boots, not caring in the least bit about them getting wet. I have more pairs. I can already picture my Catalina anchored out about a hundred yards from the shore. There's a small dock along the beach that I'll be able to use to get back and forth, and the prospect of catching some sun on the deck has my blood pumping.

"How often do you sail?" Marissa asks, pulling my attention from the water before me.

"As often as possible, though that's not nearly as often as I'd like."

"Mom said you're bringing your boat since no one has vacancies," she says, stepping up beside me, her shoes and socks tossed up on the beach and her bare feet gingerly stepping into the cool surf.

"It's a two thousand fifteen, thirty-eight foot Catalina sailboat that was built for speed. I purchased it for a steal during an ugly divorce, and there's nothing better than stretching her legs on a Sunday afternoon in the open sea," I tell her, gazing out at the water.

"Sounds nice. I've only been on a small sailboat once, but I got seasick."

"I'll take you," I tell her before I can stop the words from flying from my trap.

She glances over at me with a look. "Did you not catch the part where I got seasick?"

"Ehh, you'll be fine on *Runaround Sue*. She's big enough that you won't even feel the motion of the ocean." Total lie, and by the look she's giving me, she doesn't buy it for a second. But something deep inside me pulls hard, and the need to have her on my boat is overwhelming.

"*Runaround Sue?*" she asks, a smile playing on her lips as she looks out at the ocean. "There's a story there."

I snort a laugh. "And maybe someday I'll tell you," I reply casually, stuffing my hands into my pockets to keep from reaching for her.

"So you're going to have to stay out there, right?" she asks, pointing out into the vast mass of water.

"Yeah, I should be able to drop anchor about a hundred or hundred-fifty yards out."

"And then you'll use your little dingy?" she asks innocently.

"Well, I've never had it referred to as little before," I reply casually, biting my cheek to keep from smiling.

Her head whips around to face me as the most stunning red blush creeps up her neck and stains her entire face. Her hands come up to cover her mouth. "I didn't…I mean, that's not…Oh my God, I can't believe I just said that."

I can't help but laugh at her embarrassment and discomfort. "Yes, Marissa, I will use my *little dingy* to get from my boat to the shore. It's actually a small, portable boat, made super lightweight and versatile." And because I'm a total dog and player, I add, "And if you're ever worried about the size of my *other* dingy, just let me know and I'll be happy to show you."

Marissa suddenly bursts out laughing and takes a swat at my arm. "Oh my God, that was the cheesiest and worst line I've ever heard. Does that garbage really work?" she asks through her fits of laughter.

The smile on my face is wide and easy. I've never – and I really do mean never – felt this comfortable with a woman in such a casual situation, especially one I met less than thirty minutes ago. Hell, most of the time I'm only after one thing (and so are they). There's no small talk, no banter. Just flirting and sex.

But with Marissa, I find myself wanting to talk.

Talk.

Who the hell am I?

"Actually, most of the time, I'm not the one with the lines," I tell her honestly, throwing in a smile and a wink just for good measure.

"I don't doubt it," she mumbles and turns back to the ocean.

We stand there in comfortable silence for much longer than I would have anticipated. It's a little too cozy, though, and the need to run from the unfamiliar feelings starts to take hold. That's exactly why I need to leave. Get away from this gorgeous woman. Head into town and find someone a little more my…taste.

"Well, I should head out," I say, taking a step back and pulling her attention my way once more. I can practically tell she's shutting down on me. Her arms come up to hold themselves at her waist and her face turns polite. Almost too polite. Fake, even.

"Of course. I'll be seeing you tomorrow," she says brightly, though the green sparkle in her eyes seems just a fraction duller.

Is it wrong that I wish she were looking at me once more with that bright shimmer, that bubbly personality I try to avoid at all costs?

Yes, it's wrong.

But that doesn't stop me from wanting it.

"Tomorrow," I confirm before turning and heading back the way we came.

Just as I reach the tree line, I turn to see if she's following me. She's not. Marissa stands at the shoreline still, gazing out at miles and miles of ocean, a look of sadness on her beautiful face. Something pulls deeply in my chest as I take in her posture, her demeanor…her loneliness. It calls to me like a siren, familiar and unafraid.

I know sadness.

I know loneliness.

That's why I drop my head and turn away. That's why I practically run back to my truck to get as far away from this woman, this temptation, as possible. Because for the first time in…forever, I want to turn around. I want to wrap my arms around her petite body and make her smile that awe-inspiring smile once more. I want to wipe those smudges of soot from her cheeks moments before my lips find hers. I want…more.

And I can't have more.

Never again.

More hurts.

* * *

I open the heavy wooden door to a place called The Station. The familiar neon glow of beer signs and liquor displays surrounds me the moment I walk in. Maroon 5 plays from the jukebox in the corner, and a handful of patrons turn to see who enters. There's not too many people, mostly guys actually, and I can already sense that tonight is going to be a bust.

Walking up to the weathered bar, I pull out a stool and toss my wallet on the bar top. A woman about the same age as my own thirty-five years walks my way, a friendly smile playing on her lips. It's not flirty, nor is her gait overly seductive. I've been in my fair share of bars where the bartender swings her hips so hard I'm surprised she doesn't throw out a hip. Hell, I've even capitalized on several of those moments, enjoying the fuck out of a ten-minute 'break' in the back room.

But not this woman. Her hair is pulled back in a no-nonsense ponytail at the nape of her neck and her shirt only gives the faintest hint of cleavage. Her jeans fit her body, but don't look painted on. Before she even reaches me, I know she won't fit the bill for what I have in mind later. This woman probably has a husband at home; maybe even two point five kids and a dog named Sparky.

"What can I getcha?" she asks, that polite smile stretching across straight white teeth.

"Coors Light bottle, if you have it," I answer, omitting my standard "sugar" reference and a wink.

"Coming right up," she replies, turning and grabbing a bottle from the cooler behind her. It only takes her a matter of seconds before the top is twisted off and the bottle is placed on a coaster in front of me.

"Thanks," I say before taking a long pull from the bottle.

"I'll be back shortly to check on ya," she adds politely before walking back down to the other end of the bar.

My attention turns to the handful of men watching a baseball game on the television. They're cheering for the Braves, discussing the season thus far, and talking trash about the opponent. My kinda crowd.

In fact, it doesn't go unnoticed how comfortable I find myself feeling, not only in this small bar tucked away off the main square, but also in this town. Shit, I felt more at ease walking around the bed and breakfast with Marissa than I ever thought I would, and I was only with her for a short time.

Marissa.

That's a twist I wasn't expecting.

She's nothing like the women I usually find myself attracted to, and even though I could tell there was some attraction there, she didn't throw herself at me, which is a refreshing change. She would be a challenge, for sure, but one I shouldn't take. The only thing I should do is turn and walk in the other direction. I'm against everything she represents: monogamy, happily ever after, and a family. It's practically written all over her beautiful face, and that's the reason I need to step away.

We don't want the same things.

But…what if we did?

I shake that fan-fucking-tastic image out of my mind because as much as I'd love to engage in a romp or two with Marissa between the sheets, I just don't think it's in the cards. Even if it would be dynamic, earthshaking, and mutually satisfying (and I have no doubt that it would be), I just don't see it playing out that way. She's not that kinda girl…

I can always tell.

And that kinda sucks.

The door opens and I find myself turning with the rest of the patrons. Expecting a few more guys looking to enjoy a few beers and watch the game away from the wife and kids, I'm pleasantly surprised when two women walk in, wide smiles and full of laughter, and make their way toward where I sit at the bar.

"Mara!" the shorter of the two says as they take the two empty seats to my right.

"Well, my night just took a turn for the better…" I mumble to no one in particular.

"This seat taken, Cowboy?" a tall, leggy redhead says as she slides onto the barstool beside me.

"Only by you," I reply as her friend takes the seat on the other side of her.

"Thought you'd be here an hour ago," the bartender I now know as Mara says with a bright smile as she comes over to where we sit, two bottles of light beer already in her hands.

"Not my fault. Inventory took longer than anticipated. I have very quickly run out of space and we couldn't find two boxes of those new negligées that I just got in," the redhead says, grabbing my attention the moment she utters the word negligées.

"They were those sexy navy ones too," the friend chimes in, taking a drink from her bottle.

"Like the red one I got?" Mara says, absently wiping the bar top off with a rag.

"Yes! That one! What did Brent think of it when you showed him?" the redhead asks between drinks.

"There wasn't one word spoken, believe it or not," Mara replies, her cheeks turning pink and her grin pretty much confirming exactly what Brent's reaction was to seeing her in whatever red negligée his wife wore home.

The three girls start to giggle, but not in that fake giggle I'm accustomed to hearing. This is a shared laugh amongst friends and the camaraderie makes a smile spread across my own face.

"So, will there be a fashion show later tonight I need to sign up for, or are we just talking about the merchandise this evening?" I ask, popping a few pieces of popcorn into my mouth. All three women seem to finally realize they're not alone in their conversation and turn toward me. "I'm free later, just to be clear."

The redhead's eyebrow shoots upward before she gives me a smug grin. "I just bet you are," she teases, a wide smile playing on her plump red lips, revealing straight white teeth.

"Rhenn," I announce, holding out my hand.

"Harper," she replies, placing her slender, soft hand in my own and giving it a gentle shake. Even though she's gorgeous with a capital G, I feel absolutely nothing when we touch.

Pity.

"And I'm Free," the friend states, her bangle bracelets jingling as she reaches around Harper and offers me her hand.

"Free?"

"Short for Freedom, love. Maybe if you're a good boy, I'll let you ring my bell," she adds boldly, a playful gleam in her dark eyes. Even though her come-on is written in Sharpie marker, it's as fake as they come. She might be toying with me, but she's not really hitting on me.

"Something tells me I'd be way out of my league with you, Free," I reply, tipping my beer bottle back once more.

"I don't doubt it, love," she says, reaching around her friend and taking a handful of the popcorn in front of me. "So, what brings you to town?"

"Work."

"Of course," Free says. "What is it? Freelance journalism or espionage?"

Leaning closer to Harper, I catch a subtle trace of something sweet, with a hint of floral. I'll give it to her: she's gorgeous *and* smells good. But before I can even consider the other places that Harper might smell good, a certain blonde with dirty smudges on her lightly freckled cheeks filters through my mind. I caught several whiffs of Marissa earlier, and it was enough to drive a sober man to drink. She's like a rain shower after a long drought. She's pure temptation, which is why I'm here, trying to find a little mindless distraction.

It's also not working out for me.

While both Harper and Free are beautiful in their own unique ways, I can tell already that it's not happening. Harper looks about as interested in me as she does with the old man down at the opposite end of the bar, which is a shame, really, because she's stunning and spunky – a combination that usually gets my blood flowing south of the belt line and ensures a damn good time between the sheets. Free, on the other hand, while definitely a bit more flirty, but in that 'friend zone' way.

I hate that fucking zone.

I'm sure with a little bit of work and a little extra Rhenn Burleski charm, I could have her in my bed tonight, but that familiar desire to chase just isn't present. Why? No fucking clue, but I have a feeling it has something to do with those damn freckles I was thinking about earlier.

My mind falls back to the women before me, and I have to think hard to recall Free's question. "Espionage. Definitely espionage," I reply, leaning forward so that I'm super close to Harper. "But don't tell anyone, all right?"

Free leans just as close to her friend, her eyes squinting under the fluorescent lighting. "Or you'd have to kill me?"

"'Fraid so, Free. And I'd hate to have to kill two beautiful women such as yourselves."

Harper snorts and takes a drink of her beer. "Does that line really work too?"

"You wound me, Harper."

"I'm sure your ego will pad your fall," she sasses, bringing an instant smile to my face.

"Don't mind her. She's going through her angry at all men phase," Free offers, shoulder bumping her friend.

"It's not a phase. I'm angry at all men," Harper argues.

"What did we all do?" I ask, finishing off my beer and placing the empty on the bar.

"You all cheat. You're all horny, spineless assholes who can't keep it zipped in your pants," Harper practically growls.

"Well, you are partially right," I state, leaning toward Harper. Her light eyes turn dark with hurt and fury. Clearly this is a fresh wound and no amount of defending my species is going to rectify the situation. "We are horny and we are assholes, but most of us aren't spineless. Most of us wouldn't take the chance at hurting the most gorgeous woman in our life for a five-minute romp in what was probably a bar bathroom, no offense," I add, giving Mara a look. "That's not a man, sweetheart, that's a coward. You have no room or time in your life for cowards. So drink up, dust off those dancin' shoes, and push that loser out of your mind and your heart. You don't have the time or energy for someone who doesn't appreciate exactly what he has in front of him," I state boldly.

Her eyes fill with unshed tears, and I'm instantly sorry I said anything. It's not my place, nor do I know anything about the situation. Then there's the fact that I hate tears. H.A.T.E. them. Suzanne used to whip them out all the time to get what she wanted, and I'm pretty sure I became desensitized over the course of our long ago relationship.

"You know what?" Harper asks, steeling her back and turning to face me. "You're completely right. What kind of loser screws the known town bar whore in the men's bathroom of the joint his girlfriend's friend owns?"

I glance at Mara, who just gives me a small grin.

Wow, totally called it.

"Someone not worth another second of your time or tears," I confirm.

"You're right!" she hollers, grabbing the shot glass Mara sets in front of her. "Let's get drunk, Cowboy. Maybe, if you play your cards right, you'll get lucky in the bathroom of the bar my friend owns."

I chuckle and reach for my own shot glass. I know that if I wanted this to happen, it would. But there's something in her eyes that tells me a mindless fuck in the men's bathroom wouldn't really help her situation in the long run. Sure, an orgasm would be nice (and let's face it, I know how to provide the O's), but she'll still wake up in the morning hungover and alone.

And even though I just met this woman, that's not what I want for her.

That's why I tap my shot glass against hers, throw back the liquid, and stand from my stool. Reaching into my wallet, I grab a few bills and toss them onto the worn bar top, making sure to not only pay for all of the drinks, but a nice little tip for Mara too.

Harper glances my way, while Free plays on her phone. "You're leaving?"

"'Fraid so, sugar I have an early day tomorrow, and the last thing I want to do is something you'll regret in the morning." I should win a fucking medal for walking away from this woman. She's beautiful, but she's hurting, and I really think sleeping with her would be a bad idea.

Look at me, all grown up and shit.

She gazes up at me, studying my face. It's a bit unnerving, like I'm under a microscope or something. "Thank you, Rhenn," she says with the tiniest hint of a smile. I turn to leave, but her next words stop me in my tracks. "My sister's right. You are gorgeous."

Considering I've only met about half a dozen people since arriving in Rockland Falls earlier today (and many of them old enough to be my parents), her comment has my full attention. When I turn back around, she's watching me over her shoulder. I take a step back in her direction as she slowly turns on her stool to face me. "I'm afraid you have me at a disadvantage," I reply, placing my hands in my pockets and rocking back on my heels.

Her manicured eyebrows arch skyward and a full smile plays on her lips. "My sister just so happened to mention that she met the new electrician today. I could tell by the way she didn't really want to talk about you that something was up." Her eyes drop to my boots as she slowly peruses her way back up to my face. "Now I know why she was so flustered when she talked about you."

The corner of my mouth turns upward as I invade her personal space. I place a kiss on her cheek, much like I would a friend or family member. "Thank you, Harper."

"Don't hurt her or I'll cut off your balls and feed them to my pit bull, Snuggles," she adds, making me wince and my balls to shrivel up just a little bit.

"Sounds pleasant," I reply as I step away.

"It will be...to watch," she sasses before reaching for her beer bottle.

"So noted. Have a good night," I reply to the group before turning and heading out the front door.

The night is cool, the air a bit salty from the ocean. I can't hear the waves crashing on the shore, but I know they're there, lurking in the dark. It calls to me, which is why I find myself turning and walking the few blocks toward the sea, and not to my truck parked in the lot beside The Station. My mind is full of images, ones I've been trying to avoid all night.

Marissa.

Small world that the woman I was chatting up at the bar is the sister of the one I can't stop thinking about. Good thing I didn't shag the hell out of her in the bathroom, huh? The fact I didn't is very un-Rhenn like, but the fact I care I didn't, is even more so. Would I have? Maybe. Harper is definitely a looker, and in any other situation, I may have very well taken her up on her offer.

But the offer wasn't really on the table.

She knew who I was, and even though she offered a quick fuck to help alleviate the pain she was in, I could see it in her eyes: she wasn't really interested.

Now I know why.

Standing along the beach, I watch as the water moves tiny granules of sand, pushing them farther onto the shore and then washing them out to sea. I can't wait to get my boat. It's part of me, like an extension of my arm. I've never felt so alive as I do with my hands on the wheel and the sun on my face.

And even though I pushed the earlier thought out of my mind, I can't help but picture Marissa there with me. Sunbathing on the deck, her slender fingers gripping the wheel, a tiny bikini barely covering my favorite parts of a woman. But something tells me she's not a dental floss bikini kind of woman, and even that image turns my cock to stone in my pants.

There's something alluring and enchanting about this woman, and even though I know I should stay away, I know I won't.

I can't.

Because she calls to me just as much as the sea.

Chapter Five

Marissa

The steady beeping of a truck backing up has me walking toward the window in the upstairs bedroom I'm working in. Gazing down at the flatbed truck, I see the rest of the building supplies being delivered, including the siding and two replacement windows. The contractor and several of his workers all scramble to unload the material, but what draws my attention is the large pickup truck opposite the commotion.

Rhenn is by his pickup truck, removing large spools of wire as if they weigh merely a few pounds. His worn jeans mold perfectly to his ass and powerful thighs – thighs that promise nothing short of pure thrusting power.

I blush as those dirty images filter through the cobwebs in my brain.

His T-shirt is tight against corded muscles, leaving nothing to the imagination. I can't help but wonder if he knows exactly what kind of impact he has on the female population as a whole, or if he just wakes up in the morning, throws on an old T-shirt, and goes about his day as if nothing is wrong. As if women everywhere weren't offering up their firstborn for one chance to strip off his clothes and have their dirty way with him.

Rhenn turns, his arms loaded with supplies, and glances up at the window I'm perving from. Our eyes connect for several heartbeats before the corner of his lip turns upward in a smirk I'd normally find insulting. But on him? Totally sexy.

Oh yeah, he totally knows.

I've been successful at avoiding him all day, keeping to myself upstairs in the guest room I'm cleaning. I'm not sure how he spent the day today, but I've heard him. The heavy thump of his boots on the hardwood floors has kept me on edge, alerting me that he's near. Yet even if I couldn't hear his presence, I've felt it. It's as if my body is in tune only to him.

I back away from the window as if it were about to electrocute me, bumping into my bucket of warm soapy water. Of course it sloshes over and spills all over my foot. I mean, why wouldn't it? Now I have to either run back to my house or deal with a wet sock and shoe for the remainder of the day.

Choosing the former, I toss my sponge onto the floor and head down the hall, the water squishing in my tennis shoe with each step I take. When I reach the base of the stairs and turn toward the living quarters in back, I hit a roadblock of building material. Two by fours, OSB, flooring, and drywall. Not to mention half a dozen men moving the goods into the rooms they'll work on first.

With a deep sigh, I head out the front door where I collide with a solid chest and alluring masculine scent. "Shit, I'm sorry," Rhenn says reaching out and grabbing for my arm to steady me.

"No, it's my fault. I wasn't watching where I was going," I reply, trying to get my footing once more. When I look up, it's like taking Thor's hammer to the chest. His eyes – my God, those deep blue eyes – hold me hostage, completely against my will.

Okay, if I'm being honest, it's not completely against my will.

Like the children follow the singing witch in the movie *Hocus Pocus*, I'd clearly go anywhere, do anything this man asks, even if it was to my own death.

That's why I must initiate my Rhenn Burleski force field, keeping him and his sexy eyes and masculine scent and tree trunk thighs and broad shoulders and…

Where was I going with this?

"Marissa?" he asks, those blue eyes full of concern as they rake over my body from head to toe. A shiver slips down my spine, completely unwanted, but I can't deny how my body reacts to him.

Stupid body.

"What?" I ask, vaguely recalling him asking a question.

"I asked if you were all right," he states again, his eyes holding mine.

"Yes," I whisper, that single word a plea.

Those eyes devour me once more, leaving me with a sense of being naked and exposed. I'm not used to feeling so bare, and usually I'm not, but there's something about him – about Rhenn – that has my senses all out of sorts and my body on hyper alert.

"My shoe is wet."

Yep, I said it. Of all the things that could come out of my mouth, that's not exactly what I was hoping for. I could have gone with "Wow, your eyes are the same color as the sky" or maybe even "I love the way the ink on your arm peeks out from beneath your shirt sleeve. Can I lick it?" But no, I have to say the stupidest thing in the history of all conversations.

Rhenn glances down and checks out my shoe. When his eyes return to mine, there's a bit of a sparkle in them, one that reminds me of starry nights and fireflies. It's also the moment I realize he's still holding me. I'm pretty confident it's the reason my brain function has dropped below zero. My skin tingles and burns beneath his strong fingers, my blood pumps recklessly through my extremities. His touch is just as lethal as his smile, which is why I should take not one, but two steps back, to sever our connection and break the spell he has me under.

But as I will my feet to move, I find myself rooted completely in place. I'm trapped in his gaze, under his mysterious powers, and for a fraction of a second, I let myself just feel. Feel the way his fingers gently stroke my arms as he holds me, causing warmth to pool between my legs. Feel the way his eyes seem to watch and devour me. Feel the way his breath teases my skin, leaving goose bumps in its wake.

Rhenn looks as if he wants to say something. I'm torn between wanting him to and hoping he doesn't. It's a slippery slope we walk on, because at the end of the day, there are too many reasons why acting on this attraction is stacked against us. Too many reasons why me wrapping my arms around his broad waist and letting him kiss me is a bad idea.

The connection is broken by the slamming of a car door. I jump back as if I were being burned and stumble over my own feet. Fortunately (or unfortunately, depending on which way you look at it), Rhenn is there, his strong hands still wrapped around my upper arms, and keeps me from falling. Again.

"Hey!" my sister, Harper, hollers as she approaches the front porch.

This time when I step back, Rhenn lets me go, and I immediately feel the loss of his touch. Disappointment sweeps through me, unwanted and unchecked, as I offer my sister my biggest, brightest, and probably fakest smile ever. "Hey!"

When she reaches the top of the stairs, she glances between Rhenn and me, a smile playing on her painted red lips. It's a knowing grin, one that tells me she's trying to piece together or dig too deeply into something that isn't real.

Before I can say anything to refute whatever it is she's about to say, she speaks. "Hey, Cowboy."

"Well, good morning, sugar," Rhenn replies.

I glance between the two, as they smile at each other, and feel my stomach drop into my wet shoe. Of course. Why am I even considering that there's a budding attraction left hanging between Rhenn and I? There's nothing, not when Harper is around. She's gorgeous and exotic in a way that I could only pretend to be. Why would a man want a hamburger when he could have prime rib?

"You two know each other?" I find myself asking, though I don't really want to know the answer. They're both single – or at least I think they both are. I know Harper is, just having come out of a relationship with a loser who dicked around on her. But Rhenn? He could have a girl – or a wife – at home for all I know.

"We met last night," Rhenn says, offering my sister another smile.

I just bet they did…

My stomach takes another swan dive as I picture my sister with Rhenn, laughing and touching. Those strong fingers I've felt caress my own skin were probably tangled in Harper's hair last night. Before either of them can say anything else, I leap toward the stairs and fly down them. "Well, I have to go change my shoes. Harper, Mom's in the kitchen. I'll talk to you later," I holler in one big run-on sentence, my wet shoe squeaking as I practically run away.

I make it around back, past the sawing and hammering, and to my cute little house in record time. Stepping up onto the small porch, I open the door (it's never locked) and slam it behind me. My back sags against the hard wood, my breathing labored as I close my eyes and wish the world would just open up and swallow me whole.

They already have cute nicknames for each other…

61

I'd never begrudge Harper happiness, nor have I ever resented the fact that she looks like a freaking supermodel. It's not her fault she was blessed with *all* of the good genes. She's tall and skinny and athletic. I'm…well, not. Boys, guys, and men have always flocked to her all of her life. Even when we were younger, she was the Homecoming Queen that everyone wanted to date. She was the cheerleader who won the Scholastic Bowl tournament for our school, while wearing the quarterback's jersey. She was the woman all of the single men in town tried to impress with wine and roses.

And I was always in the shadows, watching it all play out over the top of my paperback.

One time – one amazingly, fantastic time – did I appear to win the guy over her. But I learned quickly that looks can be deceiving. Vincent was a few years older than me in school, even though we didn't hang out in any of the same circles, I knew who he was. Everyone knew who he was. When he showed up at the same coffee shop in town, not two, but three days in a row, at the same time I was getting my afternoon latte, I thought my luck with guys had finally changed. He was sweet, attentive, and hot.

He also had one eye on my sister.

Harper was in a relationship at the time, but that didn't stop Vincent from always inserting himself into my life at all the right times. It took me a while to catch on to his game, but once I saw the writing on the wall, it was clear that he wasn't into me as much as I was him. He was into Harper.

And I was devastated.

I could never be mad at her, even though I may secretly wish she'd grow a mole on her nose. Childish, yes, but if you've constantly been compared and found lacking to an older sibling, you'd understand. I love Harper, really, I do. She's an amazing woman, with a heart of gold. Unfortunately, that heart has been kicked around and walked on by more men than I care to admit. She truly is one in a million and would do anything for anyone.

But that still doesn't mean I want to picture her with Rhenn.

The man I secretly fantasized about last night when slipping between the sheets. The man I pictured running his full lips along my cheekbone as they slowly started to trek their way down my body. The man I may have thought about while touching myself long after the crickets went to bed and the owl called it a night.

The man who spent the night getting to know my sister.

I kick off my shoes and rip off my socks, tossing them somewhere into the tiny living room. I'm frustrated with myself for thinking about Rhenn as anything other than a subcontractor. I could tell the moment our eyes met that he'd be trouble, and dammit, I was right. He's a distraction I don't need, or want. I can't let his gorgeous smile and his sexy swagger pull my attention from getting this place up and running again. That's where all of my focus needs to be, not on the way his jeans seem to mold to his ass or the way his muscles flex beneath the soft, worn cotton of his T-shirt.

If he wants to screw around with Harper while he's here, then fine.

So be it.

I don't care.

But if the way my stomach plummets back into my feet is any indication, I do care. I care a lot. Because for just a few minutes, for just a short moment in time, I pictured him as mine. Not Harper's, not anyone else's. Mine. Even if the fantasy is never acted upon, it was planted, taking root and growing into something that was mine alone.

I let out a frustrated growl and grab a clean pair of socks from my drawer. I shove my feet into them as if I were angry at the poor things and reach for a dry pair of tennis shoes. Just as I'm lacing them up, my front door opens. I already know who it is. Harper never knocks.

"Hey," she says brightly as she enters my small space.

"Hey," I reply, keeping my head down and my focus on tying my shoes. You'd think I had never done it before with the amount of concentration I was putting into it.

"You okay?" she asks, coming over and sitting down beside me.

"Fine, great, wonderful. You?" I ask, offering her a blinding smile.

"I'm good," she replies, her smile not nearly as forced or fake.

The silence hangs between us for several heartbeats. Finally, I can't stand it anymore. "So, you and Rhenn, huh?" I ask, trying to act like I don't care. If the look she gives me is any indication, I already know that I'm failing miserable.

"Me and Rhenn, what?" she asks, her lips turning upward just the slightest.

"Well, you know. You guys met up last night," I reply, willing myself to stop talking. I really don't want to know.

"We ran into each other at The Station. Free and I went up for a drink after inventory, and he was there."

"Nice," I respond, messing with my socks as if they were bunched up around my ankle.

"Funny thing happened," she says, shoulder bumping me. "The entire time we visited, I felt like he was a bit distracted."

"Well, your beauty does that to guys," I reply with a smile, knowing it's completely true.

"That's not it. He was distracted by someone else. Someone who wasn't there."

Figures. Leave it to me to be completely attracted to a manwhore with a waitlist a mile long. I don't reply, just stand up and adjust my shorts. Harper follows suit and towers over me, smiling down at me with a knowing look.

"I could tell something had his attention, and it wasn't anyone in the bar. And the funniest thing when I mentioned you."

Air stops in my throat, choking me. "Me?"

"Yeah, you. As soon as I mentioned my sister, his eyes seemed to transform. He's interested," she says, shrugging her shoulders.

"Well, I'm...not."

"No?" she asks, following me as I make my way to the door. I have so much more work to do in the house, and I really need to get back to it.

"Of course not. Why would I be?"

"Because he's gorgeous? Funny? Sexy? And looks at you like you hung the moon?" That makes me stop in my tracks. "What, you don't think he notices you? I was there for about five seconds and could see it. That man is completely enamored with you."

"You don't know what you're talking about," I mumble, pulling open my front door and stepping outside.

"No?" she asks, hurrying behind me and pulling my door closed. "Then I must be reading it all wrong. You're probably right, I'm sure he's not interested," she adds, making me stop and turn toward her.

"I'm pretty sure he's not." My voice sounds small and unconvincing, even to my own ears.

"Then it must be someone else he's staring at, watching from a second floor window right now. It must be someone else's ass he can't take his eyes off of. Couldn't possibly be you, right?" Her smile is victorious and grates on my nerves just a little.

"He is?"

"Oh, he definitely is. It's probably a good thing we can't see what's going on in his mind right now because I'm sure it's deliciously dirty."

"You're bad," I reply, taking a swat at her arm before turning back to the house.

And because I'm glutton for punishment, I glance up, finding Rhenn exactly where Harper said he was. He's watching me, and even though I could argue it's her who has his attention, I know that it's not. It's me. He follows my movements from the yard to the house until our line of sight is broken by the tall shrubbery that surrounds the back porch.

I know this because my eyes watch him too.

Chapter Six

Rhenn

I spend the next two days doing the exact opposite of what I'm supposed to do: stay away from Marissa.

Instead, I find myself seeking her out, asking her stupid questions regarding the remodel and rewire that I already know the answer to or could find in the plans from the contractor. I eat lunch on the same porch as she, engaging in as much small talk as possible and soaking up as much Marissa time as I possibly can.

That's exactly what I'm doing on Friday, the last workday before the three-day Memorial Day holiday weekend. I'm working in the same guest bedroom as she is, the outlet covers all off as I change out each receptacle and light switch with new, updated versions. The rewire is going well, even though I have to climb into a nineteenth century attic that has seen better days.

Marissa has stripped the bed and the old mattress was thrown out into the dumpster. She's working on cleaning the antique wooden frame, wiping away the soot and grime left behind from the fire. It's extremely time consuming, meticulous, and takes several swipes of the sponge to clear away the remnants of the fire.

The problem that I have now is, even though the mattress is gone and I'm staring at a bedframe, the image of her lying across this very bed that she's cleaning. Call it a wish list image, if you will. No, she hasn't so much as made an implication that she'd be interested in a little afternoon delight, but the daydreams are there, nonetheless. They're bright, dirty, and there's no doubt in my mind that I'll replay them at least a dozen times tonight while I'm jacking off in the shower. Tonight it'll be the bed. Last night it was on my boat. I have a plethora of sexual fantasies starring the one and only Marissa Grayson.

"Big plans this holiday weekend?" I ask casually as I cut the protruding wire from the outlet and work on hooking up the new receptacle. I feel her eyes on me as I finish with the rewire and turn her way. She's giving me a curious look, as if she has no clue what I'm talking about. "Memorial Day weekend."

"Oh, shit. I forgot," she says absently, turning her attention back to the decorative woodwork. Lucky fucking bedframe. "No plans. I'm sure I'll be working here all weekend."

My mind wanders back to the weekend and all I have to accomplish. I have to check out of the bed and breakfast I'm staying at, drive back to Jupiter Bay, meet up with my friend Nick and his wife, and then turn around and come back on Sunday. But even when you take all of the running around into consideration, it's not a chore or an obligation. It's something I look forward to. Especially because Sunday night and Monday are mine. I'll have my boat and my friends, and can't wait to unwind in the sun and breeze. "Nick and Meghan are coming back with me," I mention.

"They are? I'd love to meet them." I glance over at Marissa who's breaking a sweat as she scrubs the ornate woodwork. Without giving it a second thought (or a first thought, really), I stand up and walk to where she's positioned between the slats of the bed that hold the box spring. My dick twitches in my pants, a subtle reminder that it hasn't seen any bedroom action in longer than he's used to. Not saying a word, I reach for the scrubber, my fingers connecting with hers. She gasps, her wide green eyes slamming into mine with the force of a Category 4 hurricane. My gut tightens, as it does every time she gazes up at me, and my breathing halts.

Marissa doesn't move, doesn't say a word, as I wrap my fingers around hers, slowly and gently removing the scrubber from her hand. She's panting, and to be honest, I'm not sure if it's from exerting herself in her quest to clean the bed or if it's from this undeniable attraction that I know isn't one-sided. She feels it the same way I do. It's written in her eyes and etched on her beautiful face.

And it takes every ounce of control I have not to taste it on her lips.

Instead, I keep with my original plan and gently pull the sponge from her hand. She lets go, her eyes never leaving mine, as her mouth falls open into a seductive little O. Fuck, what I'd love to do to that mouth. My cock is fully on board now, straining against my zipper and all but crawling from my pants.

"Grab a drink," I instruct, nodding toward the small cooler with bottles of water. She gives me a look, as if I just spoke Greek.

Turning my back, I start to scrub on the soot. It's thicker than I expect, much more difficult to clear away with a simple wipe, which surprises me a bit. I guess now I know why she has been working up a sweat. It also reiterates my thought that she could use a break, but won't take it for fear that she'll never get her tasks complete. Marissa's a hard worker, this is evident by the way she's doing all of the deep, heavy cleaning herself instead of paying a service to take care of it. That thought alone turns me on a little more.

"So, tell me about growing up in Rockland Falls. Have you lived here your entire life?" I ask, concentrating on trying to clear away the grime off the ornate wood.

I hear her finally move, walking over to the cooler to grab a drink, as suggested. I glance over my shoulder just as she props her back against the doorframe and slowly lowers herself to the floor. She looks exhausted and we're only at the end of week one. There's tons of work to be done, including the cleaning of the remaining three guest rooms, plus all of the living spaces below. It's a daunting task, even to me.

"Yeah, I was born and raised here. I've lived here at this place since I was little. Went to junior college and took some business and hospitality classes, but my real passion has always been cooking."

I stop scrubbing and follow the sound of her voice. She's looking off to the left out the window, and I'm immediately drawn to her, needing to hear more words fall from that mouth of hers. "What do you like to cook?" I ask, returning my attention to the task at hand, yet keeping one eye firmly on the beautiful woman across the room.

"Everything," she says with a smile. "I make an amazing red velvet soufflé with mascarpone cream and wild mushroom asiago chicken, but my favorite is my zesty lemon blueberry pancakes with fresh maple syrup."

My stomach growls.

The sponge falls to the floor.

Hearing this woman talk about food, the way her words ooze passion and happiness, has my insides twisted into knots and my dick throbbing in my pants. Well, more than it already was.

"Hearing you talk about food is almost orgasmic," I tell her, offering a smirk and a wink.

Her eyes meet mine, the irises dark and alluring, as a bubble of laughter spills from her lips. Those fucking lips. I almost have to bite my fist to keep from groaning. "They always say food is the second fastest way to a man's heart," she says with a shrug.

"The second? What's the first?" I ask, taking a step toward her.

"Sex."

And there it is. The one word I've prayed to never slip past her tongue. The one word that makes me want to throw out every reason why I should be staying as far away from her as possible, yet I can't seem to do just that. Instead, I make excuses to be near her, to talk to her, to touch her.

Like now. I'm standing right in front of her, and I can't stop myself from dropping to my ass on the hardwood floor. My legs touch hers, a whisper of a graze that makes my entire body rigid and hyperaware. Her green eyes follow my movements as I shift my legs to the side, careful not to disrupt her casual posture, but she's anything but casual. I can feel the nervousness and the excitement oozing from her pores. I make her anxious, and I hope it's because of this unspoken attraction and not something else.

I don't believe it's anything else.

She feels it, and so do I. The problem is that I've fought the desire to act upon said attraction, and right now, sitting here on the floor, I just don't fucking care to fight it anymore.

I want to kiss her.

I want to wrap my arms around her and pull her close.

I want to thread my fingers into that long, blonde hair and devour her mouth with my own.

I want to feel the way she writhes against me and hear the sounds of surrender spill from her lips.

I want more.

I want it all.

Reaching forward, I remove the strand of hair that is stuck to her lips. As soon as I do, her tongue snakes out, wetting the very lips I've been dreaming about. My eyes drop down, watching with fascination, as she holds her breath, waiting. I could lean in. I could steal the kiss I've been fantasizing about. By the look in her eyes, she'd be completely on board with this plan, but I know it wouldn't be enough.

It may never be enough.

I want more.

"I have an idea," I say softly, my finger trailing a blazing path up her soft cheek as I tuck the hair behind her ear.

She doesn't say a word or even a sound.

"Come with me this weekend on my boat."

Marissa blinks at me, seeming to register what I said. "I get seasick." Her words are small and wounded, as if she's sad I didn't remember that tidbit of information. But the thing is: I've not forgotten. I haven't forgotten one tiny detail when it comes to this woman.

"I remember," I say, keeping my hand on her hair. "I have Dramamine for you, and my friends are coming down this weekend. I think you'll like Nick and Meghan, your cousin. Plus, you could use a break. It's a holiday weekend, and I'd hate to see you working your tail off in the house while you could be out relaxing, soaking up the sun, and spending time with friends."

She seems to be considering my offer, and I know her answer could go either way. The possibility of her turning me down sits like a lead brick in my gut. The prospect of spending time with Marissa on my boat, in my element, has me all sorts of giddy.

And I don't fucking do giddy.

"If you start to feel lousy at any point, I'll turn around and bring you home. No questions asked."

The worry lines around her eyes disappear as she relaxes, and I know what her answer is going to be. She's about to say yes, and I couldn't be happier about it. In fact, I'm fucking ecstatic, my wheels already spinning with where we can go and what all we can do. I'm determined to make this trip a good one for her in hopes that she won't be afraid to go again in the very near future.

"I'll go…under one condition," she says, her lips turning upward into a small smile.

"Anything." I glance down and realize I'm holding her hand. At some point, when I was transfixed on her gaze, I had dropped my hands and reached for hers. I'm not sure if she realizes it yet I'm holding her hand, but if she does, she hasn't pulled away. I like it.

"I get to cook for you."

Again, my stomach growls loudly, followed by a burst of laughter from Marissa. "Deal."

* * *

My phone is ringing as I step out of the en suite shower. Holding the towel around my waist, I make a dive for the device before the caller can hang up. I smile when I see my best friend's name on the screen.

"Hey, man."

"How's it going?" he responds.

"Good. Just got home from work a bit ago. Getting ready to head downstairs for dinner," I tell him, tucking the end of the towel against my lower stomach to keep it in place.

"I was hoping I'd catch you before you went out for the evening," he says casually, though the implication is there. For too many years, my friend has watched me go out, have a few drinks, and take home whatever girl has caught my attention for the night.

The problem is that only one girl has caught my attention. I'm trapped in Marissa's web, and there hasn't been a woman since I met her. Hell, there hasn't been a woman since my best friend's wedding three weeks ago, and that's saying something. I'm not sure yet what that is, nor am I ready to dissect it. Nick doesn't need to know I'm off my game a bit or that I've been sidetracked by a beautiful blonde with alluring green eyes.

Opting to forego that tidbit of information, I reply with, "What's up?"

"Meg and I were thinking. It's silly for you to drive all the way here, just to drive your boat back down there. Plus, I'd have to drive your truck, *and* Meg would have to bring our vehicle so we can get back home Monday night."

I have to admit, it's a lot of unnecessary vehicle jockeying.

"What did you have in mind?" I ask, taking a seat on the edge of the bed.

"I'll bring the boat." I open my mouth to protest, but he continues before I can get a word out. "Before you start bitching, you know I could drive it just fine. Meghan will bring her car down, and we'll only be making one trip. You won't be going back and forth, which is completely needless."

He has a point. It's not that I don't want Nick to drive my boat down. Hell, the asshole has captained it plenty of times back home, including in and out of the marina, but he's never taken it without me. Suddenly, I feel like I'm relinquishing my truck to my sixteen-year-old kid who just got his license.

"We were talking about heading out early tomorrow morning," he adds, breaking through my thoughts. "I can be there by two."

Having my boat arrive on Saturday instead of Sunday is a plus. I could get a few hours of work in that morning while I wait for my friends to arrive. Then, we'll have Saturday and Sunday nights on the boat to hang out, plus the days to sail. It actually is a pretty good idea.

"Fine," I say begrudgingly.

"Really? I thought you'd put up more of a fight. I had an entire speech prepared to follow up with your first no."

Dick.

"I'll call the marina and have them get it ready for you. Just don't scratch up my baby or I'll have to beat the shit out of you on the mat," I reply, referring to the mats at my karate dojo. Nick and I work out together most mornings, and sparring with my friend has always been one of my favorite things to do. He's not quite to the degree of black belt as me, but he can hold his own when we face off. Being away from Jupiter Bay this week has taken a toll on my routine. If I'm not careful, I'm liable to fall into an undisciplined pattern, and that's another distraction I can't afford.

"When was the last time you beat the shit out of me?" he mouths off through the line.

"Last week."

"You kneed me in the balls," he yells.

"Don't act like you didn't love your wife fawning all over your swollen nads. She probably made it up to you five ways to Sunday that night."

Nick chuckles. "That she did, my friend. That she did. Anyway, she'll be there by noon. She wants to visit with Mary Ann and meet her cousins."

That's right, I forgot she hasn't met Marissa yet. The grandparents were here right after the fire, along with Ryan and Jaime (he's a contractor who put her in touch with some names he knew the area), but Meghan and the rest of her sisters haven't met them yet.

"Sounds like a plan. You guys can stay on the boat with me," I say, knowing that I'll give up the master suite in the below deck for them.

"I'm not in the mood to listen to you screw your way through Rockland Falls, man," he says, immediately grating on my nerves. In his defense, he doesn't know that I'm not already sleeping with half the female population in town, but the assumption still pisses me off a little.

"No parties, no women. I'm looking forward to hanging out with my friends this weekend. I haven't seen you much since the wedding." I leave out the part about inviting Marissa along for the ride.

That seems to catch him off guard. He stumbles over his words, probably because he's never heard me offer to leave extra female guests at home in favor of hanging with my friends. I almost tell him about Marissa, but decide to leave that one for later. He'll start asking me questions I'm not prepared to answer, and I'm just not ready to get into the big, heavy shit right now.

"Sounds good, man. I'll text you tomorrow when I'm getting close," he says.

"Take care of my baby." I know he will, but I feel the need to remind him.

"And you take care of mine," he replies, his words confident and full of love.

Now I'm the one to stumble.

Is he talking about Meghan or…

"Yeah?" I ask, completely surprised, yet suddenly so very happy for my best friend.

"Yeah," he says, the happiness radiating through the cell phone.

"When did you find out?"

"Right after the wedding. The honeymoon, actually. She spent the entire flight throwing up. That was our first tip," Nick says with a chuckle.

"I'm happy for you, man. No one will make a better father than you." And I mean that.

"Thanks," he says with a sigh. "I'm nervous. Scared. She's been through so much, and the last thing I want is for something to happen to her or the baby."

He's right. His new wife has been through more shit than anyone can imagine. But even though she lost her fiancé, she survived the heartbreak, and is now married to one of the best guys I know.

"Congrats, friend, and don't you worry, I'll take great care of her while you're away," I reply with a smirk, and even though he can't see me, I wiggle my eyebrows suggestively.

"You're wiggling your eyebrows, aren't you? Keep your grimy manwhore hands off my pregnant wife, or I'll have to kill you and toss your body into the ocean. They'll never find you."

I can't help but laugh. I'd never touch my friend's wife, but that doesn't mean I don't enjoy getting him all riled up every now and again. "See you tomorrow."

"Later," he replies before disconnecting the phone.

So Nick is going to be a dad, huh? That might be the best thing I've heard since Meghan agreed to marry him. He'd loved her before he let his feelings be known, mostly because she was still reeling from the death of her fiancé, Josh.

But now they're together.

Happy.

Having a baby.

And the slightest bit of jealousy bubbles to the surface.

He has it all. He was one of the lucky ones. Meghan didn't fuck him over – or more accurately – fuck his friend. She didn't try to blame him for their relationship troubles. She didn't push him straight into a new role in life, complete with different women in his arms every night, dulling the pain the only way he knew how.

He got a good one.

And I got broken.

Chapter Seven

Marissa

"I swear, you're trying to kill me," I pant as my jelly-filled legs continue to spin around and around on the stationery bike.

"This is the best kinda burn out there," my sadistic sister says with a sweet smile as she continues to pedal at twice the speed as me.

"I hate you." Sweat drips from my face; it slides down my back and into places I never thought possible.

"You love me."

"No, I don't. From this point forward, I don't have a sister. We're no longer related," I pant and gasp, trying with everything I have to make my threat come out with authority instead of choppy and weak. It didn't work.

"If you're talking, you're not working hard enough," the bubbly bleach blonde croons into the headset she's wearing, her laser eyes focused solely on me. "Come on, ladies! Work those muscles!"

"Okay, I don't hate you, but her? Yeah, I flipping hate her," I whisper over the upbeat pop music flowing from the speakers.

"Come on, Riss! This moment calls for a good F-bomb. Let it fly. I fucking hate her," she teases, pumping her legs frantically and popping up off the seat to the beat of the song.

"Jesus, are you even human?" I ask, my ass burning and my legs completely numb.

"Great job, ladies! Let's cool it down now," Miss Bubbles cheers into the headset, causing everyone to let out a whoop of accomplishment at completing the workout. Me? I'm surprised I'm even still sitting on the bike seat. In fact, there's a pretty good chance someone is going to have to carry me out of here.

"That was fun," Harper says the moment class ends. She hops off the seat, toweling off the faintest drops of sweat on her brow, and offers me a warm smile. "You did it!"

"That was the worst kinda torture I've ever experienced. Why in the hell would someone subject themselves to that, willingly?" I pant and wheeze, slowly sliding off my seat. I feel like a brand new baby deer as I tentatively take a step toward my water bottle.

"Spinning is a hell of a workout, and Staci is the best."

"She's Satan with blonde hair and perky double D's."

"Stop being so dramatic," my tall, sweat-less sister says as she wraps her arm around my shoulder and leads me toward the exit. I squirt water into my mouth, but even my jaw muscles don't seem to want to work right now. We're following in the wake of the other ladies in attendance for Ladies Spinning to Pop Divas class, held Monday, Wednesday, and Friday evenings at six. I'm pretty sure, from this point forward, I'll have something much better to do at six those nights. You know, like getting a root canal, or maybe a bikini wax from a blind man. That sounds much more enjoyable than sweating like a pig to Britney Spears and Christina Aguilera.

"I hate to say this, but you're on your own from now on, Harper. There's no way in hell you'll ever get me back in here," I say, just as she stops in her tracks, causing me to stumble over my own two feet and fall awkwardly to my left.

Hands wrap around my arms and pull me tightly into a chest. A very broad chest with ripped muscles and a manly scent. Familiarity wraps around me, warm and comforting. "Careful, Angel."

The featherlight touch of his breath on my cheek causes an involuntary shudder to sweep through my body. I glance up into Rhenn's magnetic blue eyes and completely forget where I am. Hell, I completely forget my name. It just vanishes from normal brain function. Poof. Gone. His jaw is covered in a delicious stubble that makes my thighs clench and his full lips are totally kissable and perfect. My heart starts to pound in my chest, tapping out a savory little beat, and my body leans into his just a bit more.

"Earth to Marissa," Harper says in my ear, snapping her fingers in front of my face. My cheeks flame with embarrassment, and I'm not sure what's worse: being caught openly gawking at Rhenn by the man himself, or by Harper.

"Sorry," I mumble, trying to take a step back, but finding myself downright unable to complete the task since Rhenn is still holding me against him.

Against. His. Body.

Flush together, chest-to-chest.

I can practically feel his heart pounding a strong, steady beat, or maybe that's mine. No, wait. Mine is pounding to an erratic, sporadic beat, so it must be his. I start to wonder if he even realizes my boobs are smashed against his chest when his eyes drop down, drinking in the slight spill of cleavage over the neckline of my workout tank top. His eyes dilate and darken instantly as he seems to memorize the swell of my boobs, every freckle on my flushed skin.

Yep, he definitely realizes it.

He probably also recognizes that I'm completely gross and covered in nasty post-workout sweat. Boob sweat isn't sexy, at least not on a woman like me. My cheeks are surely red from exertion and my hair, a rat's nest of chaos. No pretty messy bun, post-workout glow here, thank you very much.

"Fancy meeting you here, Cowboy," Harper says, drawing both of our gazes away from each other and toward her. Rhenn finally releases his hold on my arms, and I'm not sure if it's a welcome movement or a disappointing one; but he doesn't move entirely out of my personal space. In fact, I know I could bump my hip just a bit and connect with his body.

"Well, I've been off my routine this week, so when I was out on a walk earlier and noticed this gym, I thought I'd stop in and get in a quick workout," he says, talking to Harper, but returning his gaze to me.

I try to keep my focus on his face. It's hard, I'll admit, but I think I manage. I don't once glance down, following the corded muscles and trail of dark blonde hair that disappears beneath his tank top. Not once do I watch how his tanned skin shines with a thin layer of sweat. Never do my eyes drop below his waist to see the way his basketball-style shorts hang dangerously low on his hips.

Yeah, that's a total lie.

"Marissa?" he asks, drawing my eyes back up from his thighs to his handsome – and slightly smug – face.

"What?" I ask, digging deep in my memory bank for any recollection of what he may have been saying moments before my eyes took their southern detour down his incredible body.

Rhenn lifts the corner of his mouth in an obvious smirk. Why the hell does it look so hot on him when he does that? "I asked what class you ladies just took."

"Death by Spinning," I reply, recalling in this exact moment how homely my appearance has to be.

"She's whining," Harper adds, taking a drink from her water bottle. "She's such a physical fitness baby."

"You should take one of my classes," he says casually, crossing his arms in a manner that only highlights the veins and muscles in his impeccable forearms.

"Classes? What kind of classes?" I ask, racking my brain to think of any mention of him being a physical fitness instructor. Though, that would make sense, considering his body is a work of art that should be displayed in a museum – you know, right next to Michelangelo's *David* or Myron's *Discobolus*.

"Karate instructor, actually. I'm a third degree black belt." And just like that, my ovaries exploded.

"Karate? Bad ass, Cowboy. I'll have to call you Kick-ass Cowboy, now," Harper says, drawing a laugh from the man beside me.

"So, what do you say, Marissa? You wanna come take a class?"

"I'm not sure that would be wise," I state plainly, knowing anything with coordination isn't my strong suit.

"Marissa has zero coordination, my friend. She'd probably kick you in the balls and punch you in the eye," my horrible sister says, bringing life to my inner thoughts and deepening my humiliation.

"It's true," I add, hating the way my cheeks burn.

"If I can handle a dozen teenagers, I think I can handle one pint-sized gorgeous woman," Rhenn croons, making my insides twist and butterflies take flight in my belly. "But just to be safe, I'll wear a cup," he whispers, covering his groin with both hands.

Both hands.

As in, it takes two to completely cover it.

That means…

Well, you know.

I can't stop staring.

"You should teach her. I'm sure she'd love to lay you down on a mat and pour it to you, Kick-ass Cowboy," Harper says, smiling widely and making me wish I was the only girl. Not the first time I've wished on that particular star in my short twenty-seven years on this earth, but it's the first time I've ever thought about doing the job myself.

My mouth just hangs open – in a totally unladylike fashion – as I watch my horrible sister make plans with Rhenn to teach me karate. Or self-defense, as it so happens to be. "It's a beginner's class, so I think she can manage," Rhenn replies.

"Wait, you're serious?" I ask, glancing between my sister and the gym hottie – who just so happens to be our subcontractor and man I've secretly fantasized about no less than…well, every night this last week.

"I never joke around about karate, Angel," he replies with a smile.

"Rhenn! You're still here!" Staci, the masochist spin instructor says, sliding right in between myself and Rhenn, rubbing her massive, protruding double D's across his arm and chest as she goes.

"I'm still here," he says with a wide smile that doesn't quite reach his eyes.

"Will we be seeing you again soon? Like tomorrow?" she coos, batting her overly blackened eyelashes and all but pressing her boobs against his chest once more.

"Probably not tomorrow," Rhenn says casually, yet there's a definite flirty tone in the way he says it. It's like he can't help it.

And he probably can't.

"Shoot," she whines, drawing out that single word as if it has fourteen syllables. "I was hoping we could hang. You know, together. Alone."

"Ahhh, sweetheart, I really appreciate the offer, but my work schedule just doesn't allow much free time," Rhenn replies, grabbing the hands on his chest and gently pushing them off. But don't think I don't notice how Staci's nails try to latch on to the material, like an eagle's talons on a tree branch.

"Booo! Maybe soon, right?" Staci says, setting her head on his upper arm.

"Maybe," he says with a shrug, taking a step to the side and right into me. "Sorry," he mumbles as he automatically reaches out and grabs my arm before I can teeter and topple over.

Our eyes connect, and I wait for the moment where Rhenn blows me off. I mean, it's not like we're…anything…but no man in his right mind would ever turn down what Staci's offering, especially Rhenn. I'm pretty sure Rhenn doesn't turn down much of anything where women are concerned.

"Actually, Staci, I do have a favor," he says, keeping his eyes locked on mine.

"Anything!" she bounces on her feet just over his shoulder.

"I'd like to rent out the matted room for an hour tomorrow. Can that be arranged?"

"Of course! I can get you *anything* you want!" she practically screams, Harper drawing my attention her way when she rolls her eyes so much, I think she can see her own brain.

"Excellent. I have a few moves I want to show Marissa tomorrow. Is ten in the morning okay?"

"Marissa?" Staci asks, her eyes full of shock and, well, more shock.

"Yeah, Marissa. We have a date with the mats," Rhenn says, turning and offering me a wink. "See you tomorrow at ten, Angel," he adds as he turns and heads toward the men's locker room.

I watch him go, frankly, because the view is phenomenal, and because I'm still completely stunned over what just transpired. "Well, looks like we need to get you home to get your beauty sleep. *Someone* has a date with her electrician turned kick-ass karate instructor at ten in the morning," Harper singsongs, a too-wide smile on her face.

She grabs my hand and gently tugs me toward the women's locker room, but not before I catch one last look at the very stunned face of Staci, the spin instructor from hell. I can't help but feel a little victorious, even though it really wasn't a competition. Yet, the fact that Rhenn chose to spend a little bit of time with me on the mats instead of Staci brings a small smile to my face and a bubble of hope in my chest. He wants to spend time with me, showing me karate moves. I'll probably look like an ungraceful idiot the entire time, but I'm surprisingly excited about this new development.

Ha. Take that, Staci!

Chapter Eight

Rhenn

I worked for a few hours this morning with a big-ass smile on my face. Hell, it's the same smile I wore last night when I got back from the gym and fell into bed. I was alone, of course, and my thoughts were on only one woman: Marissa.

Surprisingly, I didn't see her this morning at the house. I thought for sure she'd be there, working in the guest rooms, but she never showed. I even thought about walking back to her little house and knocking on the door to make sure everything was all right. I didn't, though. Instead, I recalled the way she looked last night, her eyes sparkling like emeralds, when I suggested we work on a few karate moves this morning.

I have a few moves for her and none of them are related to karate.

It's almost ten o'clock and I'm walking to the gym after just checking out of the bed and breakfast I was staying at. Meghan had sent me a text a few minutes ago to let me know she's on her way, and Nick called to tell me he was just finishing his pre-sail check and ready to head out. It'll take him just a little longer to get here than his wife, but he definitely didn't draw the short straw. I'd take sailing over riding in a vehicle any day.

The air changes the moment I step through the door. Weights clank and treadmills hum. It's a pretty nice gym, honestly, and if I were in the market for one in the future, this would probably be the one I'd pick. But, I'm not in the market. I have my own small gym in the back of my dojo that I use daily, and in just a few short weeks, I'll be back to my usual life, away from Rockland Falls.

Away from Marissa.

That thought settles like a lead balloon in my stomach.

Before I can glance around the small atrium of the gym, I know she's already here. I can sense her presence, smell her sweet fragrance. Marissa looks nervous as she approaches, a cup of coffee in one hand and her cell phone in the other. "Hi," she says, coming up alongside me.

"Hey," I respond, happy she's here. To be honest, I wasn't sure if she'd make it to our little impromptu lesson. She's wearing tight bicycle shorts that leave absolutely nothing to my dirty imagination and a loose-fitting tank top. My mouth starts to water and my cock starts to stir in my shorts.

I'm not so sure this is a great idea anymore.

We head toward the matted room without saying anything, tension along for the tour. (Sexual tension, if you were wondering.) I hold open the door and wave her in, following behind as we step inside so I can check out her ass in those shorts. *Hey, I'm a guy.* Marissa stops short and I have to stifle the groan that threatens to fly from my mouth when I spy the reason. Staci is there, sitting on a bench with her legs spread, stretching from side to side.

Okay, let's talk for a moment.

Typically, the guy brain attached to my cock would have noticed. Hell, old Rhenn would probably already be fucking her on that very bench she sits on. But right now, all I want is for her to disappear so I can have an hour with Marissa to demonstrate a few self-defense moves.

Disturbing thought, considering just a few weeks ago, I let my little head make all of my decisions. Right now, little head is definitely hoping to sneak a few peeks of whatever bra Marissa is wearing underneath that tank top or maybe even brush against her ass as I hold her against my body to show her how to escape a perpetrator.

Nowhere in all of my daydreams is Staci present. Old Rhenn, hell yes! Threesome? Sign him up! But new Rhenn? This weird guy who entertains thoughts of a (whispers…relationship), well, he just wants to enjoy a little time with the woman who has piqued his interest and invaded his dreams.

"Staci, I wasn't expecting you to be here," I say casually, yet feeling anything but.

"Well, I thought that since you were offering private workouts, I'd see if you had time for one more," she replies, batting those eyelashes and arching her chest forward. It's not cold in here, but her nipples strain against the sports bra she's wearing.

Running my hand over the top of my head, I try to figure out how in the hell to get myself out of this situation. Never have I led Staci to think I was interested in any one-on-one anything, but here I am, dumbfounded for probably the first time in my adult life, and trying to figure out how to get myself out of an awkward and unwanted situation.

"Actually, Staci, now isn't really a good time. I only had budgeted a little time with Marissa, and then I have friends coming in later. Maybe another time," I offer, though wish I wouldn't have. Especially when I see her eyes light up in anticipation and feel Marissa tense beside me.

Fuck. I'm jacking this up good.

"Sure thing, Rhenny," Staci replies, her bright white teeth a contrast to the dark red on her lips. I cringe when the familiar nickname spills from her lips. I hate that damn nickname. Ninety-eight percent of the women I've screwed have called me by that fucking name, like turning it into some cutesy baby name is somehow appropriate. Most of the time I haven't minded, especially because I wasn't with them for their ability to use adult words.

Feeling like an utter ass, I hold completely still as Staci comes over and places her hands on my chest. I stop breathing when she moves in, her expensive perfume wrapping around me entire body and squeezing it to death, as she places her lips on my cheek. It feels familiar, but unwanted. There's only one set of lips I want on my body, and it's not Staci's.

She pulls back and gives me a wink before flitting away, a wide swing to her hourglass hips. I don't intentionally watch her go, at least not for the reason you may think. It's more of that shell-shocked, completely beside myself, what the fuck am I supposed to do now? kinda reasons.

When the door closes behind her, I risk a glance at Marissa.

And I wish I hadn't.

Her eyes are cast downward, but I can feel the sadness and resolution settle between us. I've never thought Marissa to be weak. She doesn't appear to be a woman who will roll over and let someone walk over her. I've seen that spunky side, with her sassy comebacks and her quick wit. But I don't see any of that now. I see a woman who finds herself second-best – and probably not for the first time either. Someone who has been compared to someone else and found lacking.

And that instantly pisses me off.

Because Marissa Grayson is the most remarkable woman I've ever met. This I can tell after only knowing her mere days – a week. She's beautiful, inside and out, and has the biggest heart of anyone I've ever met. Shit, I've never cared to see past the big hair and fake tits before, but here I am, craving to get to know someone better, to catch glimpses of the person she hides deep down from the rest of the world.

Longing for the Marissa who walked into the room, I step forward and place my finger on her chin. Without any quick movements, I raise her head and find sadness in her green eyes. This very look steals my breath and rocks me down to my core.

"Hey, you ready?" I ask, shooting for light and easy, but fearing I come across a bit too aloof.

"Yes, of course," she replies with a fake smile that I recognize immediately. "I don't want to keep you too long. You have other plans," she adds with a friendly punch to my arm. A fucking punch, like friends shooting the shit.

We might be *friends*, but the things I'm envisioning doing to her are anything but *friendly*.

Dirty. Erotic. Fan-fucking-tastic. That's what I'd describe all of the things I want to do. With her. To her.

Fuck, now I'm hard.

Locking my gaze on hers, I say the words that I know she needs to hear – the words I need to say. "I don't have any other plans except the ones I made with you." I make sure to put as much conviction as I can behind them, knowing that for some reason, this woman feels like she's so easily dismissed. Second-best.

I fucking hate it.

Determined to put her mind at ease, I step over to the bench and drop my bag. I'm already dressed for our private lesson, so there's nothing I need to get ready for our first class. "Usually, I'd have my Karate Gi, but I didn't think I'd need to bring it with me. This isn't a formal class, just a friend teaching a friend how to defend herself."

When I turn around, her eyes are staring at my legs. At first, I think they're just cast downward because of what happened earlier with Staci, but I realize quickly that's not the case. Her green eyes are wide, her pupils dilated, and a look I'm all too familiar with crosses her face. It's desire. Hunger. Longing.

My dick twitches in my pants, a reminder of how badly I want this woman, and considering the fact I'm about to have my hands all over her, I think it's safe to say she'll be well aware of that tidbit of information very quickly.

"Ready?" I ask, my own voice a little shaky and husky.

"I think so," she replies, her eyes meeting mine, filled with excitement and anxiety.

"We'll start easy. There are a few moves every woman should know. They're simple ways to immobilize an assailant, hopefully giving you the precious seconds you'd need to get away," I say, standing directly in front of her. She's so fucking small compared to me. I swear I'm about a foot taller, and much broader than her petite body.

"This first move is the open hand strike. Use the heel of your hand to strike your assailant's most sensitive areas," I state, grabbing her hand and showing her the move. I bring it up to my face. "Eyes, nose, mouth, or neck." She demonstrates the motion without connecting with my face, and practices the move a few times before offering me a warm smile.

That smile goes straight to my heart, which is pounding so hard I think even the weightlifters can hear it in the main part of the gym over the heavy metal bass pumping through their earbuds. "Good, now for this next one, you use your elbow. If needed, it could help buy you some precious seconds when dealing with an attacker. Use it to strike the face, neck, or stomach as hard as you can," I tell her, demonstrating a few hard elbow thrusts.

Marissa repeats the move, her elbow gently connecting with my stomach. "Sorry," she says, turning quickly, her wide eyes full of concern.

"You're fine. You didn't hurt me," I assure, moving so that she faces me. "Now, this one is important. Knee to the groin. Painful as fuck and will drop a man faster than you can say freedom."

She offers me a shy smile before dropping her eyes downward. My dick – as if it knows she's looking at him – starts to wave hello from my shorts. "Should we practice?" she asks, a teasing glint in her sparkly eyes.

"Definitely not. I've taken a few shots in my day, and it's not something I'm looking to repeat anytime soon."

"You have?" she asks, shocked.

"I have," I confirm. "One of the students I was working with got a little carried away. He hauled off and punch me square in the nads."

"During practice?" she asks, her eyes dropping to my shorts once more. I just pray my cock isn't standing at complete attention at this moment.

Rubbing the back of my neck, I feel a slight blush creep in. Yep, I actually fucking blush. "Uhhh, no. I was sneaking out of his mom's bedroom."

Realization sets in and Marissa begins to blush as well. "Oh."

"Yeah, not one of my finest moments," I confirm, looking to get this lesson back on track. And quick. "Why don't we try a few situations? You can practice your new moves."

"All but the blow to the balls?" she teases.

All I heard was blow and balls.

"Yeah, without that." Turning around, I will my cock into submission. The last thing I need is to walk up with a hard-on and scare her off. We're supposed to be working on self-defense, not scarring her for life because her instructor is thinking about nothing else but banging her.

"What do I do?" she asks, jumping a little when I suddenly advance. Wrapping my arms around her waist, I pull her toward the center of the mat.

Just as I'm about to tell her to fight me off, I feel her tiny body twist in my arms and almost disappear moments before I take a shot to my face. "Fuck," I mumble, staggering back a step.

"Holy shit!" she exclaims, running toward me. My hand is covering my nose and lip, the faintest taste of blood fills my mouth.

"Holy shit," I reply as she grabs my hand, moving it out of the way, and touches my split lip. "You're supposed to be running away, not tending to your assailant's wounds, Marissa," I chastise, though secretly loving the fact that she's doctoring up a fat lip.

"I hit you," she groans.

"Yes, and you were supposed to."

"But I didn't realize I was actually going to hit you. You were supposed to…block it or something!"

"I'm fine, Marissa. Not the first shot I've taken," I reassure her, grabbing her hands and holding them at her side.

It's right then and there, I realize how incredibly close we're standing. We're practically chest-to-chest, and even though she's much shorter than I am, the position feels natural and so fucking amazing. All I want to do is wrap my arms around her waist and pull her flush against me. Maybe even feel her legs wrap around my back moments before I kiss the hell out of her.

But the tender throbbing in my lip lets me know there won't be any kissing anytime soon. At least not right now.

We spend the next thirty minutes going over a few moves. I've taught karate and self-defense classes for ten years, and in all of that time, I've never had as much fun as I do with Marissa. She's attentive and quick to learn. She asks questions when I'm explaining a series of movements or stances. She teases me here and there, offering a shy and innocent grin that I think is the sexiest thing I've ever seen.

When our time is up, I grab my bag and reach for her hand. I don't know why, other than I want to feel her skin against mine. She doesn't pull away – which surprises me a bit, considering there really isn't a reason for me to hold it – so I make no sudden movements to keep from spooking her. I lead her out of the room we used, past the wall of treadmills, by the front desk where Staci beams from her stool, and right out the front door. I don't stop until I'm at the parking lot beside the gym.

Glancing around, I have no idea which car is hers. "Over there," she says, pointing to a used Chevy Malibu at the edge of the lot.

When we reach the car, she opens the back door and drops her small bag inside. She turns to face me, my heart starting to pound a strong beat in my chest. Our eyes remain locked, our fingers entwined, and I decide to make a move. I know it's a bad idea. Hell, I've talked myself out of this exact situation a dozen times since I met her.

But right here, right now? With her fingers linked with mine?

I just don't fucking have it in me to push her away.

Stepping into her personal space, I pin her body between mine and her car. I release her fingers, but only long enough to bring my hands to her face and thread them into her hair. Her breath catches and her wide eyes lock on mine. There's a bit of nervousness there, but that's not the emotion that dominates. Oh no, that's excitement. She's trying to decide which side of the fence she wants to play on: the safe side or the dangerous one.

All it would take is one little kiss to convince her, but that's not what I want. I don't want any regrets filtering through that pretty little mind of hers. I want her to be all-in, go balls to the wall, and give as good as she gets.

When her tongue slips out and wets her lips, I have my answer. It takes balls of steel not to bend down and take. Take her mouth in a bruising kiss. Take her in my arms and possess her. Take everything she wants to give and push her to her limits.

But I don't.

Jesus, as bad as I want to, I don't take.

Instead, I savor.

Keeping my eyes open until the last possible second, I witness the way her eyes dilate right before they close. I see the way she inhales deeply and holds her breath. I know the moment I won't ever be the same again, and it's right now, the second my lips touch hers.

This kiss is gentle, yet anything but innocent. She wastes no time opening her mouth for me, allowing my tongue to slide inside and taste her for the first time. I'm immediately hypnotized. I know it won't matter how many times I have my mouth on her, it will never be enough.

I feel her hands on my back, gripping at my shirt, and as badly as I want to, I muster up every ounce of willpower I have to keep from deepening this kiss. It would be too easy to get caught up in the moment, to throw her on the hood, and make her come ten ways to Sunday. But I won't. Not today.

Instead, I let my lips savor her taste, her feel, for a few more seconds before reluctantly pulling away. Her eyes remain closed, but her mouth is open, wet and swollen from my kiss. Her breathing is a light pant that fans across my face, those little puffs of air calling to me for more. Yet, I don't.

"Meghan and Nick will be here soon. You're having dinner with your family, right?"

Her eyes finally open, glossy and a bit out of focus. "Yes," she whispers.

"Will you still go out on the boat with us tomorrow? If you pack a light bag, we can stay out tomorrow night too." She starts to give me a look, and I realize how that probably sounded. "You can have my make-shift bed. I'll sleep on deck in a chair."

"I can't do that," she argues.

"I'm giving Nick and Meghan the master bedroom. There's a sofa that turns into a bed downstairs, kinda like a futon, and it's yours. I can take a chair."

Can I just stop you right there? Did you catch what I just said?

It's official. That's the first time I've invited a woman to my boat and offered to sleep in the fucking chair. This just proves my point, my brain isn't firing on all cylinders at the moment. There's a huge disconnect, and it's probably from lack of sex. But something tells me jumping into bed with her right out of the gate, while completely satisfying, would kill the progress I've made in whatever this is.

And I still have no clue what the hell *this* is.

"That still doesn't seem right, Rhenn. You're the owner of the boat and you'd be sleeping in a chair."

Sliding my hands down her sides, I feel her shudder under my touch. "Then maybe you'll just have to share the other bed with me," I reply with a low, husky voice. The last thing I want is to scare her off, but sometimes, old Rhenn rears his ugly head and I just can't hold back on the come-ons.

Marissa stares up at me for a few seconds. It bothers me that I don't know what she's thinking. She's probably about to slap me. That's what I'd do if I were her. Instead, she throws me completely off balance when she replies, "Maybe I will."

And just like that, my brain short-circuits and nearly explodes. Unable to speak words (and I'm never one for lacking those, especially in the company of a beautiful woman), I watch as she turns in my arms and reaches for her car door. I take a step back, still trying to process what she said, as she slips inside her car and cranks the engine. Before she starts to back out of the parking spot, the window rolls down. "Dinner's at five, Rhenn. Be there," she says before throwing me a wink and backing out of the spot.

I watch her go, still trying to figure out how in the hell I went from kissing her and insinuating we could share a bed, to completely giving her the upper hand. That's never happened before. Ever. And do you know what?

I fucking love it.

Chapter Nine

Marissa

Everyone is here as we watch the car pull onto the lane and toward the house. Samuel, Jensen and his son, Max, Harper, Mom, and I all wait on the porch for Meghan to arrive. What we weren't expecting was the second car that follows.

"I thought only Meghan and Nick were coming?" Harper asks as both vehicles pull off the lane and park in front of the garage.

"I thought so too," Mom replies, taking the steps down to meet our guests.

A woman gets out of the driver's seat in the first car, followed by another young couple with a baby. When the doors to the second car open, I see an older man and woman emerge from the front, followed quickly by the elderly couple that I now know to be my mom's brother and sister-in-law.

"What a pleasant surprise," Mom says as she approaches her brother and his wife.

"You didn't think I was going to let Meggy come here without tagging along, did you?" Emma asks, pulling Mom into a big hug.

I start to make my way down the stairs, my siblings hot on my heels. We join the small group and introductions begin immediately. "These are my children," Mom starts, making a gesture to each of us. "Samuel and Jensen. My daughters, Harper and Marissa. And this little guy is my grandson, Max," Mom says with love in her voice as she ruffles Max's full head of thick hair.

"Lovely to see you again," Emma says, taking the lead.

"This is our son-in-law, Brian, and his lady friend, Cindy," Emma starts. Instantly I recall hearing that Emma and Orval's daughter, Trisha, passed away from ovarian cancer when the girls were younger. Brian was her husband and with the help of Emma and Orval, raised his six daughters.

"Pleasure to finally meet you," Brian says to Mom, stepping up and giving her a warm hug.

"And these are a couple of my granddaughters. This is Meghan, who's wedding your mom attended earlier this month. Nick, her hunky dentist husband, is on his way in the sailboat. He should be here in another hour or so," Emma states. I notice immediately how Meghan blushes and shakes her head when her grandmother refers to her husband as hunky. Personally, I would have probably died from embarrassment, but after only spending a very short time with Emma, I know that this is just how she is.

"And this is AJ and Sexy Randall. You might remember him from his Playgirl spread a few years back," Emma coos, stepping closer to me, since I'm directly across from her. "That photo gave me wet dreams for days."

"Grandma," AJ groans. "Stop being dirty in front of new family."

"It's the truth! Don't tell me you didn't tickle the piano keys late at night when I showed you that photo, Alison Jane," Emma chastises, causing my sister Harper to giggle and my brother Samuel to look like he's about to stroke out.

"My husband can just be called Sawyer, not Sexy Randall," AJ says as she steps forward and shakes Samuel's hand. "No need to stroke that ego."

"As in *the* Sawyer Randall?" Jensen asks, his baseball-loving ears already piqued.

"That's me, but it was a while ago. Now I teach junior high adolescents all about physical education and listen to them complain about having to detach from the cell phones for an hour," Sawyer replies, juggling the baby boy in his arms to shake Jensen's hand.

"Pleasure to meet you," my brother replies, moving his own son so that he can shake the former pro baller's hand. "My son, Max, is about to start his first year of T-ball. He loves baseball."

"Yeah? Maybe we can throw the ball around later. Would that be okay, Max?" Sawyer asks, instantly taking a liking to my nephew. Max doesn't reply, but promptly nods his head in agreement. "Great."

"And this little cookie is my great-grandson, Nolan. Named after Nolan Ryan," she says, making AJ turn a deep shade of red in annoyance. Sawyer chuckles before he pulls her into his arms and kisses her forehead. Yeah, there's definitely a story there.

"Well, let's go around back," Mom says. She instantly starts telling the newcomers about the house, the property, and the history of the bed and breakfast. Normally, I'd be up there with her, filling in all of the gaps and sharing my favorite tidbits of details, but right now, all I can think about is the food situation. When I was preparing tonight's dinner, it was under the assumption that we'd have nine in attendance. Now, with sixteen mouths to feed, I'm not sure I planned enough.

"Everything all right?" Harper whispers when we reach the sitting area around back.

"I don't have enough food," I confide quietly.

"How is that possible? You're always prepared to feed an army."

"Well, with the power still out, I only have a portion of my refrigerator and freezer space."

"So run to the store," she says, as if it were no big deal.

My mind flashes through recipes, trying to figure out which ones I can make quickly and easily. I settle on a cucumber salad, fresh fruit, and the homemade deviled egg salad with avocado slices. Before I can ask my sister for her keys, since my car is now blocked in, my phone chimes in my pocket. My heart starts to skip around in my chest when I see the name on the screen.

Rhenn: *Do you want me to bring anything?*

My fingers fly over the letters and I fire off a reply before I can contemplate the consequences of my actions.

Me: *Yes! Come get me! We need to go to the store!!!*

Rhenn: *Three exclamation points? This must be a dire food emergency!!!*

Me: *Hurry! We have to go shopping.*

Rhenn: *I hate shopping.*

Me: *Me too, but I don't have a choice. I need more food.*

Rhenn: *Then more food you shall get, my lady. I'll be there in five.*

Me: *I could kiss you.*

Rhenn: *I like the sound of that. Do I receive my reward before or after the store?*

Me: *It was rhetorical. I'm not actually going to kiss you.*

My face flames with embarrassment. I can't believe I said that.

Rhenn: *Pity. I distinctly recall how wonderful it is to kiss you.*

I stare at the screen, having no clue how to reply. Or if I should. I definitely shouldn't. Hell, I shouldn't have even mentioned the "k" word, even in general passing. Mostly because I'm not sure that our shared kiss was a smart move. Okay, I'm pretty sure it wasn't. We do have to work together, you know. But mostly because I can't stop thinking about it. Or reliving it. My lips still tingle. My jaw still aches from his whiskers. My skin still burns from his fingers.

"Are you sure you're all right? You're all flushed and panting."

"What? I'm fine," I reply to my sister, clearing my throat and straightening my back. I thrust all thoughts of Rhenn out of my mind like they're hot and get down to business. Food. I need more food for dinner.

And Rhenn is going to help me…

I groan in frustration before I can even reel it back in.

Harper reaches forward and places the back of her hand on my forehead. "Stop it," I say, swatting her hand away.

"You're not fevered," she says just as Rhenn comes strutting around the corner.

"Ready to go?" he asks.

Harper looks between him and me, a knowing smile spreading wide across her face. "Now I get it."

"Shut up."

"You called Rhenn," she singsongs.

"Zip it," I hiss.

"He's going to help you."

"Enough."

"Even though you could have asked me to go…" she starts, but I grab her arm and pull her aside.

"Fine, yes, I asked Rhenn to help me. Stop making a big deal of this," I beg.

"Making a big deal of what? The fact that you asked a hot guy to help you? A hot guy who clearly likes you, even though you refuse to see or acknowledge it?"

"Why are you torturing me?"

"Me? I'm not. You're torturing yourself by refusing to see that the man is totally into you."

"I'm not...refusing to see it. I see it, okay? Hell, I felt it when he kissed me."

Harper gasps dramatically and smiles. "Seriously? You've been holding out on me? He kissed you?"

"Yes, now can we stop talking about this? He's standing like five feet away and can probably hear us."

"Oh, he can definitely hear you," Rhenn replies. "Your whispering skills could use a little work."

Kill. Me. Now.

"Well, since you two have an *errand* to run, I'll let you get to it," Harper says, offering me a wink before slapping Rhenn on the back. She leans in and whispers something in his ear, making him bark out a laugh, before walking away to join our family.

"Ready? My truck is running."

"What did she say to you?" I ask without moving a muscle.

"None of your business," he sasses with a smirk and a wink. That damn smirk. I hate it, yet it turns my panties into useless scraps of lace.

I also ignore the excitement that races through my blood as he reaches over and grabs my hand. He's probably just being gentlemanly. You know, like guiding me through the yard, around all of the construction remnants and potholes so I don't trip. I'm sure it has absolutely nothing to do with attraction and desire.

Rhenn's work truck is big and tall, and I almost need a running start to leap up into the monster. Instead, before I can spring into action, I feel his hands wrap around my waist. I feel his body as it comes in close behind me. I feel the sexual tension engulf me, almost as if it were its own living, breathing thing. "Up you go," he whispers, as he gently lifts me into the air as if I weigh nothing.

There's a slight tremble in my hands as I reach for the seat belt and try to secure it in place. Not because I'm worried about being alone with Rhenn – well, not unless you consider the fact that I wouldn't mind more kisses as being a worry. Because kissing Rhenn was definitely a bad idea and should definitely not happen again.

Even if I really, really want it to.

There's nothing between us except a little sizzle and spark. Attraction. But at the end of the day, I'll go my way and he'll go his. At least we will when he completes this job. That doesn't stop the disappointment from rearing its ugly head when I think about it. Even if I know that kissing him again would be bad (a very nice bad), I know it's not smart. It doesn't fall in line with what I see for myself in the next few years.

But damn, would it be a nice distraction.

And that's what Rhenn is: a distraction. Instead of looking forward, toward the bed and breakfast and the plans I have when I finally take it over, I keep finding myself glancing to the side. To him. But his presence is only temporary, I keep telling myself.

"So tell me about your friends. Meghan seems great," I say, breaking through the haze of desire that swirls around inside the too-small truck cab.

"They're the best," Rhenn says, pulling his truck onto the road that leads to town. "I met Nick back in grade school when he was a short little skinny kid. He was being picked on and I stepped in. We've been inseparable ever since.

"He met Meghan when he came back to town after dental school. She worked at the office he eventually took over. It wasn't an instant spark, considering she was with another guy. He died in a car accident a few years back and it was hell on her," he says, confirming what I had already gathered.

"That's horrible."

"It was, but eventually, after a couple of years, she started seeing Nick. It was a slow burn kinda thing, but as you can see, the rest is history."

"I'm glad she found love again. I couldn't imagine what she went through," I say absently, my stomach churning as I picture my sweet cousin struggling to get through her days.

"They went through it together and came out stronger on the other side."

"That's very astute of you, Mr. Burleski."

"I have my moments," he quips with a side grin. "What about you? What's with the rush for more food?"

"We weren't expecting as many to show up today. Not that I'm complaining, because I'm not. It's nice to finally meet more of the family we've been hearing about. Brian and Cindy seem great, and I think my brother Jensen was foaming at the mouth to meet Sawyer," I say with a giggle, recalling how starstruck my brother was to meet the former major leaguer.

"They're solid people. I knew Brian and the girls from around town, but didn't really get to know them well until Nick started hanging out with his hygienist. The grandparents are a hoot. I think I've heard them talk about sex more than I did when I was living in the frat house in college," he says, making me laugh.

"I'm learning that real quick. When we met them, Aunt Emma patted Jensen's ass. I think Samuel's head almost exploded," I reply with a laugh.

"Oh, she's a feisty one. Just wait," he says, and something tells me there's definitely more to come where Emma and Orval are concerned.

"Well, I'm happy they're here. I know my mom really appreciates it, and it makes me smile that she's getting to know her brother and his family. I just wish it wouldn't have taken them so long to reconnect, you know?"

"Definitely."

"They were making plans to have us come to Jupiter Bay for the Fourth of July," I add.

"You'll love it there. Brian's house actually reminds me a bit of your place. It's off the beaten path, kinda off by itself on a little strip of land."

"I can't wait to see it all – and meet the rest of the family."

Before I realize it, we're already pulling into the parking lot of the grocery store. We spent the entire ten-minute ride to town talking, as if it were the most natural, easiest thing in the world. That's completely not like me – if my previous relationships are any indication. I've always been more reserved, a bit shy, and never quick to share personal information. But here I am, sharing my family details with Rhenn – a man that I've literally known for six days.

As soon as the truck is parked, Rhenn jumps out and comes around to my side. No, I don't really need help getting down, but I don't decline his assistance when he reaches up and grabs my waist. In fact, I actually relish the feel of his hands on me once more and the way his arms flex under his tight green shirt.

"Ready?" he asks as he locks the truck and reaches for my hand. I don't fight it, I just go with it, and place my smaller hand inside of his much larger one.

We walk inside and grab a cart. I don't have that much on my mental shopping list, but it's enough that it would weigh down both of our arms. Plus, then I'd have to drop his hand, and frankly, I just don't want to.

Together, we head down the first aisle. Living in a small town where everyone knows everybody, I shouldn't be surprised by the amount of familiar faces I immediately see, yet I am. I guess I just thought Rhenn and I could exist in our own private little bubble, where we can hold hands without the watchful eyes of my neighbors. No such luck. The first person we come to is the town gossip, Mrs. Freeman. Her knowing little eyes lock on our hands instantly, her bright red lips turn upward in a huge smile. I can practically see the text message she's already sending to everyone in her contact list.

I greet the nosy busybody with a hello as we reach the produce aisle, and even though I don't want to, I drop Rhenn's hand. I tell myself it's because I'll need both of mine to grab the vegetables I need, but a part of me knows that I'm trying to diminish the rumors before they even start. Though, I'm not sure just dropping his hand will help. The fact that I'm here at all with him is enough to ignite the gossips in town. If they don't know the facts, they'll come up with their own conclusions.

Reaching for a bag, I start to squeeze avocados. "What can I get?" he asks as I place three greenish brown avocados in my bag.

"Can you grab six cucumbers?" I ask absently as I reach for another bag to grab a few peppers.

I throw a red and yellow pepper into the cart and turn to find Rhenn. He's standing across the aisle, holding up two large cucumbers, a devious glint in his blue eyes. "Angel, do you like them long and straight or more girthy with a slight curve to the end, like this one?" he asks innocently, yet his insinuation is anything but. A gasp sounds next to me and I see nosy Mrs. Freeman standing there, her eyes dancing as she looks on between the proffered vegetables and my wide eyes and flushed face. "And why do you need six? One cucumber isn't enough to satisfy your needs?"

I swear to all things holy, I'm going to kill him. Right here, in the produce aisle at Family Foods.

My face burns, but I try to keep from tucking my chin and crawling away. Instead of hiding, I turn to face him and raise my chin. "Actually, I have yet to find a single cucumber that is both satisfying and filling," I reply with a shrug, reaching around him and grabbing the first six cucumbers I can reach.

Rhenn chuckles behind me, dropping his loot into the bag. I feel his warm breath graze the shell of my ear as he whispers, "Maybe you just haven't found the right cucumber yet."

Why my body shutters, I have no idea. Okay, total lie. I know why, and he's standing with his front practically plastered to my back, making it damn near impossible to formulate a complete thought. How can my body crave something – or someone – it doesn't even know?

He whispers against my ear and I have to bite back the moan. "What else is on that magical list of yours, Angel?"

The amount of time it actually takes me to speak is embarrassing, so when I finally am able to say words, it shouldn't surprise me that it's something as graceful as what comes from my lips. "Fruit. I need fruit. And eggs. Lots of eggs."

Holding completely still, I feel his breath move down from my ear to my shoulder. Another shiver sweeps through as his nose faintly traces the column of my neck. It must be uncomfortable for him, considering he's so much taller than me, but I can't seem to find the urge to really care. Instead, my brain focuses on his breathing, the slightest touch of his nose, and the way he inhales deeply, as if committing my scent to memory. "You smell like jasmine. I like it."

Jesus, Mary, and Joseph, this man has the ability to render me completely speechless and utterly wanton in less than a half-second flat. I still can't speak.

"Come on, Angel. Let's get you some eggs and fruit. Then, we'll head back and you can show me how you plan to use those cucumbers," he adds, placing an open-mouthed kiss on my exposed collarbone and leaving me a pile of mush right there in the middle of the produce aisle and lusting after a man I shouldn't want.

But do.

Chapter Ten

Rhenn

This is weird in a completely domesticated sort of way.

I'm standing beside Marissa in her tiny kitchen as she prepares the extra dishes for dinner. She's humming a song I don't know, and from time to time, will add in a little hip shake. The woman is entirely in a zone as she whips through the hardboiled deviled egg salad by heart, without once looking at a recipe. That prospect alone completely blows my mind. My mom was an average cook, but she always had to look at a card or book for the instructions. But Marissa? It's like she's using some old family recipe that she keeps stored in a mental file.

It's impressive as hell.

Without saying a word, she hands me a knife and points to the bag of cucumbers. "You want me to cut them? There's no worse fate for a…cucumber."

"You can handle it, big boy," she sasses as she continues to dice the eggs.

So here I am, washing and cutting cucumbers for a salad. Like a homemade one. One I didn't order from a deli or restaurant. Careful, the sky might fall.

I make my first cut and the tip flies across the counter. By the time I have my knife ready and my hand positioned so I don't chop off a finger, Marissa has already cut another egg. She's a magician with a blade, and for some crazy reason, it kinda turns me on. I keep at it, making slow and calculated cuts with my knife, until I've finally sliced the entire first vegetable. When I glance over, she has her egg and avocado salad completely put together and is reaching for the cantaloupe.

"I can't believe how fast you are with that thing," I say, using my knife to point at hers.

She offers me a small smile. "I use one a lot. I do a ton of cutting and chopping for the bed and breakfast."

I keep one eye on what I'm doing and one eye on the beauty beside me. "You're stunning, but when you're working in the kitchen, in your element, you're incredibly beautiful." She doesn't respond, but I can feel her eyes on me. When I glance her way, she's giving me an incredulous look. "What? You don't believe me?" I ask, setting my knife down and turning to face her.

"Uhh, no," she replies with an uncomfortable chuckle, as if to blow off my statement. She turns back to her chopping, but not before I see the sexy blush creep up her cheeks.

Placing my hand on top of hers to keep from one of us losing a finger, I help her set the knife aside and turn her to face me. My fingers itch to touch her smooth skin, but I know as soon as I do, I won't be able to stop. So instead, I place my hand on her hip and pull her close. A strand of hair falls forward, and I can't stop myself from taking that strand in my hand. It feels smooth and silky and smells like flowers. "I don't know who hurt you, but he deserves to have his ass kicked."

I mean the words, even though they bite. They bite because I've been that asshole. I'm the guy who loves 'em and leaves 'em. That's all I know. Well, that's not technically true, but that's all I've convinced myself I could have. Relationships lead to pain and regret, but if I were going to give up my bed-hopping ways, it would be for a woman just like Marissa.

"He's not worth the energy," she replies with a smile, making my own lips curl upward.

"You've got that right, Angel. Now, how about we finish off these dishes so I can throw the chicken on the grill?" I ask, placing a kiss on her forehead and taking a step back. I definitely need a little space.

"You grill?" she asks, glancing at me over her shoulder as she finishes cutting the fruit.

"I'm a man. Of course I grill. It's in my DNA."

"But I thought you didn't cook." She places the final bowl in the fridge, rearranging a few containers so that the last two will fit.

"I don't, but that doesn't mean I can't throw a thick, juicy steak on the barbeque."

"We're having chicken," she sasses, crossing her arms and resting her hip against the counter across from me.

"Easy peasy."

Her eyebrow rises as she tries to decide if she believes me or not. The truth is, I'm a whiz on the grill. Hell, I've barely ever turned on the stove, but my grill gets regular use. Throw a slab of meat on, take one of the side dishes out of the fridge that I picked up at the deli, and you've got a meal. That's the only way I eat, if it's not ordered out. Well, that and cereal dinners. I hate to admit how many of those bad boys I've consumed since graduating high school, but it's a lot. Lucky Charms are my favorite, and I only have to spend an extra ten minutes on the treadmill to make up for my lack of a nutritious dinner the night before.

Totally worth it though.

"Trust me, Angel. I got this," I confirm, placing another kiss on her forehead as the door opens.

"Aww, did I catch you two neckin' in the kitchen? You know, tabletop sex is some of the best sex around. There's just something about doing the dirty where you ate your Cheerios this morning," Emma says as she sweeps into the room.

"We're not…"

"Well, not yet, darling. You're both still clothed. And I do admit, I'm a little bummed I arrived too early at the party. I've been dying to see the bare ass on this one since that self-defense class he taught. My loins were burning for hours, if you know what I mean," Emma coos to Marissa, making her cheeks fire-engine red.

I can practically feel the heat from Marissa's blush from a foot away. While I'm used to Emma's brand of sexual humor, her niece beside me isn't, and I'm pretty sure she wants to crawl in a hole right now and hide. I, on the other hand, want to talk more about this table sex…

"I'll go light the grill," I reply, whistling as I head out the door Emma just entered through.

Outside, the sun is shining and the birds are chirping. Orval is over with his sister, son-in-law, and Cindy, Sawyer is playing catch with Max and Jensen, and Harper and AJ are deep in conversation. Samuel appears to be off by himself, his stoic and rigid posture just taking it all in. Who I don't see is Meghan and Nick.

I'm pretty sure I don't want to know what they're off doing…

As soon as he arrived in my boat, I met him on the dock and went to check *her* out. Yes, I trust my friend, but yes, I needed to see with my own eyes that *she* was fine. Besides, his wife was anxious to get to him too, considering it had been a whole five hours since they last laid eyes on each other.

On the back deck of the bed and breakfast, I find two grills. A large pit-style charcoal grill and a massive gas grill. Since Marissa is almost ready with the sides, I opt to light the gas one. It'll only take a fraction of the time to heat up and we'll be eating before the coals would be ready with the charcoal unit.

"Need some help?" Samuel asks as he approaches me.

"Sure. Marissa's working on the sides, so I thought I'd get this thing ready for the chicken," I reply as I fire up all eight burners.

"She's letting you grill?" Samuel asks, his face showing as much shock as I picked up in his voice.

"That's surprising?" I ask, turning to face him.

"Well, yeah. She won't let any of us cook, even to man the grill. She's a bit territorial when it comes to the kitchen," he says, the faintest smile crossing his lips. The man rarely smiles, so I'll take this as a positive sign.

"Huh, she didn't argue with me when I told her I was coming out to light the grill. Though, I did leave her in the kitchen with Emma. She probably wasn't thinking straight with all the talk about table sex," I add with a smile.

"That woman is nuts," Samuel says, almost absently.

"That she is, but she's also amazing and generous. Hell, the whole family is amazing. They'd do anything for anyone, without so much as a question. They all pretty much took me in as an additional family member when Meghan and Nick got together."

Samuel seems to consider my words, his eyes watching and reading me. It's a little unnerving, honestly, but I don't let it show. I've always been a bit too confident and definitely a little cocky, but when I'm being stared down by Samuel – Marissa's oldest brother – I feel my armor start to slip just a little. The truth is I *want* him to like me. I want him to approve of me, and that right there is a problem. I've never wanted or needed anyone's approval for anything. I'm me, and if you don't like it, tough shit.

He seems to relax just a little. Well, as much as an uptight man like him can relax. Hell, he's still wearing a suit. To a cookout with his family. On a Saturday evening. I take that as a good sign as

I turn my attention back to the grill. "So, you're from Jupiter Bay?" he asks, keeping his arms crossed over his chest.

"Yep, born and raised. My mom still lives there."

"Dad?" he asks, my insides twisting in a familiar pain.

Shrugging my shoulders casually, I reply, "Not sure. Haven't seen him in years."

He must sense there's a hell of a lot there that I have no intention of getting into right now. "No siblings?"

"None," I answer, scraping off the grill grates, even though they're already spotless.

"Lucky," he mumbles, turning to watch his brother throw his son in the air and spin him around like Superman.

"You don't like having siblings?" I ask, closing the lid and giving Samuel my full attention.

"No, I do. We're just so different. They do shit just to piss me off," Samuel states, taking a drink from his water bottle.

I can't help but laugh. "That's what siblings are for. They're supposed to be assholes."

Samuel grunts his reply and I don't miss the way his eyes light up with laughter as he watches his nephew giggle as he spins through the air. Even though he may complain about his younger siblings, something tells me Samuel wouldn't trade his brother and sisters for the world. "So what's going on with you and my sister?" he asks, causing me to drop the grate brush I was still holding in my hand.

"What do you mean?" I ask, suddenly feeling a little hot under the collar.

He shrugs. "I've noticed you looking at her." He doesn't say anymore and waits for me to pick up the conversation.

"She's beautiful," I state honestly. Shit, beautiful still doesn't seem like a strong enough adjective to describe Marissa. "I enjoy hanging out with her," I add, not wanting to get into too much detail with this man. Frankly, it's none of his business what happens (if anything) between Marissa and me, but because I want this guy – this family – to like me, for some crazy, foreign reason, I don't just tell him to fuck off like I normally would.

"You're leaving in a few weeks." It's not a question, but a reminder.

"I am."

He continues to stare at me, but I don't back down. I keep my eyes locked on his and just wait to see what his next move is. We're practically the same size heightwise, but I have him in muscle content. He's a lean guy, but that doesn't mean he's not fit. In fact, I can tell the dude works out a bit, probably just not to my level.

We're at a standoff, both of us sizing the other up, neither of us speaking. I still just can't get over the fact that I care what he thinks of me.

What the hell?

Finally, Samuel looks away. I watch him watch his youngest sister as she comes out of her tiny little house, laughing at something Emma says. "Just don't hurt her." His words are quiet – almost so quiet that I don't hear them – but the point is obvious.

"I won't," I find myself saying automatically.

The asshole in me usually doesn't care much about that. Typically, I don't stick around long enough to see if a woman is hurt or not. Hell, they know the score. I make it very clear what I'm offering before it even advances into the bedroom. I don't want a relationship. I don't want to cuddle or spoon. I want fun, between the sheets, and that's it. Sometimes, if we both agree, there may be a few more rounds of fun, but for the most part, I'm out before there's even a chance for emotions and feelings to get involved.

Fuck, I'm such an asshole.

My lifestyle slams into me like a fully loaded semi-truck, leaving me a whole lotta breathless and stunned. As I watch Samuel observe his siblings, I suddenly find myself sliding into his shoes. What the hell would I do if I found out some jackass was screwing my sister like that? One night of crazy sex and release. No chance of more afterward. No phone calls except to hook up. No compliments or accolades, except those that are said in the throes of passion.

It's a bitter pill to swallow.

I hate it.

Damn you, Samuel Grayson, for making me feel shit I don't want to feel, see things I don't want to see.

But do you know what? A zebra doesn't change its stripes. It is what it is, much like me. I am who I am and that has never been a problem before, so no reason to make it a problem now. Even though my gut burns with something that feels a bit like shame, I push it all aside.

I won't change for anyone.

"Hey," Nick joins the conversation, coming from the bed and breakfast with his wife. Her hair is delightfully mussed, a smug grin spread wide on my friend's face, and I can't help but laugh. "What?" he asks, the smile never leaving.

"Enjoy the tour?"

"Damn straight," he states proudly. I swallow back something that tastes a little like jealousy and offer my knuckles to my friend.

"I really don't want to know," Samuel says, his voice and face void of any sort of humor. "Not only is the house a walking safety hazard, with nails, screws, and treated lumber all over the place, but there's no conceivably soft or welcoming surface left in the place. What did you do? Take her against the wall?" He looks completely mortified.

"A cabinet, actually," Nick replies with a grin.

"That's barbaric," Samuel adds, trying to act like it doesn't bother him, but I can tell by the tightness around his eyes that he's not impressed with random sex against hard objects. It's as if the only way to bed a woman is in just that: a bed. He's clearly dating the wrong kinda women.

"I just hope you cleaned up your own mess. I don't want Marissa to find it and have to deal with it, since you're unable to keep it in your pants," I add, turning the grill temperature down.

"We're in the honeymoon phase. We're supposed to be screwing everywhere, all day long," Nick boasts.

"Good thing she's already knocked up, or it wouldn't take long," I say, watching his face contort to one of pure happiness. If I thought my friend was happy before, with just him and Meghan, that's nothing compared to what I see in his eyes and written all over his face at the mention of their unborn child.

"That's right, I heard you two were expecting. Congratulations," Samuel adds, reaching out his hand before realization sets in and he quickly pulls it back. "Never mind."

Nick and I both bust up laughing. "Yeah, I'm going to head inside and wash my hands," he replies with a wink before heading off to Marissa's place. They pass in the yard, her face lighting up with laughter as they exchange a few words before going about their business.

Marissa approaches with a large tray of chicken. She sets a jar of seasoning beside the grill and turns my way. "I can do it," she says, nervousness on her face. I can tell she's having a hard time relinquishing control of her barbeque, much like her brother said she would.

"I got it, Angel," I reply, leaning forward and placing a kiss on her forehead, not even caring that Samuel is still standing beside me. "Go enjoy a few minutes with your family."

She looks torn, but eventually nods her head. She gives her brother a smile before turning and walking over to where Harper and AJ are visiting. Marissa sits down beside them, the girls instantly pulling her into their conversation. It only takes a few seconds before she's leaning over and talking to the baby. Nolan is sitting on his mom's lap, wide awake and just taking it all in. When Marissa starts to speak, his arms start to wave wildly and his eyes light up with excitement.

I know the feeling.

Before long, AJ is passing the baby to her cousin, who gingerly holds the little boy. Her movements are a bit rigid at first, but it only takes her mere seconds to warm up to the baby in her arms. She's a natural, and for some reason, that thought makes me smile. For her. I smile for her because I can tell that someday, Marissa will make a killer mom.

My heart starts to pound and an ache spreads through my chest, and even though my brain is screaming at me to look away, I can't. I won't. Because I don't want to miss a single second of the happiness etched on her beautiful face. It only makes her glow that much more. She radiates sunshine and happiness, and for the life of me, I can't figure out why she was put in my path, at this particular time in my life. I'm more of the fly by the seat of your pants kinda guy, yet here I am, feeling the need to stop and smell the roses.

Or smell Marissa.

I could definitely get on board with more of that.

Maybe a little more kissing…

Meghan joins their little group, bends down and kisses her nephew's fuzzy little head, and takes an empty seat beside Harper.

Now, she really is glowing. I've heard that pregnancy makes women glow, and I always thought that was the biggest pile of shit. You know, a way to say you're still beautiful, even though you've been throwing up for days on end or have put on a little extra weight in the neck and cheeks. But looking at my best friend's wife, I know what it means for a woman to glow. She's stunning, and my best friend is a lucky bastard. He must agree, because when he comes back outside, he just stands there, off to the side, and watches her. He smiles softly, knowing that she's his for the rest of his life.

Again, that ache I try to ignore.

I throw the chicken on the grill and lightly season the meat. There's enough here to feed an army, which is good because I've seen the way the Summer family eats. Even though we've only got about half of them in attendance today, I know that a good chunk of food is going to be put away tonight.

While the meat begins to cook, my eyes return to Marissa – completely on their own, mind you. She's taking the bottle from AJ, leaning the baby back in her arms, and placing the food to his mouth. The little guy immediately starts to go to town on his bottle, holding it with one hand as if he's afraid she may pull it away. The other hand reaches up and grabs her hair. He doesn't seem to pull it, just holds it in his tiny hand. She glances down and smiles sweetly, my heart thundering in my chest.

I have to look away.

When I do, my eyes collide with Samuel's. They're staring straight through me, as if reading every thought filtering through my brain. I need to look away. For some reason, I can't stand the scrutiny, so I do, and instantly feel guilt. "Don't hurt her," he whispers again, just loud enough that I can hear him repeat his warning.

I open my mouth to confirm, once more, that I won't, but nothing comes out. For the first time in my life, I know I can't make that promise. I know that walking away from this woman won't be as easy as it was with every woman before her. So, instead, I nod my head and turn to face the grill. I flip the chicken and ignore the rapid-fire beat of my heart and the way my breath is caught in my throat when I saw her hold the baby.

Instead, I focus on the weather and the food and push those pesky unwanted sensations (the ones that feel a lot like emotions) out of my mind. This isn't me. It's this place, this town. That's gotta be it. Once I go back to Jupiter Bay, back to my life, I'll be back in the swing of things, if you know what I mean.

In the meantime, there's no reason why I shouldn't enjoy a little extra free time with Marissa, right?

Completely untangled, uncomplicated.

Easy.

Chapter Eleven

Marissa

The sun is starting to set, but this get-together is showing no signs of slowing down. We're still gathered in the backyard, bellies full of delicious food and enjoying each other's company. I can't believe how much I've loved this evening. I've gotten to know a big part of the family I never knew, and can already feel the bonds being formed.

Even though Rhenn is on the opposite side of the yard, I've secretly kept one eye on him most of the night. In fact, every time I glance his way, I either catch him looking at me or he busts me checking him out. At first, I was embarrassed, but now? Now, I don't care. Of course, he doesn't either. Rhenn is clearly used to being ogled, and why wouldn't he be? He is stunningly gorgeous for a man, with his bright blue eyes and extremely muscular physique. He probably makes nuns contemplate tossing away the habit.

And he can cook – or grill, actually. He wasn't so coordinated in the kitchen, but the man was a wiz on the grill. Even with my anxiety at a peak, he handled the massive amount of chicken breasts with the ease of a master chef who has been doing it half his life.

Breasts. *giggle snorts* He's obviously well versed in the way to handle those…

"What's so funny?" my sister asks as she sits down beside me in the swing.

"Nothing," I reply, covering up the blush that's burning up my neck.

We're quiet for a few seconds, both of us taking in the activity around the yard. Sawyer is playing catch with Max again, showing him how to scoop up the ball off the ground and fire it back before it even really touches his glove. Max's eyes are alive with excitement in a way I've never seen before from my four-year-old nephew. He's clearly eating up the attention and practice. Ever since Jensen and Ashley's divorce, I've barely seen the little guy smile, let alone let go and have fun the way he is today.

Mom is visiting with Meghan and Nick and Brian and Cindy, while Emma and Orval have Samuel cornered over by the firepit. If the look on my poor brother's face is any indication, I'd say he's getting an earful of inappropriate comments, much like we all have throughout the afternoon. They're definitely a not for the faint of heart – or in this case, my brother, Samuel.

My eyes seek him out once more. Rhenn is standing off by the firepit after just lighting the fire. He's not engaging in any conversation, but mostly just sitting back and observing. Actually, he's observing me. Our eyes connect once more from across the fire and I hate the way my heart skips a beat. I hate it because even if I wanted to act on this attraction I feel for him, I can't. He's leaving soon.

"You might want to close your mouth or everyone will see you drool." Harper's words break through the Rhenn-laced fog in my head. Her smile is all knowing and a bit smug, which only irritates me. Stupid sister. "You should just sleep with him and get it over with."

"What?" I gape, my jaw surely hanging down to my chest.

"Oh, you heard me. Don't be a ninny."

"A ninny?"

"Yeah. A pansy, a baby, a pussy."

"Don't say that." Again, cue the blush.

"What, pussy? That's my favorite P-word. Besides, it's not really a bad word anymore. Hell, I heard Uncle Orval use it about an hour ago," Harper says, trying not to laugh.

"Gross."

"Yeah, it was in the context you'd imagine too. I almost had to throw up," she says, taking a drink from her beer. "Anyway, let's talk about you sleeping with the hot electrician."

"I'm not sleeping with him," I defend.

"Not yet, but you should be."

Exhaling deeply, I close my eyes. "I can't, Harper. He's leaving in a of couple weeks."

"So?"

Turning her direction, I see she's completely serious. "Did you hear what I said? I can't just…sleep with him, Harper. He's L-E-A-V-I-N-G soon."

My sister turns in her seat and faces me. "You know, Riss, you *can* enjoy a little casual sex every now and then. Not all sex has to be in a relationship, despite what our parents taught us when we were thirteen."

That makes me snort. "Yeah, and look how well that turned out," I reply, referring to our cheating father.

"That must have fallen under the 'do as I say and not as I do' category," Harper practically growls. Our lives were completely disrupted and shattered when his affair came out. Hell, he wasn't even doing a good job at trying to hide it. You don't take a woman half your age to a rival's bed and breakfast in town; not when the bed and breakfast is owned by one of the town gossips.

I make a noise to let her know that I heard her. Talking about our dad and his lack of decorum when cheating on our mom isn't an easy topic for any of us. Especially since he's off touring the English countryside with his new bimbo wife. Not the one he cheated on Mom with, but the one he cheated on that young homewrecker with.

These are the days of our lives…

"Anyway, let's get back to the casual sex thing," she says, a bit too chipper as she tries to steer the conversation away from the landmine-filled one that centers on our dad.

"There is no casual sex thing, Harp. I can't do that. I'm not wired that way," I tell her honestly. All of the sex I've had has been within the boundaries of a committed relationship. I've never gone home with a guy, only to have him sneak out before daylight. I've never left in the morning under the assumption that it's only a single night of passion. Hell, I've never even kissed a guy that I wasn't on at least a second date with.

Until Rhenn.

"Well, maybe you should consider it a bit more. I'm not saying that's how you should approach all sex from here on out, but that guy is clearly into you. He can't take his eyes off you, and if you're not careful, you're going to get pregnant from the 'I want to fuck you' eyes he's throwing."

I gasp. My eyes fly to the other side of the yard, where Rhenn's are clearly focused solely on me. The look in his eyes? Lust. Pure unadulterated lust, and my body shudders involuntarily. I've known there was an attraction. Hell, I felt it pressed against me when he kissed me earlier outside the gym. But this? I'm not sure I'm prepared for this.

"Listen, Riss," Harper says, leaning in closer so no one can hear our conversation. "I'm not saying you should definitely do it – though, I really think you should – but I don't think you should completely count it out. Think about it. It's a short time, I know, but think of it as a summer affair. They happen all the time around here."

"But I'm not twenty anymore. Adults don't have summer affairs," I retort.

"Speak for yourself," Harper whispers with a smile. "Remember that guy who stayed at the B&B for a week last summer? The hot writer who was finishing up that novel?"

My eyes widen and my mouth hangs open. "Seriously?"

"Hell yeah," she giggles. "He was smoking hot. Remember?"

I gulp. "Yeah, I remember."

"Well, we ran into each other in town his first night here and got to talking," she says with a shrug.

"Talking?"

"Well, we talked…at first. Then, there wasn't much talking. He said I was good for his writing; helped him clear his head," she adds with another shrug. "All I'm saying is that sometimes, people come into our lives at the right time for a reason. Sometimes those reasons are for things like fun and sex. Mark was definitely fun and the sex phenomenal, and when he finished his book and left? Well, I had nothing but a smile on my face. There was no drama, no sticky goodbyes. Only over-used lady bits and memories that help keep me warm at night."

I look at my sister as if she grew a second head. "Really? Just like that? No complications, no expectations?"

"Really, Riss. Just like that. We both went into it knowing it was just a little fun, a lot of sex, and nothing more. It was easy, but most of all, it was what I needed after the whole Joey thing." Her eyes darken just by saying his name. Last summer, my sister found out her boyfriend of a year had sex with some girl in the bathroom of Mara's bar. She was devastated, no doubt, especially because he blamed *her* for his actions.

"I don't know," I reply, risking another glance at Rhenn. He's not alone this time, but his eyes are still on me. Even through the slowly darkening sky, I can see the lust, feel the heat. My thighs clench.

"Well, just think about it. You don't have to do anything, of course, but something tells me," she starts, leaning in again to whisper in my ear, "sex with that man would be nothing short of magnificent."

Harper laughs as she gets up and walks toward the cooler to retrieve another beer. She'll probably leave her car here tonight and ride back to her place with Mom. It took a little finagling, but we were able to arrange beds for everyone here. Mom and Harper will bunk together in Harper's bed, while AJ and Sawyer take Harper's guest room that Mom has been staying in since the fire. Orval and Emma will take Samuel's guest room, while Brian and Cindy volunteered to take the foldout couch in his family room. Meghan and Nick are staying with Rhenn on his boat, which is a good thing because with Jensen only having a two-bedroom place and my tiny studio-like house, there just aren't any more beds available.

Rhenn continues to watch me watch him. He says something to Nick and slowly makes his way toward me. My entire body starts to hum as he sits beside me, the swing rocking under the weight of his large body. "I think everyone is having a good time," he says casually, glancing around at my family.

"I think so. Thank you again for grilling the chicken. It was wonderful."

He slowly starts to rock us back and forth, a gentle motion that does nothing to calm the nerves racing through my body at his close proximity. "You're welcome, though I'm sure it wasn't as good as you would have done." There's a twinkle in his eyes as he glances my way. Damn that stupid twinkle and the effect it has on my girly bits and pieces.

I don't say anything, but stare up at the early night sky. Even though I'm on edge sitting next to Rhenn, I can't help the contentment that's also present. Maybe it's the rocking or the sky full of stars, but something speaks to me in a weird calming manner. Yes, weird because I'm never one to be relaxed or at ease around guys. Even though I've dated.

"You're still going tomorrow, right?" he asks, breaking through the sound of the crackling fire and my family's laughter. Before I can speak, he adds, "I've got Dramamine."

"I'm not sure. What if it doesn't work?"

"Then we turn around and come back." He says it so matter-of-factly.

"What can I bring?" I ask, after a few long seconds of pause.

"Yourself. Your swimsuit. Something comfy to sleep in." He leans in closer to my ear, his warm breath tickling my lobe. "Unless you sleep in the nude."

"I don't," I reply quickly.

"Pity."

"You're sleeping in the chair," I remind him.

"I am, and I would be a complete gentleman if you happened to be sleeping naked. I promise I'd sleep with one eye closed," he replies with a smirk. That damn smirk.

"I just bet you would," I grumble.

He continues to use his long legs to rock us back and forth, my own much-shorter ones barely touching the ground at this point. "I thought we could pull anchor around ten. We can sail for a while, swim in the ocean, and catch a few rays."

"Why don't you guys use your little…dingy thingy…" I say, stumbling on the words and causing my entire face to erupt in flames. "I mean your…boat…the little one…" Rhenn laughs. "Stop laughing. I was going to offer you breakfast, but now I'm changing my mind."

Rhenn stops the swing and turns to face me. "You were going to make breakfast? Those pancakes you were talking about? The lemon blueberry ones?"

"Maybe? But not if you're laughing at me."

"I'm not laughing," he replies very seriously, fighting the grin that threatens to spread across his handsome face. "My dingy is small, but mighty, Angel. Just promise me you'll make pancakes."

I fight my own smile. "Come ashore around eight. We can eat and then head out," I tell him, finally giving in to the smile.

"I'll bring an extra appetite with me."

"And your friends. Bring them too. I'll make plenty."

"Hell no, I'm leaving them on the boat to starve," he says, leaning in once again. "More for me."

Something in the way he says it sounds dirty and completely naughty, and suddenly, I find my panties completely useless. I can't breathe.

"You okay, Angel? You're a little…breathless."

"Fine." It's a squeak, but I manage to speak, even though my blood is pumping and my entire body charged with electricity.

"So, eight tomorrow morning?" he asks, his eyes turning as dark as the ocean under the midnight night sky.

"Yes," I confirm, and am rewarded with a genuine smile. His smirk makes him sexy, but this smile? One that's real and natural against bright white, straight teeth? This smile is my kryptonite.

We all hang out for another hour before Max turns into a cranky little monster and baby Nolan spits up his food all over his last outfit. After that, the party quickly breaks up. Jensen and Max head back to their place, a quick bath in my nephew's future before he heads off to bed. Samuel leaves with Brian, Cindy, Emma, and Orval behind him. Mom drives Harper back to her place, as I suspected, with AJ, Sawyer, and Nolan hot on their heels. And Rhenn gets ready to walk back to the dock with Meghan and Nick.

But not before they walk around the yard and gather up the chairs and help stack them on the deck at the back of the house. I make sure the garbage is cleared away so we don't get raccoons coming up and tearing apart the trash, while Rhenn makes sure the coals in the firepit are spread out. Just to be safe, he grabs the hose and sprays them down with water. I instantly start to relax, letting go of an anxiety I never had before.

Not before the fire.

When the backyard is put back together, I head over to the walking path. Meghan and Nick are holding hands, walking a few feet ahead of me, and talking about sailing tomorrow. They both seem really excited to spend the next day and a half on the water. Well, at least they are…

Rhenn comes up beside me and takes my hand. My heart pounds like a snare drum in my chest, a heavy beat I'm sure everyone in town can hear. He doesn't say a word, just runs his thumb along the tender flesh between my thumb and index finger. I try to keep my composure, my cool, but with every graze of his finger, I lose myself a little more into the brush of his finger, his touch.

Harper's words from earlier flash back. Could I engage in a little fun, a bit of no-strings sex? With Rhenn? I'm pretty sure he'd be on board. He screams late-night-booty-call, and something tells me he'd make it completely worth my while.

"You okay?" he whispers as we approach the clearing to the beach.

"Yeah. Just…thinking." We stop when we reach the sand. It's the first time I've seen his sailboat, and even though it's dark, it practically glows under the full moon. "Wow."

"She's a beauty, isn't she?" he replies, pride in every word.

"She is."

"Wait until you see her in the light of day," he adds. I stop at the edge of the dock, watching as Nick helps Meghan down into the small boat that's tied there. "I should walk you back."

"What? Oh, no, there's no need for that. I've managed out here just fine by myself for a while now."

He watches me, those deep blue eyes boring into me. "I don't like it," he says, almost absently.

"I'll be fine. Nothing is going to get me on my own property."

Rhenn hollers to his friends, yet doesn't remove his eyes from mine. "I'll be right back. I'm going to walk Marissa back to her place."

"Okay," Nick hollers, not seeming to care that Rhenn is leaving him and his pregnant wife in a tiny boat.

I start to protest, but know immediately that it's fruitless. Rhenn pulls my hand back toward the timber, essentially causing me to fall in line with his plan. "You really don't need to do this. I've been back here a million times by myself. I know the way."

"I know that, Angel, but I just can't leave you here. It's not in me. And besides, I'm pretty sure Nick would kick my ass if I didn't. He's a stickler for escorting his employees to their cars at night. Especially after Meghan got jumped one night in the parking lot behind their office."

I gasp. "That's terrible."

"Yeah," he says.

Is it just my imagination or are his steps slowing down?

"He was on the phone and didn't walk her out. Some dick tried to take her purse and was going to hurt her. He blamed himself for a while after that," Rhenn confides in me.

Neither of us speaks as we make our way up the familiar beaten path. When we reach the clearing of our yard, the moonlight illuminates the area enough that I can see the faint smoke coming from the firepit. The light above my sink is the only light filtering through the backyard, which is still a little spooky. The large house is completely black, the electricity still out as the construction process continues.

"Thank you for walking me back," I say as we step onto my little front porch.

"It was no problem," he says, rocking back on his heels as he looks down at me. He has yet to release his hold on my hand, which, if I'm being honest, I kind of like. "I'll see you in the morning?"

Nodding, I reply, "Eight."

Rhenn gives me a smile. "I'll be here, ready to eat my fill of breakfast."

Returning his grin, I say, "I'll make sure to have plenty of big fluffy pancakes, just for you."

That seems to be exactly what he wanted to hear because when he turns the full-wattage of his smile on me, I feel it clear down to my toes. This man is lethal, and I'm not talking about his karate abilities. His smile, his build, his manners, his cocky disposition. It's all part of what makes Rhenn...well, Rhenn.

"See you soon, Angel," he responds just before his head dips down. I tighten my hold on his fingers and my breath catches in my throat.

He's going to kiss me again.

His lips tease the corner of my lip, as if testing the waters, so to speak. When I make no move to stop him, he slides his lips slowly across mine. He's gentle, as if savoring the feel, the taste of me. When his mouth is squarely over mine, I open to him, giving him full access to deepen the kiss. I shiver as his other hand comes up and cups my jaw, his finger tenderly stroking my cheek. My entire body seems to fire to life, a slow burn settling between my legs. His tongue gently slides against mine, igniting my soul and releasing the craving I've been trying to trample down.

Before I can climb him like a tree, wrapping my arms and legs around his incredible body, he releases my lips. I almost groan in protest, but keep it from spilling from my wet, swollen lips.

"Good night, Angel," he whispers, placing another kiss on the corner of my mouth, before slowly pulling away and standing to his full height. He towers over me, and all I can think about now is the way his large body would press me into the mattress as he thrusts inside me, each stroke a bit more powerful than the last.

"Good night," I manage to croak through my very dry throat.

Rhenn seems to understand exactly where my brain is: Smutville. He throws me that cocky grin, a smug little wink, and releases my hand. I don't miss the way he tries to discreetly adjust the front of his shorts as he steps off my porch and into the moonlight. My hands shake as I reach for the doorknob, my entire body alive with pent-up desire and sexual frustration. There's no way I'm sleeping tonight.

Before I shut the door, I glance over my shoulder, only to find Rhenn standing at the edge of the timber. His hands are in his pockets, but it does nothing to mask the bulge in his pants. His desire is written all over his body and his face. His eyes practically devour me as I slowly shut the door, closing him out for the rest of the evening.

As I head into the kitchen to finish cleaning up, my legs a little too wobbly for my own liking, I already know what my answer is to Harper's burning question. Can I engage in a no-strings sexual relationship with Rhenn Burleski?

The answer is a definite yes.

Now, I just have to figure out how to ask him…

Chapter Twelve

Rhenn

I barely slept a wink.

Not even the tranquil rocking motion of my boat could calm my raging hormones. All I could think about was the way she melted against me, the feel of her lips against mine, her taste on my tongue. I tried – fuck, did I try – to push her out of my mind, but I just couldn't do it. I had a taste, and now I want more.

More of her, sure, but more of all that other shit too. The touches, the lingering glances, the kisses, and the noises she makes when she surrenders in my arms. The things that felt a hell of a lot like a relationship. The things I swore I'd never want or need again.

It didn't help my situation that I was forced to listen to my friend fuck his wife, albeit as quietly as they possibly could. I can't even be mad at him because if I were in his situation, I'd be screwing my wife as much as possible too. Well, if I had a wife, that is. Which I don't.

And won't.

I tried everything. I got up and went upstairs, trying to get away from the low thump of the mattress hitting the wall. That didn't help because all I thought about was how Marissa would look splayed out on my deck, her legs wrapped around my waist, as I drove my cock deep inside her. I even tried to make some tea shit that I found in the cabinet. It tasted like ass, even after I added a few splashes of tequila.

I couldn't shower – they left the bathroom door to the main living area locked from the inside, only to access the bathroom from the master bedroom. I couldn't jack off, which was what my wayward cock needed, because I had no easy way to clean it up. Not to mention the fact that my friends could come out of the bedroom for a just-had-sex snack and find me whacking off to images of the sexy bed and breakfast owner I left up on the beach last night.

I was in hell. I was hard, aching, and craving release like no one's business.

I was craving Marissa.

As soon as the sun started to peek out, I changed into running clothes, jumped in the johnboat, and headed toward the shore. It was too early for breakfast (unfortunately), and even though I'd much rather fuck my way through this sexual frustration I'm drowning in, I opt for the second best option.

Running.

My shoes pound into the wet sand, the familiar burn in my legs and lungs settling in. I keep a brutal pace, much faster than I normally would, considering I'm running in sand. I run for a good thirty minutes down the shore before turning and heading back. My pace on the return is a little slower, mostly because I've finally found my rhythm. I try to push all thoughts of a certain blonde with alluring green eyes out of my mind, but it's impossible.

My body craves her like the sun needs the sky.

That's a problem, and unless I get it under control, she'll know exactly how much I want her when she takes one look at me. It's not like basketball shorts camouflage boners, ya know? She'll take one look at me and run away screaming.

Though, I'm pretty sure she caught on to how she impacted my body last night. I could see it in the way her eyes flickered to my shorts.

Hell. This is what hell is like. A raging hard-on with no means of taking care of it. That's probably what my headstone will read too. Here lies the sorry asshole who died because all of his blood was in one concentrated area for too long. Death by woody. Nick would love the shit out of that.

When I return to the stretch of beach that belongs to Marissa's family, I head toward the johnboat. In desperate need for a shower and a bottle of water, I climb in, only to realize that my shower really isn't an option right now, unless they unlocked the door within the last hour. Nick and Meghan are surely still sleeping, dead to the world from their marathon sex last night. Even though they'd deserve to get woken up after keeping me up half the night with their sexcapades, I don't want to be the reason they're up for no reason. Especially since she's pregnant and probably needs the rest.

Dropping my shoulders, I opt to head to my truck. I can drive into town and purchase some water at the gas station, but before I even make it two steps, I realize I don't have my keys. They're on the boat in my pants from last night.

Fuck.

Out of options, I make my way up the path that leads to the bed and breakfast. I know the code to get into the house, so it looks like I'll be working for a bit until it's time for breakfast. Checking my watch, I see I have about an hour before I'm supposed to be at Marissa's place. Not a lot of time to get anything really done, but maybe it'll help calm my racing heart and raging boner.

As I step through the clearing and into the yard, I notice a light on in the little cottage out back. Marissa's already up. When the front of her place comes into view, I notice the front door is open, her cheerful curtains all fluttering in the breeze. There's also music playing, something new and definitely pop-ish filtering through the yard.

Instead of heading to the house, I find myself stepping onto her porch and knocking. I can see her there, standing at the counter, a surprised look on her face as she glances up and finds me. "I know

I'm early," I start, not really knowing what else to say. I'm sweaty and probably a little stinky from my run, and the boner I had just finally willed into submission is starting to come back.

"Come in," she says quickly, wiping her hands on the front of the apron she's wearing.

An apron. I've never found one so fucking sexy, yet here I am, staring at her as if she's wearing some sexy negligee and beckoning me to come closer.

"Sorry to just show up like this. I was going to head into the house and maybe do a little work, but then I saw your light on," I reply, running my hand through my sweaty hair as nerves flutter in my stomach. Nerves. I'm fucking nervous.

"It's fine. I'm just cutting the lemons to juice."

I find myself walking over to where she stands, invading her personal space a bit too much for a man who hasn't showered today, and lean against the counter to watch her work her magic. "Can I help with something?"

Marissa faces me and wrinkles her nose. "This might not be appropriate to ask before breakfast, but why are you all sweaty and gross?"

I can't help but smile. "Well, you see, I had this problem. One that kept me from getting any sleep last night. So, I got up early and went for a run. After an hour or so, I realized I couldn't go back to my boat without waking up my boatmates. Access to the shower is in the main bedroom, since they locked my side of the door last night, so I thought I'd come and get some work done, and hopefully, give them enough time to wake up."

"Wait," she starts, setting down her knife and turning to face me. "You ran. For. An. Hour?"

"Yeah," I answer with a shrug.

She looks at me as if I just sprouted a second head, then carefully, picks up her knife and finishes cutting the lemons. "You know, I do have a shower."

"I don't want to inconvenience you."

"I'm thinking that you *not* showering might inconvenience me more," she sasses, the quip of her lip and glance over her shoulder going straight to my dick.

I bark out a laugh and move to stand behind her. I can feel the heat of her body as I press my front to her back. Things in the groin area are already out of control, so there's no use in trying to hide my reaction to her. "Marissa?"

Her breath catches as she replies, "Yes?"

Bending down, I take a subtle inhale of the delicate skin of her neck. "Can I use your shower? Please?"

She gasps as I set my open lips against the place where her shoulder meets her neck. "Yes."

I place another kiss on her skin because I can't seem to help myself. "Thank you. I'll be right back and then I'll help with breakfast." I use all of the willpower I possess to pull myself away from her and head off to her bathroom. It's not too far of a walk, since the cottage is so small, but Marissa stops me before I can shut the door.

"Do you have a change of clothes?" she asks, making me realize for the first time that I'll be putting my nasty clothes back on over my clean body.

"Shit."

"Hold on," she says, wiping her hands off on the apron once more and walking to her room. Since I'm curious, I follow her into her private space without being invited. Her room is exactly as I've pictured it. Feminine and clean. It's organized with everything in its place.

Marissa goes to the closet and opens the bi-fold door. On the shelf, she grabs a small stack of clothes and the hairs on the back of my neck stand up. What the fuck? I watch as she flips through the clothes, pulling out a solid blue T-shirt and a pair of gray Nike basketball shorts. "Here, they might be a little snug, but at least they're clean."

I just stand there, staring at the proffered clothes like they're about to bite me. "You have men's clothing in your closet?"

She gently puts the remaining clothes back on the shelf, grabs a pair of socks sitting beside them, and tosses them my way. "Yep."

I open my mouth to speak, but nothing comes out. A foreign sensation creeps up my spine and wraps around my chest, restricting my airway. My heart starts to pound and my head feels like it might explode. Am I having a stroke?

Realization hits me hard in the chest. This is what jealousy feels like. The thought of Marissa having men's clothing in her closet – clothes that some douche bag before me wore and evidently left behind – leaves a sour taste in my mouth. I can't even enjoy the fact that I'm standing in Marissa's bedroom because all I can think about is the dick who wore these clothes. The dick who probably had his hands all over Marissa in this very room.

I hate this.

I hate him.

I hate jealousy and the way it burns my stomach like bad Mexican food.

"Are you okay?" she asks, still holding out the clothes.

"Uhhh," I start, but can't seem to find the words. I shake my head clear and reach for the clothes. "You're giving me your ex-boyfriend's clothes?" I try to sound casual. I fail.

Marissa seems to stop moving, stop breathing. "What? Oh God, no. Those are Jensen's. They all have a quick change of clothes here for when we're working on the house."

Oh.

Fuck.

I can breathe again.

They're her brother's clothes.

"Ahh." That's all I got. I take the clothes and walk back into the main living room.

"Rhenn?" she asks behind me, stopping me once again from stepping into the bathroom.

"Yeah?" I respond, turning once more to face her. This time, I'm a little embarrassed by my reaction to the whole clothing situation. I've never freaked out like that before, even if just on the inside, and frankly, I'm not sure how to handle it.

"Why didn't you get much sleep?" she asks, leaning against her bedroom doorjamb.

"You mean besides the fact that my best friend was screwing his wife in my bed half the night?" The corner of my lip ticks.

Her face instantly blushes a dark shade of red. Marissa clears her throat. "Yeah, besides that?"

Turning to face her completely, I decide to throw all my cards down on the table. "I couldn't stop thinking about you."

Her eyes widen and her mouth drops open, but I don't hang around for a reply. Instead, I close the door, knowing I was a half second away from inviting her inside to help with my shower. Oh, the things I would do to that woman while naked and wet…

* * *

I shower just a smidge longer than normal. Why, you ask? Because her shower smells like her. The shampoo, soap, even the bright pink loofa that hangs from the rack in the corner. It's her, and I find myself completely immersed in her fragrant scent, smiling like a psycho when I scrubbed my body. My cock throbs with every inhale of breath I take. Instead of taking it in my hand, like I really want to do, I flip the water to cold.

Fucking hell!

The burst of cold liquid pelting me in the chest might help alleviate the throb, but it does nothing to calm my blue balls. Now, they're blue for another reason.

I shut off the water and grab one of the fluffy green towels off the shelf above the toilet. Running it along my head and face, I make my way down my body, careful not to whack myself in the family jewels. They might never recover.

I bring the towel up to my face once more. Would you believe that this fluffy green bastard smells like her too? And the moment I wrap one around my waist, it's like a Marissa hug to my cock.

Fucking. Hell.

I spy the clothes sitting on the sink and imagine her brother. Nothing kills a boner like picturing another dude. Worse, I don't have any clean boxer briefs so I'm freeballing it in another man's shorts. Awesome. I throw on the too-small shorts, followed quickly by the shirt and run my hand through my hair. With the socks, my dirty clothes and wet towel in hand, I step out of the bathroom, make two steps to the left, and find myself right back in the kitchen.

See? Small cottage.

"I wasn't sure where I should put this," I say, holding up the wet towel.

Marissa turns around, a bowl of pancake batter against her stomach as she stirs it swiftly. There's a smudge of flour across her cheek, which reminds me instantly of the day we met. "Oh, you can throw it in the basket in front of the washer," she says, stirring and nodding in the direction of the back door. I find the world's smallest utility room with a stacked washer and dryer, furnace, and hot water heater.

Honestly, her cottage reminds me a bit of my boat. It's close, tight quarters, which she obviously doesn't seem to mind, as long as it's well organized. Hers clearly is. I shut the door behind me and step back in the kitchen. Marissa is pouring pancake batter onto a griddle, the scent of bacon wafting through the air and wrapping around my empty stomach.

"Smells delicious," I say, coming to stand beside her. I'm not entirely talking about the food, neither.

"It'll be ready in just a few minutes. What time are Nick and Meghan coming?" she asks, expertly pouring the batter and then flipping the big, fluffy pancakes with a spatula.

Running my hand through my hair once more, I reply, "I didn't invite them."

Marissa stops and turns to look at me. "I made enough for four."

"Trust me, Angel, I won't let any food go to waste, but if there is extra, we can take it back to the boat with us. I'm sure when the lovebirds finally wake up from their night of christening my bed, they'll be starving."

She drops the spatula. "Your bed has never...you've never..." Her face turns as red as an apple.

"Oh, there's been plenty of that, Angel. I'm just saying they've never done it in my bed. At least I don't think they have," I reply, reaching down and grabbing her discarded kitchen utensil.

Why does it suddenly feel hot in here? Like the combination of oven and griddle is causing the tiny kitchen to reach hellish heat levels. The truth is, yes, there has been plenty of sex in that bed.

When I first purchased the boat, I was never alone. There was always a woman – often more than one – who wanted to go for a sail. And yes, many times, sailing involved fucking. Partying. Blowing off steam and letting loose. It was who I was – or who I am.

Present tense.

Then why does my chest ache right over my heart when I think about it?

"I'm sure they'll be some left to take to the newlyweds," she says, grabbing a new spatula and removing the first batch of pancakes off the griddle. I continue to watch her work as she adds more batter and makes a second round.

As she starts to remove the second batch, I head over to her cabinet and grab two plates and some silverware. I can't help but wonder how I remembered where everything was located, when before last night, I was never much of a details person. Hell, I never really cared to help set a table before – mostly because, before I helped her make her dishes last night – I'd never really eaten with another person. Nick, sure, but that was grilled shit. But I've never had a woman over for dinner. I've never woken up the next morning and made breakfast, and I sure as shit didn't hang around while she made me food in the morning. Once daylight hit, I was gone.

I'm silent as I set the table, retrieving butter and syrup from the fridge. Only when I open the fridge, I don't see any syrup. "Uhh, Marissa?" How the hell does she expect me to eat pancakes without syrup? Especially when she did nothing but brag about her fresh maple syrup from some syrup farm down the road?

Without saying a word, she walks over and grabs the glass bottle from the sink. It's wet from sitting in warm water, obviously warming it up so that it isn't cold straight from the fridge, and after running a towel over the container, she hands it to me. Our fingers touch. My blood boils. My cock throbs.

All because of syrup.

No, not syrup.

Because of Marissa.

When the third and final batch of pancakes is done, she shuts off the griddle and joins me at the table. My mouth waters and my stomach growls angrily as I take a quick sip of the freshly squeezed orange juice I found in her refrigerator. I've died and gone to heaven…and I haven't even eaten any of the food yet.

"Dig in," she says, placing a stack of three flapjacks on my plate and one on her own. I waste no time dousing them in syrup, choosing to forego the butter, and add a few strips of bacon on the side.

My first bite? Orgasmic. Explosions of deliciousness hit my tongue and I groan. Loudly. I do it again with my second bite, and then my third. I've never had something so amazing as zesty lemon blueberry pancakes in all my life.

When I finally look up, her eyes are wide, her mouth slightly open, and her breathing a little labored. Yes, I'm enjoying the hell out of my food, but what draws my attention now is the look in her eyes. She looks like she wants to eat me alive, instead of her breakfast, and for the sake of complete disclosure, I'd be one-hundred-percent in favor of this.

Suddenly, breakfast has a whole new meaning.

She drops her eyes quickly and takes a small bite of her food. I watch as she closes her eyes, savoring the taste of the many flavors, and slowly chews. I've never watched a woman eat before. Not like this. This is…erotic. All I can think about is drizzling that damn syrup over her naked body and licking it off.

We eat, but it's tense. Somewhere along the way, we picked up a third diner: sexual tension. It's raw and thick and makes me think with the wrong head. If I'm not careful, I'm liable to let him make all of my decisions, which no doubt, would include throwing her on the table and feasting on her body.

Every time she looks at me, I feel like there's something hanging, something she wants to say, but doesn't. At first, I think I'm just imagining it, but now, as she pushes her empty plate away from her, I can tell she has something on her mind. She's almost nervous, but I'm not sure why. It could be about our pending sailing excursion, but I have a feeling there's more to it.

"Say it," I instruct, finishing off my last piece of bacon.

She looks up, shocked and a little confused. "What?"

"You have something on your mind, I can tell. So, say it."

Marissa clears her throat and glances away. "I'm not sure I can."

Pushing my own plate away, I reach for her hand. She's wringing them both together, a nervous habit that she probably doesn't even know she has. When I hold them both between mine, I don't miss the slight tremble. "You can say anything to me. Anything. In fact, I want you to. Even if you don't think I'll like what you're about to say."

Again, she clears her throat. It takes her a few long seconds, but I sense the moment she finds her resolve. "I was thinking…"

"About?"

"Something my sister said."

Glancing down, I notice my thumb stroking over her smooth knuckles. For some reason, I really like it. "What did Harper say?"

"That…maybe we…you and I should…oh, God," she grumbles, dropping her chin to her chest and averting her eyes.

"You and I should what?" I ask, my heart pounding in my chest as I wait.

She looks up, her eyes wide, and says the words I never thought I'd hear come from her sweet lips. "That we should sleep together while you're here."

And that, ladies and gentlemen, is how I die.

Chapter Thirteen

Marissa

My mouth gapes open. I can't believe I said it. I freaking said it. I told him we should sleep together.

Oh. My. God.

What's worse than spilling those words I never should have said is the fact that he's staring at me, a lost look on his face, and not speaking. Hell, I'm not sure he's breathing.

See? This is why I shouldn't have listened to Harper. Nothing good could ever come from "just have some fun, no-strings sex with the crazy hot man. It'll be fine." She's a liar. Her nose is probably growing right now from across town!

Rhenn continues to stare at me. His hands hold mine, but they've stopped moving. I never thought I'd miss the touch of his thumb grazing lightly over my knuckles as much as I do right now. I just hope that when he takes off running out the front door, he drops my hands so he doesn't drag me along behind him. Though, that would probably be the perfect punishment for me: a little road rash and a few bumps and bruises.

Stop mouth!

"I'm sorry, can you repeat that? I was clearly hallucinating." His words are hushed as he blinks repeatedly as if to clear away confusion.

"Never mind. Pretend I didn't just say that." Oh God! Kill me!

I try to pull my hands away, but his hold only tightens. "You're serious?" he asks, his blue eyes searching my green ones.

"No."

"No?"

"Yes. I mean, I don't know."

His eyebrows pinch together as he seems to consider his next words. Oh God, this is where he lets me down easy! You know, "it's not you, it's me." Or my personal favorite, "you're really great, but…" Is it too much to ask for the ground to open up and swallow me whole right about now? My face is burning with mortification, why not just let my body go ahead and spontaneously combust?

Without letting go of my hands, Rhenn gets up. He comes around the table and drops to his knees beside me. Using one hand, he grabs the chair leg and slowly turns me to face him. The only sound is the scraping of the chair and the beating of my heart. It sounds like a foghorn blaring in my ears.

Once he has me facing him, he takes my hands in his again. "If you mean it, say it again." His eyes burn into me with question. But do you know what else is there? Lust. I can see it laced in his eyes, the ones the same color as the ocean. I can feel it in the way he holds my hands, ebbing from every pore in his large, muscular body.

It's that look, that feeling I get when his eyes devour me, that has me opening up my mouth and making him the offer I know he won't refuse. "I wanted to know if you'd like to temporarily change the status of our friendship from platonic to sexual."

Rhenn growls. He actually growls, like an animal, moments before his lips claim mine. His kiss is fierce and dominating, it makes me wrap my legs around his waist and purr like a cat.

But all too soon, he pulls his lips from mine, my mind cloudy with desire and anticipation. "You're serious, right? I mean, I'm not trying to talk you out of it, mainly because having you has been a fantasy since the moment you walked out of that house with smudges of dirt on your face, but are you sure? Really sure?"

"Yes." And I am. I'm one-hundred-percent in.

"Fuck, I can't believe you just suggested that. I thought I had actually died there for a second." Rhenn drops his forehead to mine, our breaths mingle as we both try to calm our racing hearts. When he opens his eyes, they pierce into my soul. "I really get to have you while I'm here? For the next two weeks?"

"Yes."

He closes his eyes, his lips softly caressing my temple. "You have no idea how turned on I am right now."

"I think I have a pretty good idea," I retort, flexing my hips just enough to feel the hard length of his erection pressed against my center.

Rhenn snorts a laugh before placing both hands on my cheeks and kissing me soundly. My hands wrap around his back, gripping at the tight T-shirt and holding on for dear life. My God, this man can kiss like a god. Like he majored in it in college and earned straight A's. Warmth and wetness floods my core, and I can't help but wonder if our first time together is actually going to be right here, on my kitchen table. I've never experienced table sex, and I'm a little surprised at how appealing it sounds.

"Shit," he whispers against my mouth, stopping the kiss but not pulling away.

"Change your mind already?"

"Fuck no," he growls, placing another kiss on the corner of my mouth. "I was just thinking about how bad I want to throw you down on the floor and ravish your body from head to toe, making you scream no less than five times before I've had my fill of you."

"Five times?" I gasp, my brain barely able to compute.

"Five fucking times, Angel." He places a chaste kiss on my lips before pulling away. "But not here. Not right now."

Wait, what?

"Our first time together isn't going to be on the floor or on the table."

"I'm not opposed to the counter," I whisper, apparently loud enough for him to hear.

Rhenn chuckles. "I promise you, our first time is going to be better than this," he adds, nodding toward the floor, and believe it or not, I'm disappointed by this development. "Right now, my friends are probably getting ready for our day of sailing. We're going to head back to my boat, you're going to throw on a swimsuit, and I'm going to enjoy the fuck out of watching you prance around my boat. And tonight? I'm going to love sliding into that shitty-ass fold out bed, and do you know why?"

"Why?" My mouth is Sahara dry.

"Because you're going to be beside me."

"And because you'll get sex?" I tease with a smile.

He shakes his head. "No, no sex tonight. Not with Nick and Meghan on board. When I finally have my way with you, there'll be no one else around to hear your moans, Angel. No one else will know how many times I've made you come. No one but me."

Then he kisses me again with a hunger that feels as if it won't ever be quenched. Like he might die if he doesn't have another taste. I know right then and there, I'm in trouble. I'm completely over my head with this man, which is why I must keep my heart completely out of the equation. In fact, I'm leaving it here at the house. No way am I taking it with me, allowing it to catch one glimpse of the man who kisses me like I'm the very air he breathes.

"And at the end of the two weeks, we walk away." I say the words aloud, as confirmation to him, but to me, as well. Saying them makes it true, right?

"At the end of my time here, you probably won't hear from me again." Even though those are the words I expected to hear, actually listening to him say them causes a little hitch in my heartbeat. See? That's why my heart is going to be locked in the cabinet at home and not allowed anywhere near my time with Rhenn.

"Just promise me one thing," I say, pushing aside the heavy feeling in my chest and digging deep for the girl who's engaging in a no-strings relationship.

"Anything."

"Promise me you won't fall in love with me." I mean it as a joke, as a reminder of what this really is, but I don't anticipate the catch in my breath and the slight pang of sadness when his eyes twinkle with laughter.

"No worries there, Angel. Love isn't my thing."

I should feel better. I mean, I knew going into this that there was no future, no real relationship. He made it clear way before he even said the words aloud, but I guess hearing him say those exact words makes it all the more final. Our time, while enjoyable as it may be, will come to an end.

It will expire.

He will leave.

And I'll be left here, praying I still have a heart intact long after he's gone.

* * *

I'm not going to lie: I'm a little nervous as we make our way to the small boat that's tied off to our dock. Rhenn is holding my overnight bag in one hand and my hand in his other. My stomach feels fine (thank you, Dramamine), but my head is subtly reminding me of every other time I've gotten on a boat – and puked.

"You okay?" he asks, standing on the edge of the dock.

"Yep!" I reply, a bit too cheerfully. The truth is, I'm terrified.

"Come on, Angel. You got this. Nick and Meghan will be there, so you don't have to worry about me ravishing you the moment we get on board," he whispers, his warm breath tickling my ear. "And I promise if you're not having a good time, I'll bring you back. I don't want you to be miserable."

That. That right there. Why does he have to be such a considerate guy?

"I'm sure I'll be fine," I reply, steeling my spine and taking a step down into the small boat. I take my seat quickly, holding on to the side of the chair as Rhenn gets in.

So. Much. Rocking.

He sits behind me and fires up the motor. Glancing around, I start to panic. "What's wrong?" he asks, over the sound of the motor warming up.

"Where are the life jackets?"

"There's aren't any on here. We're not in very deep water."

"Didn't you see Titanic?" I ask, one step away from jumping ship (literally) and plastering myself to the dock.

Rhenn chuckles. "Angel, I thought you weren't scared of sailing."

"I'm not."

"Then, why are you holding on to your seat like your life depends on it."

"Because it might. You don't have life jackets."

"I have them on the boat. Not in here. We're only going about two hundred yards, and the water is still fairly shallow."

"You should always have life jackets, Rhenn. What if something happens?" Why am I panicking? Seriously, I'm starting to get embarrassed *for* me.

Rhenn moves, causing the entire boat to shake. "You're right," he says, softly, reaching forward and rubbing my cheek. "I should have them on here too. I've never really thought about it since I only use this every once in a while. Next time, I'll have them."

Swallowing hard, I get lost in the sea of blue in his eyes. "Okay."

"Are you all right?" he asks, again that thumb caressing my cheek.

"Yeah."

"I promise you're safe. I'd never let anything happen to you."

There's so much sincerity and honesty in his eyes that I can't help but believe him. Nodding my head, I offer him a small smile. It feels tight against the tension in my cheeks, but when he smiles back, I relax just a little more. This is going to be okay. This trip, this relationship, or whatever you want to call it, it's going to be fine.

I'm going to be fine.

While holding on to the container of leftover pancakes as if it were going to save me in the event of the boat capsizing, Rhenn unties us and gently reverses away from the dock. We move slowly toward his sailboat (probably in light of my sudden fear of drowning), the detail and magnificence of it more evident as we draw closer. It really is a beautiful boat. Large and white, with deep blue trim. I can't wait to get on board and really check it out.

Nick and Meghan are there as we approach the rear of the boat. Nick presses a button and the back slowly drops down, making a perfect rack to store the small boat. "Seriously?" I ask absently, watching how this entire process works.

"You okay?" Rhenn asks, steering us to the ladder. "Can you climb up there? Nick will help you."

"I'm good," I reply, ever so slowly reaching for the ladder. The boat is rocking, which makes it more difficult to maneuver. Not wanting to show any more fear than I've already displayed, I grab the rungs and pull myself up. Nick places his hand under my arm and helps guide me over the edge.

As soon as I have both feet on the deck, I'm engulfed in a warm hug from Meghan. She smells of sunscreen and coconuts, and instantly hands me a cup of something cold and bubbly. "It's a mimosa. I figured you'd earned one since I know this isn't your thing."

I take a tentative drink, relishing in the cold liquid as it slides down my throat. She drinks from a glass too, but tells me hers lacks the champagne kicker. I find myself curious and carefully walk over to the edge. Nick reaches down and grabs the bags and Tupperware container of breakfast, while Rhenn expertly uses a winch to lift and secure the small boat in place.

Once it's all set, Rhenn climbs aboard and offers me a warm smile. "Still good?"

"Yeah," I reply, realizing for the first time that I really am good. I don't know if it's the anti-nausea drugs or the mimosa, but I'm really not that nervous now. The boat is much bigger than I anticipated, and the rocking is actually quite soothing, instead of frightening.

Rhenn heads over to the steering wheel and presses a few buttons. It makes me realize I know absolutely nothing about sailing, and curiosity gets the best of me. I walk over and watch as he does his thing, assumedly getting us ready to head out.

He notices my approach and waves me over. "So, this is the helm. We'll use the motors to move out of our position, and once we get into deeper, open water, I'll turn it off and we can sail for a bit."

"Can I watch?" I find myself asking.

He grabs my hand and pulls me close. "I've got a better idea. I'll let you sail."

"Wait a minute, you give me shit for days and I've been doing this with you for years, but suddenly, you're ready to hand the wheel over to Marissa? What the hell, man?" Nick teases his friend, a smile and ornery gleam in his eyes as he waits for a response.

"She looks much better in a bikini, man," Rhenn replies with a shrug. I continue to watch for a bit as he does a systems check and checks all of the sails, getting us ready to head out. Once he's done, he reaches for my hand. "We'll take a quick tour before we pull anchor."

I don't draw attention to the way my body shivers when he touches me. At least, I hope I don't.

"The deck up front is perfect for sunbathing or watching sea life," he says, pointing to the bench seating around the sides. He heads downstairs, grabbing my bag from the stairway as he goes.

As soon as I hit the floor, I stop, shocked by how beautiful it is down here. "Wow."

"Right? She's a beautiful lady," he says with a smile, gently tapping the wall beside him. "Galley kitchen with all the amenities, only slightly smaller versions," he adds quietly, pointing to the dorm-sized fridge.

"But you have coffee," I comment, noting the Keurig coffee pot sitting on the counter.

"Definitely," he replies, taking my hand once more.

We walk forward just a couple of steps and find ourselves smack dab in the middle of the living area. "Your TV is huge." It's on the one section of wall that doesn't have windows or storage and is bigger than the one I have in my own living room.

Rhenn chuckles. "Yeah, it came with the boat, not that I'm complaining. Bathroom," he instructs, pointing to the small yet nice room. Honestly, the bathroom is pretty great. It's probably fancier than my own in the cottage. "And master bedroom."

We walk into the room, which boasts a full-size bed in the middle. There's a chest of drawers that appear to be built into the wall, and a small television. The walls are a dark wood, offset by the light blue bedding and skylights. There's access to the bathroom from inside the room, as well as a tiny closet.

"We can test out that bed after my guests leave," he whispers in my ear, while running his thumb down my bare arm. Instant. Goose bumps.

"If I play my cards right?" I tease, glancing at him over my shoulder.

"Oh no, Angel. I'm a sure thing."

And cue the ache between my legs…

"You two ready to hit it?" Nick yells down the stairs.

"Oh, I'm definitely ready to hit it." Something tells me he's not referring to the sailing. To confirm my suspicions, Rhenn steps forward and presses his erection against my side. It's big – holy moly, is it big – and definitely hard. Something tells me I'm completely out of my league with this man. The room is suddenly a thousand degrees and climbing.

Before I can rip off my clothes, throw myself onto the bed, and beg him to take me three ways to Monday, Rhenn pulls back. "Why don't you get into your suit and I'll get us ready to go. You can use the drawer out here for your things," he says, stepping out of the scorching bedroom and pulling out one of the empty drawers in the living space.

I nod, unable to find words, and watch as he sets my bag on top of the table. Without a word, he throws me a wink and heads upstairs. My eyes close and a loud groan spills from my lips. How did I get myself into this mess? Well, not a mess, really. And to be honest, I'm here because I want to be. Because there's nowhere else I'd rather be in this moment. Everything else just fades away.

Making quick work of placing my personal belongings into the drawer, I grab my suit – the one I purchased on impulse and have yet to find the guts to wear – and slip into the bathroom. There's more room in here than I anticipated. There's a beautiful shower unit and a small sink. More dark built-in shelves line one wall, and natural light spills from the ceiling.

I close the door, anxiety filling my stomach as I glance down at the scrap of blue material. I knew I should have brought my one piece, but I also knew that if I had, I would talk myself out of wearing this one. Harper convinced me while I was having a weak moment that I could pull this one off. I'm not so sure I can, though. It's…well, tiny. It's all dental floss and majestic blue material, the same color as Rhenn's eyes, coincidentally.

Sucking it up, I rip off my shorts and tank top and throw on the bikini. I feel naked. I've never – and I do mean never – worn something so revealing, especially in front of another human being, let alone three others. Before I grab my wrap, I risk a glance in the mirror. I'm a little on the pale side, having no time to sunbathe this early in the summer season. Actually, I'm not sure I've spent much time in the sun for the last three summers. The bed and breakfast has taken off so much, filling every weekend to capacity, that I don't allow myself much downtime, even though my mom tries to push me out the door. There's just too much to do on a day-to-day basis, and taking an afternoon to lie in the sun isn't a luxury I've been able to afford.

I risk a glance down at the bikini bottoms. I feel like my ass cheeks are completely exposed, but I find them tastefully covered. Well, as covered as can be, all things considered. I do have a two-piece suit that I'll wear on occasion, but it has a tankini and a skirt. Not a lot of skin showing there; not like this one.

Also, it's a good thing my sister talked me into a bikini wax last weekend…

Overall, I don't look too bad, all things considering. My stomach isn't nearly as tight as Harper's but that's because I don't spend nearly as much time in the gym as I pretend to. Plus, I like home-baked goods. You know, cookies, brownies, chocolate truffle a la mode with home-churned vanilla ice cream. I make some fabulous desserts, and I'm not one to shy away from a little taste test every now and again. Desserts are life. And that's okay. Steeling my resolve, I suck in a deep breath and grab the door handle. Before I can throw on my wrap to cover up the bikini, I head upstairs, grabbing my sunscreen as I go.

The sun is bright as I join the others on deck, so I move my sunglasses from my head to my face. There's a light breeze, not enough of a chill, but enough to not feel like you're baking under the intense mid-morning sunlight.

"Hubba, hubba!" Meghan bellows before throwing in a catcall for good measure.

I can feel my cheeks starting to heat as I glance her way. She's smiling widely, wearing her own pink and yellow bikini, and sitting beside her husband on the bench seat. Nick wears a smirk, but his eyes aren't on me; they're just over my shoulder. Slowly, I turn and face the driver…errr, captain. His mouth is hanging open – like catching flies open – and his eyes are so wide, I can see the whites behind his sunglasses.

"Fucking hell," he mumbles, and I'm pretty sure he didn't mean for me to hear.

I glance down, suddenly afraid I don't have something properly covered. When I don't see anything exposed (you know, no one needs a Janet Jackson nip-slip), I take the wrap and start to bring it to my shoulder. I'm not entirely sure if his reaction is of the good variety or not, but I'm not really comfortable enough to wait around to find out.

Rhenn is moving lightning fast before I even have the sheer black material over one arm. "Don't you dare," he practically growls, low enough that I don't think my cousin and her husband heard. He rips his glasses off, the look of pure lust and desire clearly etched on his handsome face as he reaches for the wrap and tosses it over his shoulder.

Into the ocean.

"That wasn't very nice," I whisper. Meghan starts to laugh behind me, and all I can do is stare into those intoxicating blue eyes. He looks as if he's about to eat me alive, slowly and deliciously. My body is humming and I'm pretty sure my nipples are now poking through my suit.

"You're gorgeous. Please don't cover it up."

"I couldn't now if I wanted to. You threw my wrap overboard."

He smirks, not an ounce of apology on his face as his eyes slowly peruse down my body. I can feel the heat of his stare all the way to my toes. "I'm not fucking sorry." When his eyes finally return to mine, they're smiling and bright, and suddenly, the tension I felt about wearing this suit just sort of fades away.

I take the seat behind him, across the boat from Meghan and Nick. Their fingers are linked on her lap and I don't miss the way his thumb strokes her bare stomach. She's not far enough along yet to show, but knowing she's pregnant with his child and he's tenderly stroking her abdomen has my biological clock ticking a little too loudly.

Rhenn raises the anchor and fires up the engine. It purrs like a kitten, a low hum that has me excited for my first sailing adventure. When he's ready, he pushes on the throttle and the boat starts to move. As we head out to open water, the boat slowly picks up momentum, yet he keeps it at the appropriate speed. When he reaches the final buoy, he hammers down, the beautiful sailboat taking off like a bullet.

My heart is pounding in my chest, the wind whipping my hair, but do you know what I don't feel? Afraid. There's something about Rhenn at the helm that has me refraining from reaching for the nearest life vest. Instead, I try to relax a little in my seat, keep my eyes open, and enjoy the ride.

After a few more minutes, Rhenn slows the boat and turns off the engine. Once he does, Nick jumps up and, together, they prepare the sails. I watch, awestruck, as they both fluidly move about the boat. Nick doesn't do anything without Rhenn agreeing, which tells me he respects his friend and his boat. There's something almost magical about the way Rhenn moves, his taut abs flexing beneath his T-shirt and the corded muscles working on his powerful legs. And let's not forget about his board shorts. I never thought a man could look so sexy in a pair of navy and white trunks, but heaven help me, this man is pure sex appeal.

With a rope in his hand, Rhenn starts to raise the big blue sail. The moment the wind catches, we jerk forward, *Runaround Sue* finally stretching her beautiful legs. Nick and Rhenn continue to work in tandem until we're sailing at a comfortable pace. I wish I knew what they were saying, but I have no idea what aloft, jibboom, mast, or headsail mean.

The landscape starts to change as the shoreline becomes smaller. We're surrounded by vibrant water as the sun shines high in the sky, warming my skin. I close my eyes and feel. Feel the wind against my face; feel it whipping through my hair, and feel it kissing my skin. Sailing is glorious, and I'm so glad he convinced me to face my fears (well, with the help of Dramamine) and come out for the day.

And the night too.

Let's not forget that I'm staying here.

All night.

With Rhenn.

After about an hour, the boat starts to slow and eventually come to a stop. I've been lost in my own world, watching the distant landscape and the sea life that appears at the water's surface, and truly just relaxing for the first time in…forever. "Where are we?" I ask, glancing around as if some familiar landmark might tip me off.

"We're not too far from Wilmington," Rhenn says as he drops anchor. The water is littered with boats of all sizes, but they're still pretty distant. "I thought we could relax here for a while and grab a bite to eat."

"Yes, please. Baby needs food," Meghan replies, rubbing her stomach.

"Then we must feed Baby," Nick says, capturing her lips with his own.

"Do they do this all the time?" I mumble to Rhenn as he approaches and sits down beside me.

"All the fucking time. It's so gross. I don't need to see Dad maul Mom like she's his dinner. We haven't even had the birds and the bees talk yet," Rhenn quips with a smirk.

"Who do you think taught me about sex?" Nick asks without removing his lips from his wife's. "And it wasn't *Mom*."

Rhenn laughs and stretches out beside me, his arm brushing my shoulder as he places it on the back of the seat. "I believe that was *Penthouse.*"

"First time I saw boobs and got a boner," Nick adds, pulling his wife into his embrace and holding her close.

"Where did you get *Penthouse?*" Meghan asks, glancing over to Rhenn as if he's instantly the guilty party.

"Don't look at me like that. Your husband found it and showed it to me."

"Bullshit, asshole! I only found it because you told me to snoop in my dad's office."

"I told you to look for spare change to buy candy. Not porn," Rhenn blasts, giving his friend a pointed look.

"Whatever. I should have dumped your ass years ago. You were the worst influence," Nick retorts, though clearly kidding.

"I was the best influence. Your parents loved me."

"Not so much senior year," Nick adds, making them both laugh.

"Yeah, maybe not so much then," Rhenn concedes.

Nick just smiles. "Only because you told them you were the one screwing Jane Rhoades in my bedroom."

Rhenn shrugs. "They forgave me in the end, but only after I had to endure your dad's safe sex talk. Did you know that it only takes one sperm to fertilize a woman's waiting egg, Nick? One sperm."

We all laugh, even though they're clearly having their own conversation right now. "I think I have that figured out, man, but thanks for the tip." Nick kisses the top of Meghan's head and holds her close.

After several moments of quiet, Meghan finally speaks. "Jane Rhoades, huh?"

Nick and Rhenn laughs. "I told you about her."

"Was she the college girl?" Meghan asks curiously, not an ounce of jealousy in her voice.

"With huge tits," Rhenn answers for him with a head nod. "Only time I've ever been fucking jealous of your man. She was a screamer."

"That's why I got caught. Anyway, let's stop talking about our younger, stupider days. My beautiful wife is hungry, therefore I must feed her."

"There's pancakes in the fridge," I reply, finally able to add to the conversation, though I never felt like an outsider. I'm used to sitting back and listening, and Rhenn and Nick have amazing friendship dynamics.

"Wait, no there's not," Rhenn replies loudly, before turning to me. "You weren't supposed to tell them that. Then I can eat them later for a midnight snack."

"Give me the pancakes, Burleski, and no one will get hurt," Meghan demands, standing up and following her husband to the stairs.

"Fine, I'll share. You can have one. But your no-good husband isn't getting his hands on my pancakes."

"You can put your hands on my pancakes," Meghan assures him with a wicked gleam in her eyes. Rhenn and I get up to follow them downstairs, and are treated to watching Nick wrap his hands around his wife's ass and pick her up. Her legs automatically wrap around his waist and their little kiss from earlier seems to continue immediately.

Only this time, I'm not so sure they'll stop.

"We should grab our food and return to the deck. Otherwise, we're going to get another bird and bees lesson. And this one might be a visual," Rhenn says loudly to me, earning a middle finger from Nick, who never breaks the kiss.

"I'll grab the silverware. You grab the food," I reply, making quick work of getting our food and supplies and returning to the deck.

Nick and Meghan don't join us.

Apparently, pancakes can wait...

Chapter Fourteen

Rhenn

I almost stroked out when I saw Marissa standing on the deck in that blue bikini.

I've had women on here, too many to possibly count, but none of them have ever looked as amazing as she did standing in the sunlight. I wanted to grab her, throw her over my shoulder, and stake my claim.

With my cock.

But, I've never been the claim-staking kinda guy. I've been the fun, free, and easy one, and while I want to be all of those things with Marissa too, a part of me – a very unfamiliar part – wants more with her. That's why her no-strings sex offer is so perfect. I can work her out of my system – repeatedly, in my bed – and then walk away at the end, like I always do.

And the best part is she initiated it.

Talk about shocking. I didn't think she was the casual sex kinda girl, but apparently I was wrong. Actually, no, I don't think I'm completely wrong. I still don't think she's built that way, but I think she's tired of fighting this constant attraction, this crazy, fiery lust that's burning between us, and what better way than to fuck it out of our systems.

Perfect. Plan.

My dick is already anxious and ready to play. I just have to keep him under control for a little bit longer. Once Meghan and Nick head back to Jupiter Bay tomorrow, well, all bets are off.

Just like our clothes.

I have to suppress a groan as the visual of Marissa strutting around my boat all day *without* that fucking bikini fills my mind. That's another thing I wasn't expecting. Marissa gives off that one-piece vibe, or maybe even one of those little swim skirts. That dental floss bikini was a bit of a shocker to the ol' ticker. She seemed a bit timid and nervous when she appeared on deck, which tells me it definitely isn't her norm. I'm guessing her sister had something to do with it.

Remind me to send Harper a big bouquet of flowers when we return to land.

Marissa and I enjoy cubed cheese, fruit, and bottled water, while watching the waves. She hasn't complained about feeling sick, so I take it the anti-nausea meds are working their magic. Thank Christ, because even though I would have returned to shore immediately, the thought of not witnessing her in her bikini makes the sunlight seem a little less bright.

"Feeling okay?" I ask, wanting confirmation.

"Actually, I feel great. I can't believe I haven't really felt sick at all," she replies, finishing off the pineapple chunk on her plate.

"I'm glad." We're quiet for several more minutes, but it's not uncomfortable. Actually, it's the exact opposite. I don't feel the need to add mindless chatter to our day, just for the sake of talking. Instead, I just enjoy her company and her presence beside me.

When our lunch is finished and we hear movement down below, I stand up. "Ready to catch a few rays? This is a pretty good spot to relax and sunbathe. We can head out mid-afternoon and find another place for the night."

"Sounds good," she replies, standing up and stretching. She reaches for the sky, her arms extending as far as they'll go, and my mouth goes dry. Fuck, she's beautiful, and all I want to do is strip that bikini off her lush body (possibly even throwing it into the ocean like her wrap – which I really didn't mean to do, by the way) and lick every square inch of her. Every. Single. Inch.

Suddenly, her nipples pucker and strain against those little triangles, making my dick throb in my trunks. When my eyes connect with hers, I see nothing but lust. Want. I'd bet the papers of *Runaround Sue* that she's fucking wet right now. Marissa moves, taking one step closer until her knees are touching mine. She wiggles between my legs, my body burning with desire, but I hold completely still. I'm letting her set the pace here, because if it were up to me, I'd already have her spread-eagle on the deck floor, my cock pounding into her wet pussy.

She leans forward, positioning her hands on my thighs. The motion brings her tits closer, along with her mouth. Her lips are pink and wet, ripe for kissing, and it takes every ounce of self-control I didn't even realize I had to not kiss her, but I'm letting her call the shots, remember?

Then her eyes drop to my cock and her breathing hitches. My hands flex and my palms itch to touch her skin. I'm ready to sell my left nut to the devil just for one little taste. Her hands grip my thighs, her nails biting my skin through my trunks. Control is quickly vanishing, leaving nothing but a craving for this woman that may never be quenched.

I shake that thought out of my mind too as her hands slowly move toward my cock, so fucking slowly that I think I might actually die before they reach their destination. Her eyes connect with mine once more just as her hands are mere centimeters from my aching dick, and I can already tell that once she makes contact, there'll be no stopping this freight train. Once she touches me, it's all over with but the orgasms. A lot of orgasms. So many, she won't be able to walk tomorrow. And the look in her green eyes tells me she's ready.

Just as she reaches for me, voices interrupt our porno-quality moment. Marissa jumps back as footsteps ascend the stairs and my friend and his wife come into view. They both look completely sated, dopey grins on their orgasm-happy faces, and suddenly my balls are turning bluer than my eyes.

Cockblocking assholes.

They sit down across from us, Meghan placing her legs across Nick's lap as he feeds her bites of pancakes. She moans in delight, a sound that makes my internal organs twist with outrage. "Sooo goooood," she moans, licking the syrup off her bottom lip.

Nick reaches over and swipes a bit of leftover syrup off her lip, bringing his finger to his mouth and savoring the taste. When he glances my way, I try to kill him with my eyes. "What?" he asks, all innocently and smug-like.

"Fuck you. I hope you fall overboard and drown." He seems a bit surprised by my outburst before glancing down. I know my dick is still rock hard, and I should definitely be embarrassed. But I'm not. The cockblocker deserves to die.

Nick busts up laughing before returning his attention to his wife, feeding her another bite. "Bedroom's free," he says, throwing Marissa a quick wink. She turns a bright shade of pink before grabbing our trash and heading below deck. I want to follow her, I want to really bad, but I refrain. If I do, I'm liable to throw her down on the table and screw her until the sun goes down.

My friends be damned.

Hope they brought earplugs.

When she finally returns, she appears a bit more composed. Towel in hand, she glances around for a place to lay it out where she can get a little sun. I know the perfect spot. Standing up and reaching for her hand, we head toward the bow. We step around the mast to the flat area where the skylights are. "Be careful of those," I tell her, pointing to the globes that let the sunlight in below deck. "This is the best place to catch some sun."

I take her towel and spread it out, and before I can run and grab my own and lie beside her, Meghan joins her. She spreads out her own towel and tosses a bottle of sunscreen to her cousin. "Here, you do my back. I'd have Nick, but then he'd think it was an invitation for sex, and frankly, right now, I need a break," she says to Marissa, a little giggle escaping her lips.

As soon as she applies the lotion to Meghan's back, she hands the bottle over to her. "Please?"

"I'll do it," I say, my voice low and gravelly. I don't let Marissa argue as I grab the bottle from Meghan's hands, noting the smug smile on her face, and squirt a glob of sunscreen in my hands.

And then I rub her down.

Her skin is soft.

It's warm to the touch.

My entire body ignites into flames once more.

Bad idea. Very bad idea. I should not be touching her right now, yet the sadistic asshole in me can't seem to stop. In fact, I go a little slower just to draw out the torture even more.

"I think you got it there, buddy," Nick quips behind me, handing each of the girls a bottle of water.

Reluctantly, I move my hands, severing contact with her back. On wooden legs, I slowly move, allowing her room to lie on her stomach beside her cousin. They instantly start talking, completely dismissing both Nick and me. We both watch for a few minutes before returning to the main deck.

Deciding to catch a few rays myself, I toss my T-shirt onto the chair beside me, grab the offered beer, and exhale deeply. The next twenty-four hours is going to be the ultimate test of my willpower. I vowed not to do anything while we have company on board, but I'm finding it harder and harder (pun intended) to give two shits about that anymore.

Marissa. I'm completely consumed, and in this exact moment, I can't seem to find the strength to worry or care about how much I want her. I sit back, my face turning toward the sun, and listen to the sweet sound of her voice. In the past, when I've had guests on the boat, I was all about the party scene. Drinking, sailing, and sex. But suddenly, I find it hard to picture how it used to be. Instead, I revel in her voice and the calm that seems to wash over me while she talks.

"Welcome to the other side," Nick says.

I want to ask him what he's talking about, but I already know. "It's temporary." Sure, I say it to him, but to myself as well. As natural and good as it feels to have her here, I know that at the end of our two weeks, I'll be heading home and she'll be staying. I'll go back to my old life filled with random women who I barely remember the next day, and she'll go back to baking her treats and taking care of the bed and breakfast. Our worlds don't mesh.

It's temporary, right?

"If you say so."

* * *

Later that evening, Nick and I are sitting in the living area, watching the girls cook in the galley. We're drinking a beer, talking about summer plans, but both of us keep returning our eyes to the women across the way. Meghan and Marissa have quickly become friends, not just cousins, and it's hard to believe they just met for the first time yesterday.

We've been kicked out of the kitchen, neither of us allowed to ask what they're making, but it wasn't too hard to figure out, since there's only so much food in the fridge. Meghan is working on a salad, while Marissa switches from manning the portable grill I took upstairs and the range, where I'm pretty sure she's sautéing onions and mushrooms.

"When do you think you'll be finished with the job?" Nick asks, instantly making my chest tight.

"Two weeks. I've only got a bit left on the upstairs rewire, but then I have to do the downstairs, including rewiring the living room, dining room, office, and back sitting area, but also new wiring in Mary Ann's living space. It's pretty extensive, but it needed to be done. The old stuff was original."

"They're lucky they didn't have a fire before now," Nick says.

"True, but everything was still within code. Now, though, they won't have to worry about it anymore."

"I think Marissa is still freaked out," Nick says quietly, making me stop messing with my beer bottle and turn his way.

"Really?"

He nods before glancing over at the ladies. "She told Meghan she still has nightmares."

That makes me pause and sit up straighter. I know plenty of people have complained about being afraid, following a house fire, and I don't know why I didn't think more about that where Marissa's concerned. In fact, I wonder if anyone in her family has thought about it. Has she told anyone else about these nightmares? I make note to pry a little deeper into this new development. Why? Because I care and I want to make sure she's okay.

Gut check.

That realization is like a kick to the stomach, but it's true. I do care about her wellbeing, more so than I have with any other woman.

"Dinner is ready," Meghan announces proudly, bringing over two full plates and silverware to the table for her and her husband. It's small, but we'll all fit comfortably.

"I hope you don't mind I made you a plate," Marissa says shyly as she hands me a plate.

"I don't mind at all," I tell her, accepting the dish. It's heaped with fresh salad, fresh steamed green beans with bacon and grated Gouda cheese, and a steak with those sautéed mushrooms and onions.

My stomach growls.

"Meghan says you like your steak medium," she says nervously as she squeezes in the chair beside me. Okay, it's a little tighter fit with four than anticipated, but I'm not complaining considering I've got a beautiful woman pressed against my side like a second skin.

"I do," I answer, cutting into the steak so tender I could probably use a butter knife. I pop the first bite into my mouth and groan. "Jesus, that's good."

Nick takes a bite of his, moaning his own agreement, and turns to the woman at my side. "That's the most tender steak I've ever had."

"It should be. She beat the hell out of it with a mallet before you guys came down," Meghan adds, taking a bite of her own food.

"Well, it helps that they were good cuts of steak," Marissa replies, blowing off the compliment.

"And she marinated them in fruit," Meghan says between bites.

"Fruit?" I ask, giving her my attention.

"Well, sea salt and a bit of papaya and pineapple. The acids in the fruit actually help break down tough meat and tenderize it." Again, she blushes as she pokes around at her green beans.

"No shit?" I ask, surprised by this tidbit of information. "I've always just thrown the steak on the grill, sprinkled it with salt and pepper, and called it good."

"And you can do that; grilling helps tenderize meat too, but over the years, I've experimented with different ways to grill and bake. One of my old professors in a cooking class told us that certain acidic fruits will help tenderize meat. She wasn't wrong." Marissa shrugs and takes a bite of her food. She chews slowly, as if savoring the flavors, and I realize I could watch her eat all day long. It's sexy.

After dinner is finished, and Nick and I clean up the dishes, we return to the deck above to watch the sunset. We're closer to the shore than we were earlier today, off the coast of South Carolina, where the waters are calm and peaceful. Nick turns on the radio while I grab us a few more beers, and we settle in to watch the sun dip below the shoreline.

Small talk comes easy, and so do the stories. Each tale of our childhood is a bit more embarrassing than the last. We've got the girls in stitches by the time the yawns start. I admit that I really don't want tonight to end. Marissa is curled into my side, my arm slung over her shoulder and my finger brushing across her sun-kissed skin. She seemed a little hesitant at first, but eventually relented to the cuddle-ability my body promised.

"I'm exhausted," Meghan says, standing up and reaching for Nick's hand.

"That's my cue." He takes her offered hand, brings it to his lips, and escorts her down the stairs.

"If you could try to be a bit quieter tonight, I'd appreciate it," I throw at them before they escape below.

"I hope you brought earplugs," is all he says as he disappears below, a laugh following in his wake.

"Asshole."

"You love him."

Chuckling, I reply, "I do. He's a great guy. I'm lucky to have him as my friend."

"I really like him and Meghan, well, and everyone else too. I can't wait to meet the rest of the family."

"They're almost overwhelming, but in a good way," I respond as I stand up, extending my hand. She takes it instantly, her hand fitting so perfectly within mine. I push that thought aside, though, as I bring it up to my own lips. Her skin is so soft, delicate even. It makes me want to run my lips over her entire body.

I make sure the boat is secure before heading downstairs, following Marissa as I go. I shut the door, keeping the outside out for the night, and cutting off the wind noise. We can still hear the waves, still feel the gentle rocking of the boat, and for some reason, I truly hope she finds it as relaxing as I do.

"I don't think they're in the bathroom anymore. You can take it first," I tell her, noticing the bathroom door is open from our side. Thank God. Otherwise, I'd be forced to knock on their door, interrupting whatever is going on in there, and ask them to unlock this side.

Marissa heads over to the drawer I gave her to use and grabs some clothes before closing herself in the bathroom. I use the opportunity to give my dick a pep talk about how to appropriately act when in the presence of a friend. A friend that has agreed to sex, but a friend nonetheless. We haven't hit that phase in our friendship yet, but my dick doesn't seem to care. I told her I'd wait, so I wait.

Dammit.

I grab a pair of shorts from the drawer I threw my clothes in while Nick and Meghan are here. I'd much rather sleep naked, but that's not the best option for tonight. I don't want to scare Marissa away before we even have an opportunity to test out this whole friends with benefits option. Since she's still in the bathroom, I step into the small storage room beneath the stairs and change out of my trunks. They're not wet anymore from today's swimming adventures, but there's no way I want to sleep in them tonight.

When my shorts are on and my trunks thrown over the pile of kitchen supplies, I glance around the small space. It was meant to be a second bedroom, only enough room for a twin size bed, but the couple who owned the boat before me didn't have it finished that way. They didn't have kids, therefore didn't feel the need for a second bed. It sure would be coming in handy right about now. Hell, it would have come in handy from day one. Usually I take the bed and Nick is forced to sleep on the tiny fold out couch that he's way too big for.

I should finish this room.

When I step out of the room, Marissa's standing in the living room. She's wearing an oversized T-shirt that hits mid-thigh and her face is free of makeup. I can't help but notice she looks just as beautiful without the little bit of makeup she wears as she does with it. In fact, with her standing in that sleep shirt, I think she's even more gorgeous.

The only thing that would make this scene better is if it were *my* shirt she was wearing.

I head over, releasing the table from the floor, and move it out of the way. Opening the cabinet above the drawers, I pull out two blankets and pillows, even though I'm pretty sure I won't be using one tonight. Dropping the bedding in the chair I'll try to sleep in, I unfold the couch into the futon bed. I can feel her eyes on me while I lay a sheet down, toss the pillow toward the head, and drape the blanket over the rest. When our eyes connect, sexual energy zips through the air, zapping my fraying nerves. This is a bad idea. I can tell. There's no way I'll be able to sleep with her mere feet away, not when I've already seen what her body looks like in a bikini and not when all I want to do is rip off that nightshirt and have my wicked way with her.

I can feel my cock growing, thickening like he's ready to play. Instead of giving in to the urge to touch her skin, I motion for the bed. I can't even find words.

"Thank you," she says, grabbing the blanket and sliding underneath. Of course, I catch a glimpse of smooth thigh and pink panties before she's able to cover herself.

That image is now burned in my retinas.

"Well, good night," I say, turning off the light and grabbing my own blanket. I throw it around like I'm angry at it, but in reality, I'm angry with myself. I'm angry at the way I react to her, even though I don't want to. I don't *want* to want her as badly as I do, but fuck, I can't help it.

"Night."

I toss and turn for ten minutes, trying to get in a comfortable position, but that's hard when you're sitting up. And have a boner. The pillow is useless, just as I expected, and does nothing to keep my head from falling back. There's too much space between the back of the seat and wall, so that doesn't help. My legs are extended out in front of me, occasionally coming in contact with the futon bed.

And to make it worse? I can hear her. Her breathing. Her skin sliding against the bedding. Her soft little sighs as she tries to get comfortable too. I. Can. Hear. Her. And it's driving me absolutely wild.

"Rhenn?" she asks, my cock pulsing in my shorts at the way she says my name.

"Yeah?" I ask, my voice hoarse and my throat thick.

"Will you please come over here and sleep beside me. I know you're not comfortable, and I'm not sure I'll ever be able to sleep knowing that."

May Day, May Day!

Bad idea, Captain!

"I'm fine," I reply tightly.

"You're not fine." In the moonlight spilling from the skylights, I see her sit up. "It probably won't be comfortable here either, but at least you'll be lying down." And then she goes for the kill. "Please."

That's the moment I know I'll never be able to deny her anything, as long as we both shall live. I'll do whatever she wants, whenever she wants it, and I'll do it with a smile on my face. She owns my body, sure, but something more. She just pushes her way right on in, staking her claim on something I haven't given freely or willingly in a decade.

Knowing it's fruitless to fight her, I get up and slip behind her on the futon. She's turned on her side, facing away from me, so that we both fit. I instantly feel the heat of her body and willingly let it envelop me in its immediate comfort. Lying on my side behind her, I'm able to extend my feet onto the chair I was trying to sleep on.

Marissa moves back, the globes of her perfect ass pressing against my swollen cock. I'm pretty sure she doesn't mean to, but we're so close that it's impossible for us not to touch. See why this was such a bad idea? My brain says abort, but my cock says free me now. She adjusts again, the soft material of her panties sliding easily against the material of my shorts, and a moan of pure torturous pleasure threatens to spill from my lips. I have to grab her hip to keep her from moving. I'm not sure I can take much more.

"I really think you should stop moving, Angel." My words are tight again, just like my shorts.

She pauses, a small gasp filling the cabin. But then my little vixen does exactly what she shouldn't do – not if she wants to keep this little spoon-fest PG-13. She arches her back, firmly pressing her ass against my aching cock.

My mind blanks.

My cock starts to cry with happiness.

My body bursts into flames.

"What if I don't want to stop moving?" she asks, not in the least bit innocently.

"This is a dangerous game you're playing. I want you too much right now, Marissa," I whisper, my hand squeezing her hip.

"Rhenn?" she asks, my control a thread away from breaking completely.

"Yeah?"

"Touch me."

And just like that, she throws a can of gas on an already raging inferno. "You sure?" I ask, timidly moving my hand from her hip to her bare stomach.

She quietly whimpers as my fingers flex against her skin. "God, yes. Please," she begs, wiggling backwards until her ass makes contact with my cock again. She grinds against me, making me quickly realize I'm two seconds away from blowing like a virgin. I've wanted her for too long, fantasized about this very moment, and I know if I don't put a little distance between us, I'm going to do something embarrassing.

Instead of letting my dick call the shots, I slide my hand between her legs. She's already wet. I can feel it through her panties, and my mouth waters to taste. But not tonight. Tonight, I'll give her the release she's craving, without completely mortifying either of us if my friends come out for a drink and find me with my head between her legs.

Though, it would be their fault for not knocking first.

Instead, I opt to move my hand beneath the wet material. Her skin is smooth, with just a small trail of hair. Next time, I'm tracing that trail with my tongue. Gently, I slip my fingers between the lips of her pussy, her clit already swollen and pulsing under my touch. And she's wet. So fucking wet right now that it makes my balls ache. She coats my fingers as I tease and toy with her, little gasps of pleasure spilling from her lips.

She grinds against my cock and I know it would only take a quick second to remove the clothing barriers between us and slide home. She's ready, and I'm so fucking ready it hurts. But that's not what's going to happen tonight.

My fingers tease her entrance and she lifts her leg, throwing it over mine. She's giving me access, begging to come. With one finger, I gently push inside her warm, tight pussy. So. Fucking. Tight. I instantly feel her clench around it. She's already that close. "God, do you feel good, Angel."

Marissa whimpers, rotating her hips and taking what she wants. When I add a second finger, I know she's mere seconds away from coming. Her gasp is the sweetest sound as I thrust both fingers into her tight body and rest my palm against her clit. The contact causes her to clamp down, her entire body tightening with need. "Let go, baby. I got you," I whisper as I grind my palm and plunge my fingers into her pussy once more.

Her release is amazing – there's no other way to describe it. She shudders against me, rocking her hips and riding out wave after wave of pleasure. She's so tight that I can't even move my fingers anymore, so I just lie there, slowly moving my palm and reveling in the feel of her pulsating around me.

Best. Fingerbang. Ever.

Chapter Fifteen

Marissa

Best. Orgasm. Ever.

I can't breathe. I can't think. I can't feel my toes.

I'm also pretty sure I'll never be the same. No orgasm will ever compare, will ever amount to what I just experienced with Rhenn. By his magical hand. The hand that is still cupping me, his fingers still buried between my legs.

"That was magnificent," he growls into my ear as he slowly starts to retract his fingers. I want to ask him for a repeat, but frankly, I'm not sure I can move right now. I open my eyes and glance over my shoulder. His blue eyes are alive with desire, his body hard in all the right places. But what he does next? Well, that has me ready to throw in the towel, beg for mercy, and worship at the altar of Rhenn.

He puts those two fingers in his mouth.

And sucks.

I almost orgasm right then and there.

"Delicious."

And I shiver again.

I have no idea what to say, but I know what I want to do. I've never been big on going down on a man, but I can't let go of the desire I have to do so right now. I need to feel him in my hand and taste him in my mouth. A part of me likes to remind myself that I'm not very experienced at this and he'll probably be bored after the first ten seconds, but I want to try.

I need to try.

Before I can offer, Rhenn rights my panties, pulls down the T-shirt, and turns us both so that we're lying side by side. He has his arm slung over my waist, but that's it. I can no longer feel that impressive erection grinding against my butt, and I actually kinda miss it. I try to scoot back, but he holds me still, not allowing me to make contact.

"Don't move. If you move, I'll never get it to go down," he grits through clenched teeth, his hand flexing against my stomach. Even through the shirt, I can feel the heat of his touch.

"What if I help it go down?" I ask boldly, pushing aside all the uncertainty I felt just a few moments ago.

"That's not why I did what I did, Angel."

Glancing over my shoulder, my eyes connect with his. "Why did you do it?"

"Because not touching you wasn't an option. I needed to feel your pussy, feel you come, as much as you did. It was as if I couldn't breathe until I experienced getting you off," he practically howls in my ear.

I find myself turning, and this time, he lets me move. His hand is still draped over my hip, but now we're face-to-face, and I can see nothing but hunger in those amazing blue eyes. "I want to experience that. Will you let me?" To prove to myself I am brave, I go ahead and palm his erection in my hand, which extends well past my fingers.

Rhenn makes a choking sound. I'm not sure if that was supposed to be words or not, but I take it as his approval to keep going. With my eyes locked on his, I gently slide my hand into his shorts, getting my first real feel of what this man has been packing in his pants.

And holy hell is it impressive.

Wrapping my hand around his cock, I slowly move it upward until my palm hits the head, making him hiss and thrust. I move down the smooth, tight skin until I've reached the root. I swear he grows thicker as I speak – errr, think. My mouth waters to taste.

I inch my way down, my lips finding the hard plains and muscles of his stomach as I go. His breathing is almost erratic when I come face-to-face with what I've been holding in my hand. It's like a hammer. Thor's hammer – large, hard, and probably going to rip the hell out of me.

That makes me giggle.

"That's not good when a woman is staring at your dick and starts to laugh," he whispers hoarsely.

"I was just mentally comparing you to Thor's hammer," I confess, moving my hand from the root to the head of his cock, earning me another moan of pleasure, this one a little louder than the last. I glance over my shoulder, hearing no stirring from the other room, and decide it's time.

I move my mouth, letting my tongue slip out and taste him for the first time. I swipe it along the thick head, tracing the pulsing vein that runs down his shaft. "Holy fuck," he huffs, grabbing my head and holding on tight.

Taking him in my mouth, I hollow out my cheeks and go down as far as I can – which is surprisingly farther than I would have expected. I take my cues from him, licking when he groans and sucking when he gasps, and the entire time, I move my hand up and down his length.

"So fucking amazing," he mumbles, causing me to look up and connect with his eyes. There's something heady about staring up at him while giving him pleasure. The look on his face is one of pure ecstasy combined with a bit of trust and awe. "Close. Can pull out," he rasps, his hips starting to thrust, as if completely on their own.

"Don't. I want to taste you," I instruct without removing him from my mouth. I'm not sure if he actually understood what I said, but when his eyes flare with fire and his shaft jerks in my hand, I'm pretty sure he got the gist.

I suck hard, taking him as far in my throat as I can, making my eyes water, but I don't stop. I stroke his balls with my free hand, feeling them tighten, until he gives me the signal. "Coming," he tries to warn me, giving me one last opportunity to remove my mouth.

But I don't.

His release is warm and thick as he empties everything he has into my throat. Rhenn is making noise, moaning with each thrust of his hips, but I don't think he cares. I don't think he even knows. When his body finally stills and he falls limp against the futon, I finally release him from my mouth, savoring the last taste of him on my lips.

"You okay there, champ?" I ask, taking one last swipe of his shaft with my tongue and making him shiver. I can't believe he's still rock-hard. My previous boyfriend was more like a bottle rocket. Shot up hard, exploded quickly, and fell just as fast with little to no fanfare.

"I can't open my eyes. I'm not sure I'm even breathing right now. Am I breathing?" he pants, one hand draped across his chest and the other thrown over his forehead.

"I believe talking is a good sign of breathing," I tease him, snuggling into his warm body.

Rhenn moves his arm until it's under my neck and pulls me close. "That was pretty amazing."

I feel the blush and am grateful it's dark in the cabin. What am I supposed to say? Thank you very much? Your cock makes it easy because it's as yummy as an ice cream cone on a hot summer day? Yeah, I should probably not say any of that.

Even if it's true.

"Turn on your side," he instructs softly, gently moving me until I'm facing away from his body. One arm under my head and one thrown over my waist, he settles in behind me, his body pressed against mine. I hear him inhale as he nuzzles his nose in my hair, and feel his arm start to get heavy as he relaxes. "I like to spoon with you."

My throat feels thick and it's hard to breathe, but I find the strength to answer him honestly. "I like to spoon with you too."

And I do.

Maybe a little too much.

* * *

It's warm. Very, very warm.

It's not the blanket tangled around my legs so much as the man draped around me like a mink coat. We're in the same position we fell asleep in last night, proof neither of us moved after we fell asleep, post-orgasm. It's been a while since I've had my world rocked so hard that I basically became unconscious, only to wake up eight hours later, completely refreshed and ready for the day.

Okay, so maybe I've never actually had that happen. Not in real life. I've heard about it– mostly from my sister – but never actually experienced that complete nirvana, the mindless slumber that can only be induced by amazing orgasms.

I feel eyes on me, but they're not Rhenn's. He's still lightly snoring behind me, holding me tightly against his body as if I might somehow try to slip away. Holding completely still, pretending to sleep, I hear a muffled voice, followed by giggling and what sounds like a slap on the butt. Obviously Meghan and Nick are awake. I notice immediately when Rhenn starts to stir. Actually, I feel the moment he starts to wake. Remember that hammer from last night?

It's fully hard and ready for action. Seriously, this man has some impressive morning wood, and even though it's not the first time I've felt it pressed against me, it's the first time I've felt it post-blowjob, and well, I suddenly wouldn't mind another round of bedroom hammer throwing.

Nick and Meghan move on to the kitchen, the smell of coffee percolating filling the entire cabin. "You awake?" I ask, wiggling my butt against his crotch.

Rhenn tenses and groans in my ear. "Stop that, Angel, or I'm going to be forced to do something about it."

"That doesn't sound like much of a threat," I tease. Who is this bold vixen and what has she done with shy Marissa Grayson?

"It's more of a promise," he says, pulling me close and kissing my jaw. "Did you sleep well?"

"Like the dead," I confirm, reveling in the feel of his arms wrapped around me.

"Me too. I can't believe I slept until," he starts, lifting his wrist and glancing at his watch, "seven forty-five. I never sleep in that late. I'm usually up with the sun and getting in my morning workout."

"Me too. Well, minus the workout. I'm usually up at five so I can start preparing breakfast."

I should get up and move, definitely get up to pee, but I find myself snuggling in deeper into his embrace. "I have an idea," he whispers, running his nose along the shell of my ear.

"I'm listening."

"Stay with me tonight."

I suck in a breath, but not because I'm shocked or afraid. Because I'm excited. Because I know what will come of me staying another night on the boat with Rhenn. This time without my cousin and her husband on board.

Just us.

"Okay."

"We can go to town and have dinner, if that works for you. Then, we'll come back to my boat. I promise to get you back to the house before the contractors and your mom show up in the morning."

Oh God, my mom. It would be bad enough to do the walk of shame with a half-dozen construction workers running around, but my mom? Total mortification. She always comes and has coffee with me when she arrives at the house. Could you imagine if she showed up at my cottage and I wasn't there? And then when I do show up, I have bedhead and look like I was ravished all night long? Try explaining that.

"I like that idea," I tell him, running my fingers along his forearm.

"Yeah?" he asks, leaning up so that he can see my face, which of course, blushes.

"Yeah."

Rhenn bends down and kisses my cheek before sliding out of the bed. He carefully heads to the bathroom, watchful not to flash his tented pants to the others lurking in the galley. I risk a glance their way, my eyes immediately connecting with Meghan. She raises an eyebrow and gives me that questioning look. I shrug my shoulders, which earns a smile and a wink in return. She knows, but I'm grateful she chooses to not vocalize her discovery.

I sit up, wrapping the blanket around my legs since I'm wearing only a T-shirt, and head into the kitchen for a cup of coffee. "That looked cozy," she mumbles, handing me an empty mug.

"He had nowhere else to sleep. He was too big for the chair," I reason, knowing it was so much more than that.

"So you just happened to make a spot for him in your bed?" she asks over the rim of her mug. I don't have an answer for her, so I just shrug. "Just be careful, sweetie. He's a great guy, but not one for sticking around too long." Her eyes are sober and honest, and her confirmation of what I already know just makes my throat tighten a bit more.

"I know. He's gone in two weeks."

"And you're okay with that?" she asks quietly, trying not to draw the attention of her husband, who is throwing a few eggs on the griddle.

"I am," I reply with resolve, throwing in a decisive head nod to confirm. "I know what I'm getting myself into."

She watches me for just a moment, before answering. "Good," she says with a smile. "Now, we have a few hours of sun and sailing left before we have to head home and back to our everyday lives, so how about we let the men cook up breakfast and we head up to see if we can spy dolphins," she adds loudly.

"I'll use the restroom and meet you on deck."

* * *

The rest of the day flies by. We sail for a few hours, enjoy lunch on deck under the gorgeous sun, and finally make it back to my place around three in the afternoon. Meghan and Nick have already gathered up their belongings and are ready to disembark the boat, the bedding they used stuffed in a bag. I offer to take it up to my house so that it can be washed, along with anything else Rhenn may need cleaned. He argues at first, but then seems to relent when I tell him it would be easier at my place than at a Laundromat in town.

"I don't want to inconvenience you," he says quietly, placing his lips on my sun-kissed shoulder.

"You won't be. You run a load or two, and then we can go out to dinner. It's simple time management, Rhenn," I tell him with a smile.

"Time management, you say? Like you get to hang out with me while your washing machine cleans my drawers?"

"Exactly. Then, when your clothes are all clean, we come back here. To your boat. For the night."

"I'm so hard right now," he whispers deadpanned. He's also not kidding. He proves his point by flexing his hips and running his erection against my lower back.

"Ready?" Nick asks, interrupting our little moment. Probably a good thing too, since I'm liable to beg him to take me downstairs and have his wicked way with me.

"Yep," Rhenn replies, tightly, before he whispers, "Grandma, Grandma, Grandma."

I can't help but giggle as he eventually gets his hard-on under control and heads to the back of the sailboat to release the small boat we'll use to get to shore. "I'll take them up first and then come back for you and my dirty drawers, okay?"

Nodding, I watch as he helps his friends get into the small boat, their luggage piled on their laps, and takes off for the dock. It doesn't take long at all to drop them off and come back for me. He helps me down into the boat, handing me a lifejacket as he does, which makes me smile. "I think I'll be okay."

"Trust me?"

More than I probably should. More than he'll ever know. Neither answer is one I should give, so I go with, "Yes." Rhenn nods, grabs the rest of the laundry and tosses it on the small space of floor between us. With my bag on my lap, we head to shore.

Nick helps me out, while Rhenn secures the rope, and before we know it, we're back on land and off to the house. I'm surprised to see most of the family there, having a good time and carrying on.

Aunt Emma notices us in the clearing right away. "Hey! They're back!" she bellows loudly, drawing everyone's attention.

We make our way to where everyone is congregating, my mom pulling me into a hug as soon as she can. "You survived," she says with a smile.

"Yeah." Huh, I just realized I didn't take any more Dramamine since yesterday morning and never once felt sick. "It was fun."

"Well, good. I'm happy you had a good time and got to spend some time with Meghan. She seems really sweet."

"She is. We've agreed to stay in touch," I tell her as Rhenn comes up and takes my bag from my hand.

"I'll just drop this at your place," he says, offering me a quick wink before he goes. I follow his movement with my eyes as he takes my stuff, along with his bag of dirty clothes and sheets, and heads into my cottage.

"How did things go with him?" Mom asks, a knowing tone laced in her voice. When I glance at her, she's smiling wide and her eyes twinkle just a little too brightly.

"It went…fine." I should probably leave out the orgasm part.

"Just fine?" she asks, her eyebrows shooting heavenward. "I'd say by the way your face is practically glowing and you can't take your eyes off him that it went a little better than fine."

And cue the blush…

"I agree, Mary Ann. That look right there is one of a woman who let the captain plunder her treasure last night," Aunt Emma interrupts, making me gasp with mortification. She steps closer and adds, "That man's ass is finer than an expensive bottle of wine."

And to make matters worse, she steps closer yet and whispers, "I bet that man could really make you whine. Or moan. Or scream. Am I right?"

I choke. I start sputtering and coughing, trying to catch my breath. Finally able to suck in a deep breath of sweet oxygen, I glance her way, tears streaming down my face, and all eyes on me.

"You okay?" Harper asks, patting my back as a mom would to a small child.

Before I can answer that I was going to make it, Emma speaks for me just as Rhenn returns, a concerned look on his face. "Oh, she's fine. She gave away her booty to the boat captain. Does that make you the wench or him a pirate?" she asks, glancing around for an answer to her question.

Harper busts into fits of laughter, while everyone else just seems to ignore Emma's completely inappropriate question. Maybe they've already spent too much time with her on this short visit? Her granddaughters, while offering looks of pity, are clearly much more immune to her incorrigible behavior than we are.

"I'm going to start a load of laundry, and then I'll help you pack up your car," I say to Meghan, who is fighting a smile. I ignore everyone around me, and quickly retreat into my place. Bathed in quiet, I hear everyone start to speak again, all conversation of Rhenn and me and my...treasure all but forgotten.

"Need help?" Rhenn asks when he comes inside.

"I think I can manage," I respond, grabbing his bag and taking it into the laundry room.

"I'm sure you can, but since it's my stuff, you shouldn't have to do it." To prove his point, he very effectively moves me out of the way and places some of the dirty items from the bag into my washing machine. He grabs the bottle of detergent from the shelf, measuring out the appropriate amount, and dumps it on the bedding.

He selects the correct setting on the machine, closes the lid, and turns my way, leaning his hip against the washer.

"So you've done that before."

"I've managed to care for myself for thirteen whole years, thank you very much," he teases with a wink.

Rhenn steps forward, all traces of humor wiped from his face, as he wraps his strong arms around me, pulling me close. His lips tease mine, the faintest of kisses placed along my jaw, and his hands dropping to grip my rear.

"We should probably get back outside to say goodbye to everyone," I manage to say, albeit completely breathy.

"We should," he says, sliding his tongue along the seam of my lips.

"Maybe after one more kiss?"

He doesn't even respond, just plasters his lips to my own, drawing me into his large frame and holding me tight. His tongue delves inside my mouth, tasting and seducing me with every passing second. Finally, after thoroughly kissing me, he pulls back. "One more kiss may never be enough, Angel."

Oh, he's definitely a smooth talker. I'm putty in his hands when he says things like that to me. Even though I know he doesn't necessarily mean it because eventually, our kisses will be enough. The end is on the horizon, bright and shining like a beacon in the night. That's why I need to forget all about the sweet and sexy things he says to me.

One day, he'll be gone.

And I'll be nothing more than a memory, a good time.

But I'm afraid, if I don't keep this thing in check, he's liable to be so much more.

Chapter Sixteen

Rhenn

"One more kiss may never be enough, Angel."

Truer words have never been spoken.

Her eyes darken and I can practically see the internal war in her head. I shouldn't say things like this, not when the end is drawing near with every passing minute. The fact still remains, our relationship has a deadline. It will come to an end, whether either of us are ready or not. Yet, even though I shouldn't say it, I can't make myself stop. Because at the end of the day, I know that it's true: one more kiss will never be enough.

Needing to change the direction of our thoughts, I go with, "Let's head outside before they all leave."

"Sounds good," she says, steeling her back and turning.

She doesn't make it far before I wrap my hand around her upper arm, and I gently turn her. Her eyes are full of surprise, but it's quickly replaced with heat. "Later, I'm totally ravishing your booty."

Marissa's eyes burn darker and her lush, freshly kissed lips turn upward. "Does that make me your wench, captain?" she teases, her words going straight to my cock. I've pretty much been a walking hard-on for more than a week now. I should probably be concerned about some long-term damage.

Reaching down and grabbing her ass – because it really is fucking phenomenal – I pull her against my body and revel in the feel of her tits pressed against my chest. "Argh." Marissa laughs, places a quick, chaste kiss on my lips and turns to head out the door. I let her go, even though I don't really want to. "I'll just be another minute," I holler after her, watching the sway of her hips as she exits her house. "Once I get this boner under control," I grumble to myself.

"I'd offer to help, but we're on our way out, dear. You'll just have to take care of your lovestick solo," Emma says from behind, startling me.

"Jesus, woman, how did you get in here?"

"I slipped in the back door. If you two were bumping uglies, I wanted to make sure you were doing it right," she adds casually with a sweet grandmotherly smile.

Yet, no grandmother I've ever met is like Emma.

"You're a dirty ol' woman," I snort with a laugh, shaking my head.

"You speak the truth, Rhenn Burleski. Now, come give Emma a big hug so I can pinch your ass one last time before we go," she says, approaching with her hands out.

I should run the other way, but I know she means it in good fun.

Horny ol' woman.

She does, in fact, pinch my ass, as I give her a parting hug. "Come on, let's go find your husband. I bet he's anxious to get everyone on the road."

"He's more disappointed that we're riding with Brian and Cindy. Road-head used to be one of his favorites," she replies with that ornery gleam in her eyes.

I laugh. "Back when you were younger?" I bet they have stories for days.

"Younger? Shoot, Rhenn. Last Tuesday."

* * *

196

After the third load of laundry is pulled from the dryer and folded, I put all the clean clothes back in the bag, minus the khaki shorts and polo I've changed into for tonight. It's just after six and I'm starving. Not only for food, but for Marissa. She's been in her room, packing another night bag and getting ready for dinner. There's a small steakhouse in town that Jensen said was good, so I plan to take her there. Then, we'll come back here to grab the bags and head off to my boat.

For the night.

Just as the last towel is placed in the bag, her bedroom door opens. Marissa steps out wearing a light pink sundress that hugs her curves and dips dangerously low between her tits. She's wearing a bit more makeup than normal and a pair of silver strappy sandals on her feet. Her hair is pulled back from her face, yet spills down her back in long blonde waves. She looks like an angel.

My Angel.

I whistle the moment she steps fully into the kitchen. She offers me a happy smile and spins around one time. The back of the dress is hard-on inducing, with much of her skin exposed. "Damn," I groan, taking in a long, appreciative perusal of her appearance.

"Thank you," she replies, stepping forward, a small white sweater in her hand.

"You look amazing." I place a kiss on her cheek, careful not to get too close to her lips. I'm liable to throw our entire evening plans out the window and take her right here on the kitchen floor.

She runs her hands up my chest, my body already responding to the way she touches me. Yeah, I've had women fawn and grope all over me before, but there's something different in the way her hands feel. It's as if my body is recognizing the person who was made to touch it.

NO.

Stop right there, brain.

You're getting way out of line here. Yes, her touch feels different, but that's probably because I haven't gone this long without sex in my entire life. Well, not since college. As soon as I figured out how many women are willing to fuck for fun, I haven't exactly had a shortage of bedmates.

And now I just feel like the biggest pile of shit ever.

"You okay?" she asks, pulling back and gazing up at me with big, trusting eyes.

Clearing my throat, I reply, "Yeah. You ready?"

She nods and takes my hand. My heart starts to pound at the small gesture, and I can't even begin to understand why. I haven't even slept with this woman yet, and she has me tied in knots. That's a sign that I should leave. I should get back on my boat and sail into the fucking sunset.

But I won't.

I can't.

Yeah, I might be confused about these pesky feelings that keep trying to push to the surface, but I'm not confused about one thing: sex. She asked for a no-strings relationship, and if there's one thing I'm good at it's that. I can give her exactly what she wants, and at the end of our time, walk away with a smile on my face.

And plenty of memories burned into my mind that I'll never forget.

She doesn't lock her house, something I've noticed she rarely does, as we head out. My truck is still parked in the driveway, right next to her small car. I help her up in the cab – like all good gentlemen do – never once copping a feel. Okay, lie. I totally brush my hand over her delicious ass as she climbs up. The knowing look on her face tells me she felt it, and the naughty grin lets me know it didn't bother her one bit.

It doesn't take long to arrive at the place her brother recommended. It's a small restaurant with well-worn tables and chairs, and a comfortable atmosphere. There are plenty of open tables, probably in light of the fact that today's Memorial Day. "Have a seat anywhere," the bartender says from behind the bar, a handful of patrons parked on stools.

"Over here," Marissa says, heading away from the few tables with diners and toward the dark booth in the back.

A waitress comes from the kitchen area, bringing us menus and glasses of water. "Oh, hey, Marissa. How are you?" the tall brunette says, setting down our glasses.

"Good, Felicity. How are things with you? When did you move back to town?" Marissa says, her smile just a tad tight as she gives the waitress her attention.

"Oh, everything's good. I just got back a few weeks ago. I heard your sister opened up a shop down the street?" the waitress coos to Marissa.

"She did," Marissa confirms, glancing down at her menu and not elaborating further.

"I'll have to stop in. I haven't seen her in forever," Felicity says, drawing out the last word and flipping her long hair over her shoulder.

"I'm sure she'd be delighted." Only I can tell Marissa doesn't think her sister would be all that happy to see Felicity drop by for a visit.

"Are you ready to order?" I ask Marissa, trying to steer the conversation to safer ground.

She orders a steak and fries, while I choose the steak and baked potato. We both order a beer, and while our waitress goes off to grab our drinks and salad bar plates, I reach for her hand and rub the tender skin over her knuckles. "So what was with Felicity?"

Marissa rolls her eyes. "She hated my sister in school. They competed for everything. Head cheerleader, class president, the quarterback, everything."

"So her asking about Harper and wanting to stop by was bullshit?"

"Probably. She just wants to be nosy and see what Harp has been up to," Marissa says quickly as Felicity returns with our beers.

"Here ya go. And if you need anything, just let me know," Felicity says with a big smile, winking at me before she turns to leave.

I ignore her parting comment and return my eyes to my date. "So? Who won?"

Marissa sets her bottle down on the table and gives me a questioning look. "Who won what?"

"Head cheerleader, class president, and the quarterback."

"Oh," she laughs, her eyes sparkling with mirth. "Harper won it all."

I laugh. "Of course she did. She's the bomb."

"She won because she was the whole package. Harper has always been beautiful, charismatic, smart, and outgoing."

"Well, Felicity back in town might make things a bit more interesting," I say, taking a drink of my own beer.

"Definitely. I have no doubt there are no good intentions where she's concerned."

A few seconds of silence hang between us. Marissa scans the room, checking out the other diners, while I take the opportunity to check her out. Her eyes are a bright green, very similar to those of her cousin's. Her cheekbones are high and swiped with a hint of pink, and her lips have a light sheen of nude colored gloss. I almost wish they were painted a deep red so I can smear it all over her face with my lips.

Felicity returns with plates for the salad bar. We make our way to the opposite side of the room and fill up on salad, pasta, and fruit. Marissa wastes no time diving in the moment we get back to the table. I love the fact that she isn't afraid to eat.

"Tell me more about your family." The words are out of my mouth between bites before I can stop them. I never want to know family details. Never. But with Marissa, I find myself wanting to know everything about what makes her *her*.

"Well, you've met them all. Samuel is a mortician at one of the funeral parlors. He's the oldest, never married, and probably showers in his suit." That makes me laugh, because, frankly, I think it might be true. "Harper is next and owns a lingerie store in town."

Leaning forward, I set my fork down and drop my voice. "Do you own anything from there, Angel?"

Her eyes meet mine, a slow burn filling those emerald orbs. "Maybe."

"Maybe I can see them sometime?"

"I'm pretty sure that if you continue to play your cards right, you'll be seeing them in about an hour," she adds with a flare of sass that goes straight to my balls.

I playfully gasp. "You're wearing something from her lingerie shop right now?"

"It's quite possible," she says with a shrug.

"Let me see." I reach for the tablecloth and bend down to look under the table.

"Stop!" she whisper-yells, swatting at my hand with her own.

"I'm not going to be able to sit here and eat, knowing you're wearing something dirty under that beautiful dress."

"I'm sure you'll survive."

"Probably not," I add sadly, picking up a piece of lettuce with my fork. "Unless…you wanted to just give me a little hint?"

Marissa shakes her head, a joyful smile on her face. "A hint, huh? Like if I just mention that they're blue like your eyes, that'll get you through until the later part of our evening?"

Blue like my eyes. Holy shit, this woman is doing a number on me. "What about the material? The color is a delightful detail, but if you told me the material, I'm sure I'd be able to survive the next hour."

"You're incorrigible."

"That I am, Angel. That I am," I answer, offering her a smile and taking a bite of my pasta salad. She doesn't say anything for several seconds, and the silence suits us just fine. I'm comfortable with her in nearly any situation, and I love the fact neither of us feels the need to add mindless chatter.

When I push my plate away, I see she's already finished her salad. She glances my way, a smirk toying on her lips. "Satin with lace. Thong." Without saying a word, I toss my napkin down on the table, reach for her hand, which she reluctantly and with a lot of question in her eyes takes, and haul her to her feet. "Where are we going? We haven't eaten dinner?"

I place my lips to hers. "We're taking it to go, Angel."

"But you asked for a hint," she counters.

"Yeah, but now the picture is so vivid in my head, I need to know if the real thing is just as fucking phenomenal as what I'm imagining."

Her eyes dilate and darken, even beneath the low lighting of the restaurant. Felicity returns to the table, a plate in each hand, and gives us a questioning look. I'm sure I look like I'm about to throw this woman over my shoulder, our destination unknown, but one fact remains: I want to fuck the hell out of her. All. Night. Long.

Marissa keeps her eyes locked on mine as she says, "We'll take those steaks to go, Felicity."

Guilt sweeps in, and I open my mouth to protest. This isn't how a date works, at least not a proper one. I should be able to control my cock for an hour so that we can enjoy a nice meal together. The end of the evening is already pretty much a guarantee, but that doesn't mean I should turn all caveman-like on her and forget my manners.

Before I tell our waitress to leave the food and take my seat in the booth, Marissa goes for the kill. She grazes her hand over my hard cock, essentially cutting off what little blood flow I had to my actual brain, and says, "Check please."

She turns and winks at Felicity, who's standing beside us, mouth gaping open and shock written all over her face. Then, because this woman is hell-bent on stepping over every line she's ever drawn in place for herself, she threads her hands behind my neck and pulls me down, her lips meeting mine in a fierce kiss.

A kiss that's a prelude.

A promise.

Best. Date. Ever.

Chapter Seventeen

Marissa

I have no idea who has taken over my body, but I think I like it. This bolder, wilder version of Marissa Grayson is a force to be reckoned with, that's for sure.

I can't keep my hands off him as Felicity goes back to box up our meals. We're not inappropriate, but we're teetering close to the borderline. Rhenn has his hands on my ass, slowly inching the back of my skirt up my legs. With each passing second, I feel a bit more air hitting my overheated skin. Thank God we're in the back of the restaurant, and no one seems to be paying us much attention.

Once she returns with our boxes and the check, Rhenn throws a handful of bills on the table, grabs my hand, and we bolt for the door. He's practically dragging me behind him, but I don't care. I'm just as anxious for this next part of our evening as he is. When we reach the truck, he spins me around, making my skirt flare out around me, and pins me against the steel. With my back flat against the truck, he kisses the air straight from my body. It's only when a car passes and honks its horn do we startle apart.

"I can't seem to control myself when I'm around you," he pants, warm breath peppering my forehead.

"Personally, I like you out of control," I tell him, my voice just as breathy as his was.

Rhenn glances down, his dark blue eyes meeting mine. "What do you say we head back to the boat?"

"I'm ready."

And I am. So ready.

Without saying a work, Rhenn helps me into the cab of his truck, hands me the bag of Styrofoam containers, and places a quick, chaste kiss on my lips. Then, he practically sprints around the hood of the truck and jumps in the driver's seat. I'm not sure how many laws we break on our ride back to my place, but I know there were a few.

Rhenn drives up the empty driveway, parking his truck beside my car. My seat belt is off and the door is open before he can even meet me around to my side of the vehicle. I take his offered hand, grabbing the food as I go, and slide out of the big truck. Before my feet hit the ground, his lips are on mine, hungry and full of desire. He presses me against the metal, my legs instantly wrapping around his waist. The food falls to the ground, but neither of us care. Right now, his tongue is claiming my mouth and my sanity.

"Damn, you drive me so fucking crazy," he growls as he nips at my jaw and grinds into the apex of my legs.

My response is a loud groan that would make a hooker proud. My panties are soaked, ruined probably, but I don't care. I'm still throwing myself at this man, practically begging him to take me right here, against the side of his truck. Rhenn's ability to read my mind works wonders right now, as his teeth pull at my bottom lip and his hand moves from my rear. My skirt is already balled up around my waist, which makes it easier for him to slip his hand between our bodies and connect with my core.

"So wet and ready," he groans, his lips devouring the sensitive skin on my neck. I'm pretty sure he's going to leave marks, but I don't care. Not one bit. As long as he doesn't stop…

"I won't stop," he whispers, confirming I have no control over my own mouth and clearly said the plea aloud. Rhenn slides my panties to the side, teasing my clit as he goes, and I'm about to lose my mind. "Is this what you want?" he asks as he slowly presses a finger inside my body.

My response is another groan. I'm physically unable to form words right now, and when he applies a bit of pressure with his thumb to my clit, I practically detonate like a bomb. It's quite embarrassing, actually, how quickly he makes me come, but there's no time to revel in my shame, since his fingers are currently stroking every last bit of my release from my body.

"Fuck, I could watch you come all day long and never tire of it," Rhenn says, taking my mouth with his once more. This kiss is a bit slower, as if he's drawing out and savoring my orgasm. When my shaking stops, he gently pulls his fingers from my body, picks up the discarded bag of food, and strolls with purpose toward my cottage.

I reach down and open the door so he doesn't have to move his hands from my butt. Plus, I don't want him to break his concentration because Rhenn is able to kiss my lips and neck, while still navigating through the yard without looking. It's a talent of his, I'm sure. This man was built for seduction and sex, and he just continues to prove it over and over again.

When we slip inside my cottage, he kicks the door closed and tosses the bag of food on the counter. With quick strides that eat up the floor, he moves to my bedroom. At the doorway, he says, "Maybe just one more before we hit the boat?"

I can't help but chuckle. "I'm not sure it's possible, but you can try."

As we reach the bed, he gazes down at me, his eyes so intense that I almost choke on oxygen. "Oh, it's definitely possible, baby, and pretty much a guarantee. I'm going to show you what every fuck before me should have been giving you."

He drops me on the bed, but comes down with me, my legs still wrapped around him. Rhenn lifts himself up and gazes down at the apex of my legs. My dress is hiked up, panties slightly askew, and wetness coating the entire area, definitely from the fingerbang I was just awarded.

"One more," he confirms, licking his lips before dropping his head between my legs.

His tongue slides slowly over the panties, sending post-orgasmic shockwaves raking through my blood. A loud gasp fills the room, one that doesn't even sound like it could come from me, and it only seems to spur him on. His tongue – oh, his magical, unbelievably talented tongue – toys with my clit through the material. The friction adds something I never expected, something that seems to awaken the woman who's lain dormant inside of me my entire life.

Rhenn grabs the panties at my hips and slowly brings them down, cool air kissing my exposed bare skin. He helps lift my legs straight up in the air, removing my underwear as he goes, and peppering open-mouth kisses on the backs of my thighs, knees, and calves. When he tosses them somewhere into the room, he allows my legs to fall open once more. Rhenn stares down at my center, his hands gently spreading my thighs farther apart.

"You have the most beautiful pussy I've ever seen." I shiver at his dirty words, not even caring that he's admittedly seen his fair share of them. "I've never wanted to bury my face in one as badly as I want to yours, Angel. I'm going to lick, suck, and fuck this pussy until you're screaming my name."

I whimper in anticipation, the determined look in his eyes lets me know he's about to do just that. There's no way a man like this would leave me anything less than completely satisfied.

Then he moves. His mouth descends on me, his tongue connecting with my bare, wet skin for the first time, and I almost see stars. Rhenn demonstrates just how well versed he is on the art of oral, teasing and sucking on my clit, drawing me closer to another impending orgasm. His tongue delves into my center and my hips start to rock against his face. He holds my thighs open and continues to devour me with nothing but his amazing mouth and tongue.

The orgasm is building, I can feel it gathering in my toes, ready to consume my entire being. Rhenn moves his mouth back to my clit, his fingers finding my wet pussy. He slowly pushes two fingers inside while his mouth clamps down on my swollen clit, making me see stars and gasp his name. His fingers work their way in, stretching my body to accommodate them in the most amazing way.

My hands grasp his head, my fingers pull at his hair, as my hips move in a frantic rhythm on their own. I'm like a wild madwoman, hell-bent on riding out this epic orgasm that's threatening to erupt from within. When he curls his fingers upward, hitting that magical little button deep inside of me, I detonate. Rhenn sucks hard and licks frantically on my clit while his fingers pump into me, as I scream my release.

As I start to feel my body coming down from the epic high, Rhenn continues to lick and work his fingers in my pussy, clearly not ready to end his play. The gingerly strokes to my G-spot combined with his warm tongue lapping at my pulsing clit sends blood rushing to my center. I can feel the second one building before I can even think about stopping it. And why would I?

"Again," he growls, removing his fingers and quickly replacing them with his tongue. He plunges his tongue deep inside repeatedly as his fingers find purchase with my clit. Rhenn pinches and caresses it, basically playing my body masterfully like a violin.

The result is another orgasm that leaves my body completely boneless, with no life or energy remaining.

Rhenn curls up next to me on his side, his head in his hand as he gazes down at me. "You okay there, sweetheart?" His trademarked smirk is back, and if I had any energy left in my body, I'd probably smack his smug ass.

"Fine." It comes out a pant.

"Ready for round two?" he asks, bending down and slowly kissing my lips.

When he finally allows me a moment to catch my breath, I respond, "Wasn't that round two?"

"Hell, no. That was a really long, continual round one. Round two takes place on my boat. And we'll both be naked." His words are low and dirty, and believe it or not, my body responds. I have no idea how, but it does.

"We should grab the food," I say, turning to my side and facing him. I slide my fingers through his hair, loving the way it feels.

"I'll definitely be feeding you. I need you to keep up your strength. I'll even let you catch a catnap between rounds two and three," he replies, waggling his eyebrows suggestively.

"Three?"

He bends down and grazes his lips over my jaw. "I told you, Angel. I won't stop until you've had five."

* * *

The boat ride is silent as we make our way to the bigger boat anchored offshore. Both times I was on this little thing, it was broad daylight, but now, it's quite dark, which adds a little creepiness to the ambiance. There's a bag of clean clothes on the floor between his bench seat and mine, an overnight bag on my lap. Do you know what else is riding shotgun in this boat?

Sexual tension.

We've got it in spades, that's for sure. As soon as Rhenn got up from my bed (after thoroughly kissing me until I was breathless once more), he was gathering my bag for tonight's excursion. He tried to mask the discomfort he had going on in his pants, but it was fruitless. He was hard and aching and ready for what's next.

We approach the boat and he heads straight toward the lift on the back, which he lowers with a small remote control. "Are you okay on the ladder?" he asks, gently maneuvering us alongside it.

"Sure." I got this.

"Leave the bags and I can throw them up when I secure this boat," he says, shutting off the trolling motor and grabbing the rungs of the ladder. When he has us steady beside the boat, I make my way up the rungs and onto the deck. After a couple of successful ascents and descents, I feel like an ol' pro at this whole boat thing.

On deck, I head over to where Nick stood the other day, ready to help Rhenn secure the small boat to the back. But Rhenn is obviously more than equipped with the knowledge and tools he needs to do the job solo, because before I know it, it's secured and in place, he's setting the bags on the deck, and climbing over the railing.

The moment his feet hit the ground, he pounces. Rhenn hoists me into his arms, my legs once more returning to his waist, and his lips are kissing me soundly. He bends down and grabs both bags in his hand, not even for a second breaking our connection, and heads toward the stairs. "One of these nights, I'm going to take you on the deck under the moon and stars."

Rhenn secures the door, finishes carrying me down the stairs, and walks me straight back to the bedroom.

Where we realize we still have to make the bed.

He groans his frustrations (probably most of it sexual), and slowly lowers me to the floor. I lose my balance just a hair, stumbling to the side as the boat gently rocks. "Careful there, Angel," he says as he reaches for my arm to help me balance.

"I'm not much of a seaman," I tease, wondering if I'll ever get my sea legs.

Rhenn throws me a smirk and replies, "Good thing for you I have the semen covered. Lots and lots of semen."

The burn sweeps up my cheeks as a bubble of laughter flies from my lips. "Cocky much?"

"Soooo cocky," he grumbles, flexing his hips and reminding me just how *cocky* he is when it presses against my side.

"You're unbelievable," I giggle, turning into his embrace as his hand grips my hip.

"I'll take that as a compliment."

"I had no doubt that you would. Come on, let's get this bed made so we can dirty it up again."

His eyes dilate and flare. "I love it when you talk all dirty-like." With a chaste kiss on my lips, he pulls back and grabs the laundry bag, pulling the clean sheets out.

We make quick work of making the bed. I've made beds with a partner before – Mom and I tag team chores all the time at the bed and breakfast – but this is the first time I've ever made the bed with a man. Especially for us just to rip it all apart once more. My heart rate starts to kick up a few beats per second as realization sets in. Before, I wasn't able to think – only feel and react. But now I have all this time to really think about what we're about to do – what I want to do.

It's exhilarating.

Yet, a little bit scary to step out of my comfort zone.

"Change your mind?" he asks, breaking through my thoughts.

"What? No."

Rhenn seems to visually look relieved. "Good. You just seemed like you were thinking awfully hard for a second. I just wanted to make sure we were still on the same page."

"We're definitely on the same page," I confirm, glancing down and realizing the bed is completely made. The comforter and sheets are folded down, just the way I do when we're turning down the bed at night for a houseguest.

"Did I do it wrong?" he asks, glancing down at the bedding with a worried look on his face.

"No, you did it just right. That's the way I do it when a guest is arriving late after a long trip."

He nods his head and reaches for my hand. I place mine in his without hesitation. Rhenn pulls me against him and slowly brings his head down to meet mine. Tilting my face toward him, our lips meet once more, soft, yet with a bit of urgency gathering beneath the surface. I can already feel the build, can already taste exactly how amazing this is going to be – and I have no doubt that it will be every ounce of just that.

"I'm going to take off your dress," he whispers, grazing gentle kisses across my jaw and down my neck.

"Yes, please," I reply, making him chuckle.

"So polite," he says as he grips the hem of my dress and slowly brings it up my body. "So sexy," he adds as he gathers it over my head and drops it on the floor beside us. "So beautiful," he states, his eyes devouring every inch of my exposed body.

I'm wearing a strapless bra that matched the panties that are still lying on my bedroom floor, and nothing else but my sandals. With an expert flick of his fingers, Rhenn removes the bra, leaving me standing before him completely naked. Even with the lights off, I feel completely exposed. I can see every facial expression, every emotion under the bright moonlight.

Taking me in his arms once more, Rhenn carries me to the mattress and gently sets me down. My heart is beating erratically in my chest as I watch him stand up tall, his head barely clearing the lower ceiling of the cabin, and pull his polo shirt from his shorts. His eyes are locked on mine as he removes the shirt, exposing his incredibly chiseled chest. The thump of his shoes hitting the floor fills the room, but my eyes are glued to his waist. With long, thick fingers, Rhenn slowly unbuttons his shorts, followed quickly by the bite of zipper teeth.

I hold my breath as he pushes his shorts and boxer briefs down his waist, past his tree trunk thighs, and drops them on the floor. His erection is every bit as hard, thick, and long as I remember last night, only this time, I'm getting a full picture of everything else too. Warmth floods my center, and honestly, I'm not sure how I can be wet again, especially after three back-to-back orgasms, but here I am, wetness practically spilling down my thighs and my body begging for him to make me come again.

Without saying a word, he joins me on the bed, reaching over to the cabinet on the side and pulls out a strip of foil packets. He tosses them on the bed beside me and crawls up my body. We lie together, completely naked for the first time. I wrap my legs around his waist and reach for his neck. My short nails bite into his skin as he presses his lips to mine. Our tongues entwine, our lips dance, as we bring our bodies in line. I can feel the hard press of his erection against me, and all I want to do is grind against it.

So I do.

Rhenn threads his fingers into my hair, his kiss turning more bruising with every passing second. Finally, he pulls back and growls, "You're going to make me lose my mind," he says, reaching for the strip of condoms.

My only reply is a pant as I watch him rip it open and slide it over his cock. As soon as he's completely sheathed, he positions himself between my thighs, brings my legs up to his waist, and starts to press forward. There's a slight burn, a sweet ache, as he stretches me farther than anticipated. "Are you okay?" he asks, stopping his movements and gazing down at my face.

"Please don't stop," I beg, flexing my hips to encourage him on.

"Fuck," he mumbles as he closes his eyes. His chin drops to his chest as if to gather his thoughts. The moment he opens them again, he looks down at where we're joined, a fierce look crossing his face. "Ready?" he asks, stretching over the top of me and kissing my lips once more.

"Definitely."

As soon as the word is out of my mouth, Rhenn springs into action. He positions himself on his knees and uses his leverage to slowly pull from my body. When he's almost completely out, he glances my way once more. He gives me no warning, but pistons his hips, filling me completely.

I gasp, the stretch and ache quickly replaced with pure desire. He sets a fast pace, pumping into me with everything he has. His hands roam my body, teasing my nipples and holding me by my hips. Rhenn moves his hand above my hip, changing up the angle as he continues to drive into me with force and determination. He lifts my right leg, hitching it over his hip, which aligns him up perfectly to hit just where he needs to.

I can already feel the familiar stirring of another release. Where it could possibly be coming from, I have no clue, but I'm not about to turn it down. Instead, I encourage it, spreading my legs wider and gripping his back. His lips find my neck once more as he kisses and sucks on the sensitive skin. My entire body is alive and begging for the release it craves.

Rhenn must sense how close I am and brings his body down on top of mine. He's buried so deep that I'm not sure where he ends and I begin. Our mouths come together, our kisses frantic and wild. "I can tell you're about to come. I can feel your pussy tightening on my cock," he whispers, driving himself into me once more.

"So good," I whimper, locking my ankles around his waist.

"You ready to come, Angel?"

"Yes," I pant, that one word a plea.

Rhenn grunts and flexes his hips, grinding himself against me. "Come now."

And as if my orgasm was somehow connected to his words, I fly over the cliff, soaring with the birds in a sea of tranquility and bright lights. I don't even realize I'm saying anything until he says, "Fuck, I love hearing my name on that sweet tongue of yours while you're coming. Say it again," he demands, his body tight and his moves more frantic.

"Rhenn," I moan, my body reaching the peak and slowly starting to float back down to the ground.

"Fuck," he replies just as his body stills completely and he lets go. Rhenn pumps fast little short strokes as he releases himself inside me. His lips are immediately pressed against my neck, my jaw, and my lips, as his hips start to slow and his body begins to relax. His weight starts to push me into the mattress, but I don't mind. There's something oddly comforting about him pressing me into the bed, his cock still nestled within me.

When Rhenn finally rolls over, he takes me with him, my body half lying on his, half on the mattress. "Are you okay?" he whispers, holding me tightly against his chest.

"I'm better than okay," I answer honestly, my heart rate finally starting to approach normal level and surprised by how comfortable it is to relax on his chest.

He turns so that he's facing me and takes my head in his hands. His kisses are sweet, with less urgency than before. Now it seems more of a savor than a devour. "I'm going to run to the bathroom and grab a washcloth. Stay right here," he says, slowly untangling his body from mine and getting out of bed. I can't help but watch his rear as he walks into the bathroom and takes care of the condom.

When he returns, he places a warm washcloth between my legs and wipes away the remnants of moisture. I can already tell I'm a bit sore, but that's to be expected when the man you're sleeping with is packing a Louisville Slugger in his pants. After he has me cleaned up, along with himself, Rhenn slips back into bed, pulling the comforter up and over us as he goes. He tucks me against his side, gently pushing my hair back from my forehead, and places another slow kiss on my lips. I hope he never tires of kissing me. They're pretty much magical.

My body is tired and sated and suddenly, I'm not sure I could keep my eyes open another second. I feel his arms tighten around me as I relax my hand on his chest. "Good night, Angel."

"Good night, Rhenn," I reply, unable to open my eyes.

As I start to drift off to sleep, I realize that it's not just the gentle rocking of the boat or the light sounds of the waves outside. It's not even the warmth of this man's embrace or the record-breaking four orgasms he drew from my body. It's a combination of all the above that has me more relaxed than I've been in a long time, if ever. It's Rhenn and everything that goes with him that has me so grateful I took a chance on him. No, there's no future in our forecast, but maybe that's okay. Maybe this – this casual, carefree hook-up – can be exactly what I need in my life right now.

It better be, because at the end of the day, that's the only offer on the table.

Table.

Hmm, maybe we could try something dirty and fun on the table next?

Chapter Eighteen

Rhenn

I startle awake, trying to recall exactly what I was dreaming about. I remember taking a blow to the chest, and maybe one to the jaw, as I think back to what karate class I was rewinding in my dream.

But I come up blank.

And then I come under attack again with an elbow to the gut.

"Mom," Marissa whimpers, her hands reaching and tugging at something that isn't there.

"Marissa?" I whisper, not wanting to startle her. She thrashes to the side, nearly punching me in the balls. "Angel, honey, wake up. You're having a bad dream." I try to keep my voice calm and even, gently shaking her shoulder to try to rouse her without fright. Reaching up, I tenderly cup her cheek, stroking her jaw with my thumb.

She startles, her eyes flying open and connecting with mine. "Hey, beautiful."

Marissa looks around, trying to catch her bearings before returning those deep green eyes to me. "What's going on?"

"You were having a bad dream."

Her eyes fill with tears. She doesn't have to say a word for me to know whatever she was dreaming about affected her deeply. And then I remember Nick telling me about a conversation Marissa and Meghan had, about how she's having nightmares about the fire.

"Do you want to talk about it?" I ask, rolling to my side and taking her with me. There's something wildly comforting about holding her in my arms at two in the morning. I try to ignore it, but I can't. When have I ever woken up at two and offered to *chat* with a woman? Never, that's when.

Marissa is silent for a bit, her face pressed against my bare chest. I run my fingers up and down her spine in a reassuring manner, rather than a sexual one. I feel the wetness of her tears hit my skin before I hear the sniffle. My gut tightens painfully as I think about her upset enough to cry. I don't like the feeling, not one bit.

"I keep having the same dream over and over again," she says quietly, her voice timid with emotion.

"What's it about?" I ask, reaching down and swiping away the tears on her cheek.

She swallows hard. "I can't get her out. My mom is trapped in the house when the fire breaks out and I can't save her. I can hear her screams," she whispers, her hushed voice full of pain and fear, as another tear spills from her eyes.

Not really knowing what to say, I hold her close and continue to rub her back. "Can you tell me what actually happened? You mom wasn't even there when the fire broke out."

"You're right, she wasn't. We had two couples staying that weekend, and Mom was on the fence about going to see her brother after so long. We convinced her to go, especially since the bed and breakfast wasn't full. I could definitely handle two couples for two days.

"So she went and I took care of business. After dinner was cleaned up and everyone had retired to their rooms for the night, I went back to my place. It was a beautiful night, one of the first real warm ones of the spring, so I went for a walk on the beach. I was gone, maybe forty-five minutes, when I came back up the path to the house. I remembered that Mom had left a few windows open in her part of the house to let the fresh air in so I went back up to the main house to close them. As I approached, I could smell the smoke. It was this horrible burnt plastic smell." She looks up at me. "I'm not sure I'll ever get that smell out of my head."

"It's definitely not pleasant," I confirm, having smelled it plenty of times in my line of work.

"Anyway, I went running inside and into her wing of the house just as the sparks jumped from the outlet in the wall and the smoke alarms went off. I called 911 and grabbed one of the extinguishers we have in the house, but by the time I got off the phone with them and could engage it, the outlet had flames shooting out of it, the fire starting to devour the old plaster and wood in seconds.

"They say that the extinguisher definitely helped it from getting worse, but it wasn't able to completely put it out. It was in the wall, which is why they had to remove so much of her bedroom and bath outer wall."

She takes a deep breath and continues. "The couples upstairs had come down to find out what was going on and pulled me from the house. When the fire department arrived, they were able to contain the fire to Mom's bedroom and bathroom, and a bit of damage to the ceiling. I don't want to think about what could have happened had I not been out for a walk that night," she adds, shaking her head.

"How did it start? I haven't read the report."

"Hairdryer. It was plugged in and the fire marshal says it was caused by dust. Dust. Can you believe it?"

"Actually, I can. I've heard it happening more than you think, especially in older homes. The wiring and receptacles aren't quite as good as the newer stuff."

"We had updated everything in the kitchen when we bought the place, but were told the rest of it was fine."

"And it was. It probably could have been fine for a lot more years, Marissa. It was a fluke thing that happened, and there was nothing you could have done to prevent it or change it," I assure her.

"I know that, I do, but I can't help but think 'what if my mom had been home?' Every time that thought enters my mind, I want to throw up."

"Understandably, but you need to remember that she wasn't home. You did what you were supposed to do, had extinguishers handy. Most people don't even have extinguishers, let alone know how to use them." I bend down and kiss her forehead. "Everything happens for a reason, Angel. You mom wasn't there because she wasn't meant to be." I'm quiet for a bit, enjoying the feel of her skin against mine. Finally, I open my mouth to speak. "The reason I named my boat *Runaround Sue* was because I caught my old girlfriend, Suzanne, screwing one of my frat buddies."

She gasps in shock and looks up at me. "That's horrible."

"Yeah," I laugh humorlessly. "It wasn't fun." Deep breath and swallow. "I thought I'd marry her one day, you know? I thought she was it. I had a ring picked out and everything."

"How long did you date?"

"More than two years. We were nearing the end of our senior year and starting to make plans. Plans that involved us being together."

"Holy cow, Rhenn, I'm sorry. What a shitty thing to do."

"Yep," I say, tightening my arms around her. She's nothing like Suzanne. Even the way she feels against me is different. Better.

Marissa exhales again and relaxes against my chest. Her hand is resting beside her head, right over my heart, and I can't help but wonder if she feels how hard it's beating right now. Can she tell how she impacts my body, just by something as simple as a touch?

"Thank you," she yawns, her entire body starting to unwind from the stress and guilt she's carried.

"You're welcome, Marissa," I reply, kissing her once more on the forehead.

"I like it when you call me Angel," she whispers, almost inaudibly.

"Good night, my Angel."

My throat thickens with emotion as I try to swallow. Why does she make me feel so…alive? So wanted? So good? So free? I feel completely free to be me, but not really the old me. This new version of me who enjoys talking and laughing with a woman as much as I enjoy fucking her.

Because it's her.

I know it.

I'm just not anywhere near ready to understand what that means.

* * *

The sun is peeking through the window, and I'm pretty sure that means Marissa is already running late. She's used to moving and working before anyone else, making sure her guests have fresh coffee and breakfast before they head off to whatever adventures call to them for the day.

Today, work calls to us – cleaning, more accurately. I'm slowly making my way through the upstairs bedrooms' rewires, a job that I could have already had completed, yet find myself wanting to slow it down just so I can spend a few more minutes with her.

Glancing over, I find the most beautiful woman in the world sprawled out in my bed, using my arm as a pillow. I don't want to rouse her from sleep, especially since she looks completely stunning naked in my bed, but know her mom will be arriving soon for their morning coffee and visit, as well as to get the day's schedule for work ironed out. The last thing I want is for her to be late, all because I couldn't keep it in my pants again.

Besides, I already hit my target with five orgasms when I woke her up about an hour ago and insisted she take a shower, all so I could dirty her up again. Now, here I am, achingly hard cock and an unquenchable appetite for a certain blonde, and instead of taking what I need (like I usually would), I want to make sure she gets as much rest as possible, especially since I know she'll be sore today.

I want my girl to rest a bit, is that so wrong?

Nope.

"You're staring at me," she mumbles without opening her eyes.

"Because you're beautiful," I state honestly.

"Why is the sun out?"

"That usually happens around this time every morning," I quip, pulling her into my arms and sliding my nose along the column of her neck.

"Smartass," she replies, fighting a smile. "What time is it?" she finally asks, opening her eyes and glancing around.

"After six."

"Shit," she grumbles, throwing the blankets off her naked body and trying to get up.

My arm snakes out around her waist as I pull her back into bed, covering her with my entire body. "Where do you think you're going?" I ask.

"I need to get up to the house. The guys will start working at seven, and I need to make sure I'm there. I need a quick shower and some coffee, and get ready to work."

"But we took a shower a bit ago," I remind her, nipping at her left earlobe.

"Yes, but that wasn't really a shower. That was really wet sex," she says, making me laugh.

"That was really wet, amazing sex," I confirm. "And it's a good thing I'm such a gentleman or I'm liable to take you back into the shower and fuck you against the tile instead of kissing you good morning and sending you on your way."

Her cheeks flush. "That actually doesn't sound so bad."

"I think it sounds pretty fucking great, myself, but I don't want to hurt you."

"You won't," she replies, my stubborn, determined goddess.

"Well, I've already decided to be a gentleman. So you're just going to have to settle for a good morning kiss. And maybe an ass grab. Your ass is phenomenal naked," I say, wiggling my eyebrows and sliding my hands beneath her body to cup her ass. Her giggles go straight to my cock, who is completely on board with the whole wet sex thing.

"Let's go start some coffee, and then you can jump in the shower," I say, kissing her chastely on the lips.

"Alone?"

"All alone, Angel. Otherwise, I'll never let you leave."

"That would make it hard for me to get anything done," she teases.

"So hard."

Marissa reaches down and palms my dick. "Yes, so, so hard."

Then she does something I'm not expecting. She shimmies down my body, pushes me onto my back, and sucks my cock down her throat. Instantly, I see stars.

Apparently, we're both going to be a little late today.

Chapter Nineteen

Marissa

I'm rushing up the path toward my cottage, my hair still wet from the shower we took together, and my bag in my hand. I should have been up here an hour ago, and maybe I would have been if not for the morning blowjob, followed by the most amazing oral by his magical tongue in the shower. Have I mentioned before just how wonderful his tongue is?

I have. I know.

I can't help it.

It's worth mentioning again.

Rhenn is currently running up the beach. He decided to get in a short run (and by short, I mean a quick three mile, eighteen minute run) before taking another shower (this one solo) and working on the house. He's going to use my shower though, so he doesn't have to go back out to his sailboat. It's a huge timesaver to just come up to my place and jump in the shower, you know? I'm all about helping out and saving a little time.

Plus, I really hope to catch another peek at him naked.

I step inside my cottage, drop the bag on the floor, and smell it.

Coffee.

Mom is sitting at the table, a knowing smirk on her face as she sips from her cup. "Have a good weekend?"

My face flushes red as I make my way to the coffee pot, doing everything humanly possible to avoid eye contact. "Sure."

She doesn't say anything while I fix up my own cup. It isn't lost on me that she made a full pot either. It's like she knew there would be a third person drinking it. "Rhenn well?"

How to answer that loaded question? Do I confirm he's fine (three orgasms in about eight hours will do that to a man) or do I go the opposite way and risk it looking like our night wasn't any big deal. Because it most certainly was a big deal – and I'm not just talking about what the man is packing in his pants. Plus, there's the fact that I'm the worst liar ever and Mom will see straight through me and any lie I try to pedal.

"He's...good."

Oh my God, did she turn on the heat? It's stifling in here.

Mom actually laughs at me. She looks me straight in the eye and laughs. "Good? Are we talking about how he is or how he...*was?*" she asks as she wiggles her eyebrows.

"Mom!" I gasp, almost dropping my coffee mug.

"What? You think I don't know the look of a woman who enjoyed her night with a handsome man? I mean if the walk of shame home at seven in the morning wasn't going to tip me off, that blush you've had since the moment I mentioned his name sure did it." And then, she shrugs and takes another sip of coffee as if she didn't just call me out.

I take a seat across from her and eye her over the rim of my cup. "Technically, it wasn't a walk of shame. I'm in fresh clothes."

That makes her laugh, which in turn, makes me grin. "It's good to see you smile. It's been a while."

"I'm enjoying spending time with him," I add with a shrug.

"I'm glad, sweetheart."

"How was it this weekend, spending time with your brother?" I ask her, diving into our comfortable morning chitchat.

"I wish we hadn't been so stubborn all those years ago. It's hard to believe we let so many years pass without contact, but I was young, as was he, and our lives just took us in opposite directions."

I reach across the small table and grab her hand. "Well, now you can make up for all those lost years. They all seem great. I had a wonderful time on the boat with Meghan."

"She and Nick seem great, as do AJ and Sawyer. To think, we have a former professional ballplayer in the family."

Taking one last drink of my coffee, I reply, "I think Jensen and Max were in heaven this weekend."

"Oh, definitely. Sawyer signed a baseball for Max before he left yesterday. Jensen called first thing this morning to say he slept with that ball tucked under his pillow," Mom says with a warm smile.

"I can't wait to meet the rest of them," I add, referring to the rest of Aunt Emma and Uncle Orval's granddaughters.

"We were talking about making a trip there for the Fourth of July. I know we should be open in a few weeks, but maybe we can hire a few helpers to oversee this place for a few days."

We've done that before, the weekend Jensen got married about six years ago. Even though both of the ladies had worked in a bed and breakfast in town in the past, they sure did make a mess of things in a short amount of time. They managed to ruin my oven and overflow the washing machine. Even at the ripe ol' age of twenty-two, I had learned a valuable lesson about hard work and respect.

"I can see your wheels turning. It won't be like the last time. Free said she'd be happy to help," Mom chimes in. "Mrs. Gillenwater said she was always available to assist too." Mrs. Gillenwater owned a B&B in town for more years than I've been on this earth, retiring and selling her place a few years back. Mrs. G was the woman who helped Mom turn this house into what it is today, providing countless hours of support and advice to a young mother of four with a dream to own a bed and breakfast.

"I'm not sure taking time away so close to reopening is smart, Mom," I answer honestly. Not to mention that if I went back to Jupiter Bay to meet the family, I'd probably run into Rhenn. How is that going to work after our fling expires? Will he have someone else there with him? Or worse, what if he acts indifferent, as if I was just someone to help pass a little bit of free time?

Sadly, I know that's exactly what I am.

What I offered to be.

Because nothing more can become of *us*.

There is no us.

"Just promise me you'll think about it, okay? I'd love to have my entire family there to meet everyone, but I don't want to create more stress for you after we reopen."

I nod without verbalizing an answer. My heart starts to pound in my chest, a loud rhythm I'm certain Mom can hear across the table. The thought of going and meeting the rest of my cousins is an attractive offer, but I'm just not sure I'll be ready to run into the friend that's likely to be invited and show up.

We sit in silence for a few minutes before I get up to clean the coffee cups. I'm rinsing the mugs and placing them in the drainer when she speaks again. "I ran into your father last night."

Well, I wasn't expecting that.

Grabbing a fresh cup from the cabinet, I set it in front of the pot and turn to give her my full attention. "Where?"

"The grocery store."

"Was he alone?" I hate to ask, but I know if Mom would have run into Dad with his new wife, it would have upset her.

"He was. He was buying a frozen pizza and that broccoli salad." Mom makes a face because we all know that while the deli in the grocery store has delicious broccoli salad, it's nothing compared to Mom's famous salad. She glances at me. "Have you seen him?"

I come over and sit across the table once more. "It's been a while. He called right after the fire," I confirm.

"He asked me about the remodel, wanted to know how it was going."

"And?"

"And I filled him in." That's all she says, though, and it's the way she says it: so casually. "Why are you looking at me like that?" she asks.

"I don't know, I guess I just expected a bit more animosity." And that's the truth. When my mom found out about my dad's affair, she wore her anger like a coat. It went everywhere with her, especially when both of our parents were required at the same place at the same time, like our high school and college graduations.

Mom blows a big puff of air from her lungs. "I'm too old to hold grudges anymore, Marissa. If anything, I kind of pity him. I mean, he's aging horribly, he's lost the rest of his hair, and apparently touring the English countryside didn't help his knees any. He was walking with a limp."

I can't help but smile at her reply. Even though he devastated and embarrassed her in town with his affair, she seems to be in a much better place than before.

"Besides, Everett Johnson invited me for coffee, and I think I'm going to take him up on it."

I blink repeatedly, trying to process her words. "Really?" A smile spreads across my face and I find myself leaning forward to hear more.

"Well, he has always been such a handsome man, you know. Plus, he has a nice ass."

And that's when I almost fall off my chair. I start snickering, which triggers her giggles. "Mom!" I chastise through my fits of laugher.

"What? It's true! Don't act like that, Riss. You know what I'm talking about. Your own young man has a mighty fine ass too. Don't deny it. I can see the truth beneath that blush."

Before I can say a word, my front door opens and the man with the fine ass walks into my tiny living room, a knowing smile on his face and his shirt slung over his shoulder. I'm pretty sure he overheard our conversation, and if the way he's grinning is any indication, I'd say he's pretty proud of himself right now. "Good morning, Mary Ann. Marissa."

"Good morning, Rhenn. I made coffee," Mom says with a big smile, nodding toward the coffee pot.

"Thank you," he says, grabbing the mug I placed on the counter and filling it to the top.

"How was your run?" Mom asks, drawing my eyes to his sweaty, yet still incredibly sexy body. His hair is standing up and his chest is wet. My tongue practically dangles from my mouth as I watch droplets of moisture slowly slide down the eight distinct grooves of his abs.

He places the pot back in the machine and gives Mom one of his full-watt smiles, a trail of wetness disappearing into the waist of his shorts. "It was refreshing to say the least," he replies as he brings the cup to his mouth. His totally kissable, sexy mouth.

"Well, I may not agree with the refreshing part, but I can respect someone's commitment to it. I was never a runner, but Colin, my ex-husband, used to run 5K's back when the kids were born."

"I've run many 5K's. There's nothing like the rush of running distance," Rhenn says, leaning back against my counter as if he owns it. Damn, he looks good there.

"Rhenn thinks running is fun," I gasp to Mom, making a disgusted face to prove my point.

"And Marissa obviously doesn't agree," Rhenn laughs, throwing me a wink.

Mom stands up and takes a few steps to the front door. "I'll let you kids get to your day. Rhenn, it was good to see you." Turning to me she adds, "Thank you for the coffee. I'm going to head into the office and grab a few things. I'm going to work from Harper's shop today and start confirming reservations."

"Do you have a date?" Rhenn asks, referring to the date where the inspector says we can occupy the house again.

"We have a timeline of three weeks to final inspection. As long as everything passes inspection, we'll reopen in four."

"I'm happy to hear it," he says, and I can tell by his smile that it's genuine.

"Call me if you need me," Mom hollers over her shoulder as she heads out the door, leaving Rhenn and me alone in my kitchen. He's staring at me, a wicked gleam sparkling in those blue eyes as he smirks over the rim of his cup.

"What?"

He sets his cup down on the counter and takes a predatory step my way. "I was just wondering how you got so dirty," he states, never taking those eyes off mine.

I glance down, looking for the source of his comment. "I'm not dirty," I say, checking over my arms. It's not uncommon for me to find flour or food remnants on my arms from preparing meals or desserts, but I haven't done anything but drink a cup of coffee.

When I glance back up, confused as to what he's talking about, I know I've been played. Warmth pools between my legs and my nipples pebble against my shirt as my confused eyes meet his hungry ones.

"You're not yet, but you're about to be," he says just before he crouches down, puts his shoulder into my stomach, and tosses me over his shoulder. I squeal as he stands and walks toward the bathroom. In reality, it only takes him about three steps to reach the room, but I enjoy the hell out of the view, and even say as much with a friendly slap to his hard rear.

Mom's right: he has a fine ass!

* * *

"You gonna take a break soon?" Rhenn says as he enters the guest bedroom I'm working on. I'm hot, with sweat running down the back of my shirt, but I'm determined to finish this room today. I fell behind schedule now that I spent the holiday weekend with Rhenn, but I wouldn't change it for anything. We only have two weeks together, and three to four before we reopen.

I need to focus.

But my focus is shot to hell when he comes strolling in wearing jeans that mold perfectly to his legs and a tight T-shirt that, while showing very little signs of sweat, looks good enough to peel off his body…with my tongue. Can a tongue peel off a shirt? I'm willing to prove that it can.

"What?" I ask. He's smirking at me and waiting, clearly already knowing that my mind was in the gutter.

"You tell me. I want to know what you were thinking about. All of a sudden, your eyes dropped to my chest and your breathing hitched," he says as he slowly approaches. Even his walk is sexy.

"Did not," I mumble. It did.

"Oh, it most certainly did, Angel. Your eyes kinda widened just a little and then turned a few shades darker. They're like cut grass after a rain shower. Have I ever told you green was my favorite color?" he asks as he approaches. The scrub brush falls from my hand as he wraps one hand around my lower back and pulls me against his chest.

"You have all the lines," I reply, blowing a strand of hair off my forehead.

Rhenn grabs that piece of hair and pushes it behind my ear. "It's not a line. It's the truth."

"Well, then, by all means, tell me again," I say, offering just the faintest smile as I gaze up at him.

"Tell you how sexy I think your eyes are? And these tiny little freckles on the end of your nose," he adds, slowly running a finger down the bridge of my nose, "are my fucking undoing." Then his finger reaches my lips. "And these lips? I dream about these pink, plump lips."

I'm panting, my lips falling open just a hair. "What do you dream about?" I ask, letting my tongue slip out and touch the tip of his finger, basically just throwing the match in the bucket of gasoline.

His eyes flare hot with desire and he pulls me tighter against him. "I think about how amazing they look wrapped around my cock and how they fall open when you're coming on my dick."

I gasp, so not used to a man as brazen as this one. But do you know what? I like it. A lot.

Just as his lips descend closer to mine, my name is called from the stairwell. "Marissa? You up here?"

"Crap," I mumble, jumping back like a teenager about to be busted by her parents. Rhenn lifts his eyebrows and gives me a smirk, which I ignore, but doesn't take a step back. I'm unable to move back anymore, since the bed is there, which only makes Rhenn smile further. He has me caged in. "Stop it," I grumble, trying to move him out of my way so I am not standing in what could be construed as a compromising position when my brother walks in.

"In here," Rhenn hollers over his shoulder, earning a slap to his shoulder. That only makes him laugh further.

Jensen walks into the bedroom and stops just inside the doorway. "Oh, sorry. I didn't mean to interrupt."

"You're not," I assure at the exact same time Rhenn says, "You did."

Again, I slap him on the shoulder and give him a good solid push. He moves, but only because he wants to, not because I was strong enough to move him. Taking a step away from Rhenn, I give my attention to my brother. "What can I do for you?"

He glances between Rhenn and me, probably trying to figure out exactly what he walked in on. Rubbing the back of his head, he says, "I'm going to work in the yard for a bit, and then I thought I'd come help clean for a bit. Ashley got Max from school, so I have some free time."

"Oh, that would be great. I'm almost done with this room and was planning to start across the hall next," I answer, trying to ignore the way Jensen continues to glance back and forth between Rhenn and myself.

"I can help too. I'm almost finished with my stuff for today. Why don't I grab some beers and food and we can all knock out that room together," Rhenn offers, making me look down at my watch. Now I know why he asked if I was going to take a break anytime soon. It's almost four.

"I could definitely go for a beer," Jensen says, throwing Rhenn an appreciative grin. "Long day."

"Then it's a plan. I'll finish the wiring in the bathroom in room three, and then run out and grab some food and drinks. We can have a cleaning party when I return," he says, taking a step toward the door, which just so happens to be toward me as well.

"See you soon," he says, kissing my forehead before he steps away and exits the room, nodding to Jensen as he goes.

"What was that?" my brother asks, his tone a little annoyed.

"What?" I ask innocently, knowing exactly what he's referring to. I just don't know that I want to talk about it with my brother. Harper, sure. She's a girl. Hell, she's the one that told me I could handle this no-strings sex thing, but Jensen? I really don't want to have this conversation with him.

"You. Him. That," he says, motioning his hands between me and the empty doorway.

"It's nothing," I mumble, grabbing my discarded sponge and heading back to the wall.

"A kiss on the forehead is not nothing. Plus, it felt like I was interrupting something when I walked in."

"You weren't," I assure him, lying out my butt, of course, and scrubbing hard on the light green wall.

"Marissa."

"Jensen," I mock, dropping my sponge and turning his way. I cross my arms, mirroring his stance. "We're friends, okay? We've been hanging out."

"Friends? He kissed you."

"On the forehead."

"And that's all that's happened?" he asks in total big-brother mode. When I stumble for words, he adds, "That's what I thought."

"Don't patronize me. I'm a big girl. I know what I'm doing," I say, turning back to the wall and scrubbing.

"What are you doing?"

"We're having sex, okay? Is that what you wanted to hear?" I practically holler, knowing he can probably hear me in the room he's working in.

"Eww," Jensen grumbles, looking down.

"You're the one who has been pushing it, so now you know. That's all it is, that's all it can be. I'm tired of defending myself and my choices to you people," I mutter.

He approaches slowly and takes the sponge from my hand. "*You people* are your family, and we care about you. We just don't want to see you hurt."

"Well, you won't. I knew what this was when I entered into the agreement. He's here for a short period of time and then will move on. I know that."

He reaches over and sets his hand on my shoulder. "Okay, I'm not trying to upset you. I just wanted to make sure you were both on the same page, Riss. I don't want to see you hurt."

I want to reply that I won't be, but I'm pretty sure that'll be a lie. Watching Rhenn walk away is going to hurt, no matter how much I plan and prepare for it, because at the end of the day, I care about him. I've come to appreciate the friendship he offers. I enjoy talking with him, and he makes me laugh. A lot. Not to mention the things he makes my body feel. "I appreciate it," I end up saying instead.

Jensen pulls me into a quick hug. "Give me an hour to mow and trim the back, and then I can help you clean."

"Thank you."

He nods as he walks out the door. I can hear him talking in the hallway, and when Rhenn's voice speaks up, my ears strain to overhear their conversation. With the construction commotion downstairs, it's too hard to hear their words, but just as the saw stops running, I catch a statement. My heart hammers in my chest as I think about what Rhenn said to my brother.

I don't want to hurt her. I've come to care for Marissa.

And that's when I feel myself start to fall.

Only I know that when I reach the bottom, it's going to hurt like a bitch.

Chapter Twenty

Rhenn

Listening to Marissa and Jensen carry on over the last three hours has a permanent smile on my face. They've been recounting numerous stories of growing up in this house, sharing details of their life together with two other siblings, and giving me a peek into their past. With three of us helping, we knocked out the fourth bedroom upstairs, and I'm not sure why they haven't all gathered together sooner to take care of it. Other than Marissa being a bit of a control freak when it comes to the bed and breakfast, and wanting to do it herself. Harper even showed up as soon as we sat down to enjoy pizza and a few cold beers on the back patio to celebrate the completion of our task.

"On your way home?" Marissa asks her sister between bites.

"Yeah, it was a busy day. I don't know why women always feel the need to touch every piece of lingerie in the place," Harper says, grabbing a beer from the cooler and taking a big pull. "I bet I've refolded some of those pairs of thongs five dozen times."

I glance back and forth between Marissa and Harper as they carry on about women's fucking panties (yeah, it's as sexy as you'd think), while Jensen just shakes his head. "You okay?" I ask their brother.

"I don't know why they feel the need to discuss fucking thongs in front of us all the time."

"Panties are part of life, killjoy. Everyone wears them," Harper defends.

"Not everyone," I reply casually, thinking about the moment I ripped Marissa's fancy panties off her body and devoured her sweet pussy. She went without them for the rest of the night, not that she needed to wear them.

"Really?" Harper asks, her facing lighting up as she glances to her younger sister. Marissa blushes a thousand shades of red.

"Knock it off before my brain hemorrhages," Jensen mumbles, taking another drink.

"Seriously, maybe you need to get laid. You and Ashley have been split for two years now. Please tell me it hasn't been that long since you dipped the pen in the ink," Harper says, making us all burst into laughter.

"Where did you hear that?" Marissa asks.

Harper shrugs. "I overheard Aunt Emma chastising AJ about making sure she was servicing her husband's...pen."

Marissa snorts. "She's definitely...unusual."

"That she is," Jensen interjects. "I thought Samuel was gonna pop a blood vessel when she started offering blowjob advice."

That makes us all laugh. "You should have heard the time she threw a divorce celebration for her granddaughter Lexi, and her now husband Linkin ended up as the stripper." I spend the next ten minutes recounting a tale I've heard several times over.

We sit there in silence for a few minutes finishing up the beer we each have in our hand. "One more room upstairs?" Jensen asks, tossing his second empty in the trashcan.

"Yep, one more bed and bath, then on to the downstairs. The living room is definitely bad, but the kitchen and dining room are horrible," Marissa confirms, curling up on her side in the lounge chair. My dick starts to harden as I picture taking her from behind right there. (Preferably without her family around us...)

"I'll have Max, but if Mom will help watch him for a bit, I can help for a while Saturday. We can work on the furniture in the shed. I bet Samuel can lend a few more hours too," Jensen offers, standing up and stretching. Just as he puts his arms down, his cell phone rings. I watch his face as he glances at the name on the screen, his features tightening in irritation. "Hello?"

We all try not to listen, but it's hard, considering he's standing in the middle of the three of us.

He's quiet for a few minutes, his jaw tensing. "So sit with him for a bit," he says, not even bothering to mask the bite in his voice. "Ashley, I don't understand why there's always an issue at bedtime. Max has no problems falling asleep when he's at my place." Again, he listens, and so do we. "Fine. I'll stop by on my way home." Quiet. "Yeah, see you in a few." Jensen pushes on his screen with a bit too much force and jams the device into his pocket.

"Let me guess, Max won't fall asleep for her?" Harper asks, her own disdain evident in her words.

"Again. You forgot to say…again," Jensen replies, exhaling deeply. "I'll talk to you guys soon. I'll text Samuel and see if he can help Saturday."

"I can help after the shop closes," Harper adds.

"Thank you, guys," Marissa says, yawning from her chair. I feel a little guilty for keeping her up so late last night (and early this morning), but then I recall exactly *why* she's a bit tired today. My cock is already primed for another go.

Harper leaves just a few minutes later, and after making sure the house is secure, Marissa and I head to her little cottage. My bed in the boat is a bit bigger, but frankly, sometimes the smaller bed is the way to go. Now she won't be able to get too far away from me when we're naked and lying together beneath the sheet.

* * *

We continue to work on the remodel and renovation of Grayson Bed and Breakfast, sometimes side by side. Marissa puts everything she has into cleaning, redecorating, and getting each room ready to be occupied. It's been pretty fucking cool watching the process throughout the week.

Speaking of occupied, since the weekend, we've occupied either her bed or my own. We've enjoyed dinners on her porch and a few on my boat, and even went sailing on Wednesday night during sunset. I'm still choosing to ignore the way my heart sped up with her in my arms and the way the moonlight illuminated her blonde hair, making it somehow shine even brighter than the stars in the sky. I'll ignore it because, at the end of the day (or specifically, the end of this job), it won't matter that I really just like spending all of my free time with her.

It's Friday night and we're heading to one of her favorite places in Rockland Falls. We both cut out of work just a little early, but with all the extra time we've been putting in throughout the week, we're still ahead of schedule.

Let's not talk about that fact right now either…

Marissa climbs up in my truck, her legs in a pair of jean shorts and a purple and gray flowy tank top showing just a smidge of stomach when she lifts her arms. Compared to some of my previous *dates*, she's modestly dressed in a comfortable and casual way. But do you know what? It's sexy as fuck.

Even her Nike tennis shoes are hot.

"Where are we going?" I ask when I hop in the driver's seat and pull down their lane.

"It's a surprise," she says happily, her smile easy and infectious.

"Well, you will tell me how to get there, right?" I reach for her hand and set it between us, our fingers linked. That's another thing I chose to ignore, mostly because her hand feels like it was made to fit within mine.

"Of course, silly. Head left on the highway and drive through town. When you get to the McDonald's, turn left."

"I can handle that. Why don't you find some music?"

It only takes her a few stations to find the one she's looking for, and I have to admit, I'm a little shocked. Blaring through my speakers is Godsmack. Glancing over, I find Marissa bobbing her head in beat to the heavy music, her lips moving ever so slightly with the words. She looks my way, seemingly feeling the weight of my stare, and says, "What?"

"Godsmack?"

"Yeah. You don't like them?" she asks, getting ready to change the station.

"Like them? I love them. You just don't seem like a Godsmack kinda girl," I answer honestly.

Marissa shrugs her shoulders and gives me a shy smile. "I guess I'm full of surprises."

"I guess you are," I say, keeping my eyes on the road and enjoying the music. It only takes us a few minutes and I'm turning left at the McDonald's, as instructed.

"When you get to the next stop sign, make another left. You're going to follow that road around the river for a few miles," she instructs, jumping right into the Breaking Benjamin song now playing. It still shocks me. I wasn't necessarily expecting classical or jazz music, but I definitely wasn't envisioning this. Maybe country or pop. Not rock.

The road we're on starts to wind around the river as we drive farther from the ocean. Trees are in full bloom, bright green and full, and the sun still sits high in the sky. It's the first of June and already indicating that the summer months will be warm ones. We pass a few houses, but there's plenty of distance between them, nothing that would constitute neighbors.

As we approach a heavily wooded area, Marissa sits up and watches. "Slow down. You're making a right up here. It's almost hidden, so be ready to turn."

She's not kidding. I almost miss the turn, but as soon as I do, I'm completely stunned by what's in front of me. The road is dirt, well worn, and completely tree lined. There's plenty of room for two vehicles to pass, but appears to be somewhat deserted. I don't say a word, just drive slowly down the road, ready to make my next move.

"Up here on the left will be a parking area," she says, pointing to the clearing in the trees. It's a gravel lot with one other car parked there. I steer my truck to a spot in the corner and turn off the ignition. "Ready?" she asks, tossing off her seat belt and sitting up high in the seat.

"I'm not sure what I'm ready for, but you seem super excited, so let's get to it." I jump out of my truck and head to the passenger side, helping Marissa down. I go ahead and take the opportunity to steal a kiss while I'm there, making sure to leave her completely breathless. "That should tide me over for a few minutes."

She doesn't respond, but I've noticed she doesn't do that often when she's flustered, and my kisses definitely get her all worked up. Much like me. Right now, I'm definitely *up*.

"Come on, pokey." Marissa takes off at a fast pace, heading toward a walking trail. It doesn't take me long to catch up with her, considering my legs are much longer than hers, and when I do, I go ahead and take her hand in mine once more.

The farther we head up the trail, the more serene our surroundings. There are a few critters running around and a bunch of sticks and branches. Off in the distance, I hear what sounds like water running, and I can't help but notice that her pace picks up just a bit. When we meet the occupants of the other vehicle on the trail, we all offer a quick greeting, but continue on our way. "That was the mayor's son and his wife. She just had a baby a few weeks ago." I nod in acknowledgment, but keep my mouth shut and my legs moving. "Almost there." She's practically bouncing in her tennis shoes.

After a few minutes, we reach a clearing. I have a pretty good idea where we're going, considering how noisy it is now, but what I wasn't expecting was for it to be as beautiful as it is. Marissa stops in her tracks, me right beside her, and together, we gaze up at the most beautiful little waterfall I've ever seen.

"Rockland Falls," she whispers, a smile spread across her face.

I tighten my grip on her hand and lead her toward the impressive sight. There are large boulders surrounding the falls, and a large pool of blue-green water at the base. "So I guess this is where your town got its name."

"The first settlers used to call it Rocky Land because of the large boulders that surrounded the waterway. If you follow it up or downstream, you'll see those boulders for miles. When Rockland Falls became an actual town, they took that name and shortened it."

I gaze up at the waterfall, completely in awe. At the top, the waters rage, almost angrily and loud, and at the bottom, it seems almost calm and peaceful. "This place is awesome," I tell her.

She smiles up at the falls. "It's probably my second favorite place in town, after the bed and breakfast, of course."

"Of course." I pull her to me, lining up her body in front of me. Her back is pressed to my front, and believe it or not, I'm not thinking about all the ways I can make her scream my name. Okay, fine. I'm a dude. I'm still thinking about all the wonderful ways I could make her moan, but I'm mostly thinking about how special it is that she brought me to one of her favorite places.

We stand there, my body supporting the weight of hers, as she leans back against me, both of us gazing at the waterfall. No words are spoken, but they're not needed. I can see why she loves this place so much. The falling water is almost soothing, and I'm damn lucky to have this opportunity with her.

Something about the ambiance makes you sit back and reflect on your life. Mine may not be exactly what I expected it to be, but I'm not complaining. I have a job I'm damn good at and a karate studio that's thriving. My friends are loyal and just a call away if I need them, and I'm never lacking for female companionship when I want it.

My chest tightens and so do my hands as I think about the past, present, and future. My past isn't horrible, but it's filled with a few bumps in the road. The biggest bump is the reason I don't do relationships anymore. She fucked me over – and fucked one of my roommates – and pretty much sealed the coffin on the idea of ever having a relationship again.

Until now.

The present.

The woman in my arms who makes me laugh and want to be a better man. Me. The man who has spent the better part of a decade screwing his way through more zip codes than he cares to admit. Light, carefree, and easy. That's what I've always wanted. But here I am, actually considering having something more with Marissa.

Except, I can't.

I'm leaving in nine days. A week from this Sunday, I'll be pulling up anchor, never to return to this sleepy little bed and breakfast town. I'll never again lay eyes on this site, or any of the others I've come to enjoy around Rockland Falls. But worse, I'll never see Marissa again either.

And that thought pains me.

"What do you think?" she asks, glancing over her shoulder, a small smile playing on her lips. Totally kissable lips, that is.

"I think I want to kiss you," I answer, pushing all other thoughts out of my head.

She doesn't say anything, just turns in my arms and wraps hers around my waist. "Then, I think you should definitely kiss me."

"I should," I reply, slowly dipping my head toward hers. I love this moment – this time right before I kiss her – where her breath catches and her eyelids get all droopy. I take a mental photograph of how she looks right now, wrapped in my arms with the raging waters falling behind her. It's this exact image I'll carry with me when I return home to Jupiter Bay.

Then my lips taste hers. I keep the kiss leisurely, knowing that if I deepen it too much, I'm liable to take her up against one of the boulders. She doesn't seem to mind, though. Marissa wraps her arms around my neck and threads her fingers into my hair. Her tongue is sweet against mine, a slow and deliberate dance. It's crazy to think it, but it's perfect.

She's perfect.

When I pull back, her eyes are glassy and her lips swollen. Personally, it's one of my favorite looks on her, especially knowing I put it there. "Come on," I say, grabbing her hand with mine and leading her to one of the big boulders. She yelps when I grab her by the waist and lift her onto the rock. Then, I hoist myself up and sit behind her, my legs framing hers.

I sit back, my arms poised back and supporting my weight. Marissa sits on the edge of the rock, her feet dangling and swinging as she watches the water. And I watch her. Someday, some bastard is going to hit the fucking jackpot with her. My gut clenches and nausea stirs when I think about it, but I already know I'm not that man. And I'm man enough to want her happy and loved, even if that man isn't me.

She glances back over her shoulder again, a beautiful smile on her lips, and I feel it. Somewhere near my heart, right there in the middle of my chest, I feel the armor I've had in place for a decade start to crack. She chips away at every layer of protection I've ever had in place, and she does it with a simple smile. A gorgeous, never to be forgotten, smile.

"You okay?" she asks, a look of concern on her face.

I clear my throat, but my words still come out hoarse. "Yeah, I'm good." I sit up and wrap my arms around her waist, pulling her back against my chest. "Thank you for bringing me here."

"You're welcome," she says, relaxing in my arms and making my heart pound hard against my chest.

We sit like that, talking for hours. It isn't until the sun drops behind the trees and the singing birds start to quiet for the evening that I realize how late it is. We actually just sat there for over two hours and talked. About everything. Our childhoods, lives outside of the job, families. We covered college and even exes. I even told her more about Suzanne, and I never talk about that shit. But do you know what happened while I was talking about it? While her soft green eyes gazed up at me with so much sadness and outrage for my pain? I felt it start to slip away. The pain I had been holding on to. The grudge too. It all just…fell away, leaving me with a woman in my arms who I could seriously see myself falling in love with. Maybe even spending the rest of my life with.

But can't.

Chapter Twenty-One

Marissa

I spend a little time on Saturday morning cleaning the living room and picking out a few new paint colors. Since we have the room disassembled, Mom and I decided to go ahead and give everything fresh coats of paint. I mean what's a few extra days of painting, right?

Actually, the cleaning process is going very smoothly, and much quicker than I thought it would. Once I got a system down, I was able to power through the bedrooms and bathrooms, leaving the downstairs. I'll admit I've been taking my time on the project. Yes, because I wanted to make sure it was done right the first time, but also because of a huge distraction. You know, a six foot one karate instructor, with ocean blue eyes and a smirk that turns my insides to jelly.

He's out this morning, having to run to another town to pick up a few extra supplies. While he was there, he was planning to meet up with his boss's brother, who's also an electrician, and who technically Rhenn is working for while in North Carolina. He explained last night while we were sitting together on the boulder that his original license is for Virginia, but he also carries one for North Carolina. The brothers each own their own businesses, one in Virginia and the other in North Carolina, providing electrical work for residential homes and businesses all over two states, and work together often. It was neat to hear more about the work he does and the family-owned companies he works for.

"Anyone home?" Harper hollers from my doorway.

"In here," I yell, placing a few items of Rhenn's in the washing machine, along with my own.

"Why are you inside? It's perfect outside."

Shutting the lid and turning on the machine, I turn my attention to my sister. "I was catching up on a few chores before Rhenn gets back."

"You should be working on your tan. Your Casper-white legs blind me," she teases, holding her hand up to shield her eyes.

"Shut up," I retort. "I was able to get a little sun last weekend on the boat, and we're taking it out again tomorrow."

"Oh, are you going to do a little topless sunbathing on the boat? I'm so jealous," she says. "The shop keeps me super busy and I don't have time for that as much as I used to."

"Topless sunbathing? Seriously?" Though, I really shouldn't be surprised in the least.

"You've never done it? Oh my God, Riss, it's the best. So relaxing," she adds, helping herself to a bottle of water in my fridge.

"Why would you sunbathe topless? You know what? I don't want to know." I grab a bottle of water from the fridge too and take a seat at the table.

"You mean besides the fact that you don't get bikini lines? It's quite freeing and relaxing, actually. I miss coming here and laying out." Harper shrugs her shoulders and takes a big drink of water.

"Wait, here?" I swear, I almost choke.

"Sure, where else would I lay out topless? My nosy neighbor would be filming me, probably selling that shit on the Internet or keeping it in his digital spank bank on that laptop he's always carrying around." Harper shudders.

"He's so weird," I mumble, getting completely distracted by her weirdo neighbor.

"That he is. Now, back to the topless sunbathing. I think you should do it. It's the perfect day, and you don't have to worry about anyone happening upon you since there are no guests."

I stare across the table at my brazen sister. "Has that happened?"

She giggle snorts. "Oh yeah, a couple of times. The old geezers never complain, though."

"And you think you know someone," I gasp with a tease. I mean I knew she would go back and lay in the sun, but I had no idea she was taking off her bikini top while doing it.

"Seriously, though, you should go do it. Enjoy some sun. Take a book. Relax."

My ears perk up at book. How long has it been since I read a book? Weeks. Everything with the house and remodel after the fire has kept me super busy…and stressed. It wasn't until Rhenn came along and offered to…de-stress me for a bit, but still, I miss reading. I used to read almost every night on the porch after I was done with the house chores.

"You know what? I think I'm going to."

"Good!" she chirps, clapping her hands dramatically. "You won't regret it, I promise." Harper gets up and tosses her empty water bottle in the recycling bin. "Well, I'm off to sort and sell underwear."

"You're not staying?" I ask, not that I want my sister to see me topless, but it would be kinda nice to spend a little one-on-one time with her.

"I can't. Free opened the store for me today, but I have to close. Saturdays are always busy so I don't want to leave her too long by herself." I nod as she heads toward the door. "I'm coming back though to help with the downstairs cleaning. Jensen called me the other night and said we're all pitching in and getting it done."

"Yeah, Samuel texted me earlier and said he'll be here after the Hanson funeral."

"He has such a weird job. Who wants to be surrounded by death all day?" she asks aloud, but I can tell she isn't really looking for an answer. It was more rhetorical. But I also agree with her one-hundred-percent. I don't even want to think about some of the stuff that goes on behind that "Employees Only" door…

"Anyway, I should be here a little after three. Do I need to bring something for dinner?" she asks as she steps out the front door.

"Mom said she and Max are taking care of it," I reply, joining her on the porch and immediately loving the warm, June sun.

"See you soon." Harper slides her sunglasses on her face and heads around the house to her car.

I'm left standing there, all alone on a late Saturday morning, and wondering what I'm going to do with my time. Jensen isn't coming until one to start working on the house, and Rhenn thought he'd be back early afternoon. That leaves me with about two hours to myself and nothing to do. Sure, I could go inside and get started on the living room, but now that I'm standing in the sunlight, Harper's suggestion has started to grow roots.

Should I take some time to go enjoy the sun on the beach?

Can I even do what she proposed?

A few months ago, I'd say hell no. But now? Well, a coy smile takes over my face as I think about taking this big step outside my comfort zone. I picture a certain bed hog with dark blond hair and alluring eyes, and suddenly, it seems like the best idea ever.

But I'm not doing it for him. No. I'm doing this for me. I'm doing this with my newfound confidence that I didn't even know I had, and maybe that's inspired by Rhenn, sure, but this leap is all me.

Running back inside, I throw on my tiny bikini, grab the book I had started weeks ago and haven't picked up since, a bottle of water, and a towel, and head out the door.

To sunbathe.

Topless.

* * *

I've been reading for about fifteen minutes, or at least trying to read, but really I'm just conjuring up the courage to pull that string. But I'm nervous and a little scared. I haven't seen anyone on the beach since I arrived, so I really don't think anyone's going to find me here, but there's just something a little terrifying about being almost nude in public.

And then I picture Rhenn. The way his eyes light up and darken when he's aroused (he's like that a lot). He looks at me as if I'm the only woman he sees, that what he sees is enough. At least enough for now. He gives me the confidence I didn't realize I desperately needed.

So I pull the string.

Tossing the bikini top beside me, I continue to lie on my stomach, making sure all of my girly bits are covered. The sun is hot, causing little beads of sweat to gather on my body, but do you know what? Harper's right. It feels liberating and a little naughty, and I have a huge smile on my face.

I read for a good thirty minutes, relaxing and enjoying the warmth, and feeling at ease for the first time in too long. My eyelids start to grow heavy and I find it hard to focus on the words. Setting my book aside, I turn over so I don't burn my back. Using my shirt as a pillow, I let the sun calm my body further, lulling it into sleep. I must immediately start to dream, quite possibly about being on

Rhenn's boat, because I hear a splash. My eyes fly open and I glance around, realizing I'm still on the beach.

And I'm not alone.

Chapter Twenty-Two

Rhenn

I made an early morning trip to Harriston to pick up a few extra supplies and meet Jeff, my boss's brother. I guess, technically, while I'm working in North Carolina, Jeff's my boss too. They're both electricians and own thriving businesses in both states. We all hold the certifications we need to cross state lines and work wherever the brothers may need us. When I arrived in Harriston, Jeff called to let me know his youngest was sick, so he couldn't meet up with me. So, after grabbing what I needed from the shop and one quick trip to the electrical supply store, I headed back to Rockland Falls a bit earlier than expected.

Marissa was at her place when I arrived, and even though I thought about heading to her place for a bit (preferably naked), when I realized her sister was there, I decided to just head out to my boat for a bit. I really haven't been alone much since I arrived. I've spent a lot more of my free time than I would have anticipated with Marissa. First, just because I enjoyed spending time with her, but now, we're enjoying a lot of time together in bed too.

A lot.

My healthy sex drive is certainly appreciating this work trip.

I'm planning to head back to shore in a bit to help Marissa and her siblings work on the house. The electrical work is on track, and if I were being completely honest, could be completed as early as Wednesday. But I won't let that happen. Any other job, I'd be jumping for joy at finishing early, ready to head back home. Not this one. The idea of completing the job early makes me feel like someone drove a butter knife into my chest. Hurts like hell. Instead,

I'll draw out those last few days, making sure to soak up as much of Marissa as I can.

Then I'll leave.

And won't look back.

Knowing she's coming home with me tonight has me running around, picking up dirty clothes and washing the few dishes in the sink. Almost all of the time I've spent on here in the last week has been with her, and the last thing I've wanted to do when she's with me is clean. Balls deep inside her sweet pussy has been my favorite pastime, though I realize how much of a dog that makes me sound like. I don't know what it is about her, but she's different. I know it, and at least now, I'm acknowledging it too.

When the downstairs no longer looks and smells like ass, I head back on deck. We're taking the boat out tonight, heading down the coast a short ways to a little island area, and I want to make sure everything is ready to set sail. Even with the short twenty minute sail, I still want to feel her to stretch her legs in the open sea. And when we arrive at our destination, I might be able to feel Marissa stretch her legs too.

Speaking of Marissa, I automatically glance toward the shore. I'm not sure what she's doing this morning, and even though a big part of me is anxious to get up there and spend more time with her, I refrain from jumping in the johnboat and heading to shore. It will do me (and her) a bit of good to spend a few minutes apart. I've been up her ass (figuratively, that is – unfortunately, not literally) since the moment she proposed our little two-week friends with benefits arrangement, and it won't hurt me any to start to pull back.

There's something on the shore that pulls my attention.

Actually, it's someone.

Someone is lying in the sun on the beach not too far away from the Grayson dock. Even though I can't see who it is, my blood starts to zing through my body and pool at my dick. It's like I already know who, I'm just not sure why. Is she hurt? What the hell is she doing on the beach?

Grabbing the binoculars from beneath the captain's chair, I point them in her direction to make sure everything is okay. I realize right away, she's face down, but the moment I see the towel, book in her hand, and bottle of water beside her head, I realize that she's not injured, but sunbathing.

I step up to the railing, in total stalker fashion, and quietly observe her smooth, clear skin as she reads a paperback. She's wearing that tiny blue bikini – the one she says reminds her of my eyes – and her body is covered in a fine sheen of sweat. My cock is already hard and aching in my pants, and it's probably a good thing I'm a short boat ride away, or I'm liable to take her right there on the beach.

And then I notice her back.

Or what's missing.

There's no bikini strings.

"Fuck," I growl, loving the shit out of the way the sun is kissing almost every square inch of her body.

I lean farther over the railing, the biggest douchiest douche of them all as I perv on the sexy woman on the beach. I should stop. I should put the binoculars down and walk away, head downstairs. Jack off. There will definitely be some of that. But I should not be the man who watches a woman while sunbathing topless on the privacy of her own land. But she *is* out in the open where anyone could happen upon her. A boat could come in, a jogger run by, one of the contractors come looking for her. My blood starts to boil as I imagine someone finding her like that, nearly naked with her soft skin so exposed for everyone to see.

See, I'm not perving, I'm protecting.

Right?

No, you're right. I'm totally perving.

I'll walk away.

Just give me one last moment to memorize this image of her like this…

Then she turns over.

"Holy fuck," I gasp, leaning over just a little too far.

And that's when I fall overboard.

Hitting the water is a shock, but so is the mouthful I take in before I can close my wide-open trap. I come up sputtering and gasping, somewhere between falling and hitting the water, dropping my three hundred dollar binoculars into the ocean. Thank Christ my phone wasn't in my pocket, but then I think about the wallet that is.

Embarrassed, and slightly irritated by my stupidity, I swim over the ladder and hoist myself up. As soon as my feet hit the deck I turn toward the shore, praying with everything inside me that she has fallen asleep and doesn't know what just happened. Unfortunately, my eyes meet her very wide, very concerned ones. Even from the distance, I can see her shock as she clenches the towel to her chest, covering up all the good parts I was just ogling.

Head hanging in shame, there's no way I can sweet talk my way out of this one without coming across as the biggest asshole on the planet. Hell, I can't even talk to her now anyway considering we're about two hundred yards apart. Resigned to head downstairs, dry myself off, and deal with my wallet mess, I turn to head below. Just as I do, a loud whistle grabs my attention. Turning back around, I find Marissa now on the edge of the dock, waving. At least she's not pissed, right? She doesn't seem pissed. I mean, it's hard to tell from this distance, with a huge body of water between us, but if she were upset, she surely wouldn't wave at me.

Right?

I'm horrible at this. Yes, I, Rhenn Burleski, manwhore who knows his way around a woman's body blindfolded and drunk, am admitting I'm not so good with reading women when it's not about flirting and sex. That I can do. But this? Whole new territory, filled with murky, shark-infested waters.

I throw her a wave, a wide smile cresting my face, and get ready to head below deck. Just before my feet move, she does the one thing I would never, ever, *ever* in a billion years expect her to do.

She drops the towel.

Instantly, my cock is hard and raring to go in my soaked shorts. I stand there, gawking like the perv I've proven to be, and watch (a little helplessly) as she smiles wide and turns, the sway of her ass hypnotizing me as she goes. Yeah, she totally won that round. Marissa collects her belongings on the beach and heads up the grass lane that leads to her place. Before she disappears from sight, my little vixen glances over her shoulder, her pearly whites visible even from the distance.

Game.

Set.

Match.

* * *

After a long shower and a change of clothes, I head to shore, ready to help clean the downstairs with Marissa and her siblings. When I tie off the boat, I'm surprised to see her step from the lane and onto the beach.

"Hey," she says, heading my direction.

"Hi."

She meets me on the dock wearing a pair of shorts and fitted tee. "So, did you have a nice swim?" Her eyelashes bat innocently, but her smile screams wicked woman.

"Yeah, it was great," I reply, wrapping my arms around her waist and pulling her into my chest.

Marissa runs her hands up my chest. "Feeling a little…hot, were ya?"

I almost groan. "You have no idea."

Wrapping her hands around my neck, she looks up at me with full pouty lips and dark eyes. "I think I do, actually," she says, moving one hand down and palming my erection.

"Fuck, I've been hard since I saw you on the beach," I confess.

She continues to drive me wild, stroking me through my shorts and cutting off any and all blood flow to my actual brain. "I didn't know you were there."

"To say I was shocked was an understatement," I gasp, trying to focus on her words and not her hand. But it's hard…so, so hard…

"Did you watch me?" she whispers, her eyes locked on mine as she moves her hand down to cup my balls.

"Fuckshitdamn," I grumble, feeling them pull up tight as she caresses them with her magic fingers.

"Did you?" she asks again.

"Fuck yes," I groan, grabbing her hips and flexing mine. My cock rubs against her stomach.

"You've been very naughty." She moves her hand back up to my dick and strokes it long and slow. I'm about to come in my shorts like a teenager.

"As have you, Angel," I finally say through gritted teeth.

"What are we going to do about that?" she asks all innocently, but I can tell her mind is exactly where mine is.

"I'm going to show you how naughty I can be." I lift up her hips, her legs instantly wrapping around my waist, and I carry her off to the timber. "What time is your family going to be here?" I ask, lifting her shirt up and over her head as I go.

"About fifteen minutes," she pants, sliding her center against my erection.

"I'm going to fuck you out here, Angel. Are you ready for that?" I ask, pausing to make sure she's on the same page as me.

"Yes, please."

I growl. "Always so polite." Then my lips devour. I consume her, taking her mouth and kissing her until we're both breathless. "Are you wet?"

"Yes." That one word comes out a pant, a plea.

"Did you get wet knowing I was watching you earlier?"

Her face flushes a little deeper and she drops her eyes. "Yes."

"Good. I was so fucking hard. I told myself to walk away, to not watch, and then you flipped over and I thought I had died and gone to heaven."

"Is that when you fell overboard?" she asks, a teasing smile on her plump lips.

"Yep," I confess, setting her on a downed tree and stripping off my shirt. I place it on the tree and move her so that she's sitting on it. "This might be quick and hard, baby," I admit, unbuttoning my shorts and letting them fall down to my ankles. I reach for her shorts, but she's already shimmying them down her legs. I practically rip off my underwear and reach for my wallet.

My wallet.

Fuck…

"Dammit," I groan, closing my eyes and trying to breathe through the pain of impending blue balls.

"What's wrong?" she asks, her sweet, angelic voice summoning me to open my eyes. She's sitting on the tree (which is perfect height for fucking, by the way), and bare. Her pussy is glistening, her clit swollen, and I almost start to cry at the irony.

"I don't have my wallet. It was in my pocket when I fell overboard and I left it on the boat so everything could dry out." It almost causes physical pain to say those words.

"And if you don't have your wallet, you don't have a…"

I nod, grabbing her thighs, but keeping myself from stepping between them.

"Rhenn?" she asks, drawing my eyes back to hers. "I'm on the pill."

My heart pounds in my chest, my cock practically weeping with joy. "Are you saying what I think you're saying?"

She doesn't hesitate. "Yeah."

I close my eyes and just breathe for a moment, the scent of her mixing with earth and dirt filling my senses. "Are you sure?" The words are tight. It's hard to breathe.

"Definitely sure," she says, reaching out and grabbing my aching cock. She starts to stroke it, toying with the beads of liquid that spill from the head. "I want you to fuck me bare. I trust you."

Her words. Her dirty, magical words come barreling through every layer of protection I've built around my heart. They beat down all of my defenses, and I know right then and there: it's not that I *could* fall in love with her, it's that I *am* falling. Falling so hard and fast that I don't know what to do, what to say.

She takes all of my decisions out of my hands as she pulls me forward, her warm little fingers wrapped around my dick, and leading me to where she aches for me. Where I ache to be.

"I'm clean, I swear. I never do this without a condom. Ever."
I don't know why I feel the need to say it, but I do. Maybe it's
because she knows about my past, my lack of commitment when it
comes to the opposite sex. Maybe it's because I trust her as much as
she seems to trust me. Maybe it's because my feelings for her
outweigh everything shitty from my past, leaving only the good and
pure pieces behind.

Like her.

She's my good, my pure.

"I know." The honesty and openness in her eyes is almost
enough to bring me to my knees.

Marissa shifts her weight and leans back just a bit, guiding
my cock to her pussy. I already know she's wet, but when I feel that
hot wetness wrap around my dick, I lose all ability to think. My
brain just shuts down. Inch by glorious inch, I slowly make my way
inside of her, unsheathed and unprotected. Exposed. Her eyes are
wide with desire, and I'm pretty sure she's holding her breath.

Grabbing her hips, I keep pushing until I'm completely
seated within her body. My balls are already tightening, reveling in
the feel of being inside her without anything between us, but I power
through. No way am I letting this end prematurely. "Ready?" I ask,
waiting until she gives me the green light. When she nods her head,
I pull out and slam back in. The force causes her to slide, so I grab
hold of her hips tighter, and thrust once more.

Marissa wraps her arms around my neck, holding on for the
ride. And what a ride it is. It doesn't take long and I can feel her
starting to tighten around me. My body drives into hers, guiding her
toward release. My own is full of tension and ready, but I push past
it, determined to make sure she gets off before me.

When she detonates, it's the most beautiful thing I've ever
seen. My name spills from her lips as her pussy clamps down on my

dick and milks it for everything it's worth. I see stars as I finally let go, giving in to the orgasm that has been knocking on the door since the second I slid inside her body. My head drops to her shoulder as my body pulses and shutters through the last bit of my release.

"Wow," she whispers, turning her head and kissing my neck, her hands gripping my upper back.

"Mmm," I reply, unable to formulate words.

My lips find hers. The kiss is slow, yet demanding, as we both come down from our release. She tastes like sugar and desire, a heady combination that I'll forever associate with her. Gently, I pull from her body, feeling my cum slip out too. Grabbing for something to help with the mess, I shove her shirt between her legs, determined not to let the mess get all over.

"Well, this will make for an interesting trip to my place," she says, noticing that the shirt she wore is now covered in her and I. And something about that makes me smile.

"Oops," I laugh. "I'll throw on my clothes and run up to the house and grab you something."

"Okay," she replies, wiping away all traces of our short little interlude and handing me the soiled shirt. I use it to clean myself up as best I can, but it doesn't do much good. I'm definitely going to be paying a visit to her bathroom before we go to the house to work.

I pull up my boxer briefs and shorts and turn to the grass path. "Be right back." I place a hard kiss on her lips and then make my way up the lane and to her cottage. The shaded air feels good against my overheated skin, and even though I should probably be wearing a shirt, I'm a little glad not to be. At least I was, until I step into her cottage and find not one, but both of her brothers standing there, along with her mom.

Awesome.

Chapter Twenty-Three

Marissa

It takes him a little longer than anticipated to return with a fresh shirt for me to wear. While I'm waiting, I go ahead and slip his over my head, instantly wrapped in a Rhenn-scented hug. The shirt is big and soft, and I can't help bringing the material to my face for a quick sniff.

When I finally hear the rustle of his steps on the path, I glance his way, immediately knowing something is wrong. "What?"

Rhenn rubs the back of his neck and then his chest, which only draws my eyes to the magnificent view. "My eyes are up here," he teases.

"I know, but this is quite impressive," I state, stepping forward and running my hands up his bare chest. "If only we had more time…"

"Yeah, about that," he says, handing me the shirt.

"What?" I ask, pulling his over my head and tossing it his way.

"Your mom was there." He slips his shirt over his head, little pieces of bark stuck to the chest.

"Where?" I ask, stalling my motions, my shirt half on. "At my place?"

"Yeah," he says, diverting his eyes. "But she wasn't alone."

Dread fills my stomach. "Who else was there?" I ask, already knowing the answer.

Please don't say Samuel, please don't say Samuel…

"Jensen was there with Max," he says, and I instantly relax. Jensen knows there's something going on, but isn't going to give me too much grief over it. At least, he hasn't thus far. "And Samuel."

"Shit."

"Yeah, he wasn't too happy to see me show up without my shirt," Rhenn says, shrugging.

"So, what did you tell them?" I ask when he steps forward and helps me pull my shirt into place.

"That we were relaxing on the beach and you got something on your shirt. You didn't want to walk around without one so I volunteered to run up and grab a clean one."

I snort a laugh. "Something got on my shirt."

"Your mom just started laughing and smiled. I'm pretty sure she wasn't buying it. Anyway, they were going to head up to the house and start in the living room."

"Great," I mumble, making sure my clothes are straight. "How do I look?"

"Freshly fucked." My eyes widen as I look his way. Rhenn starts laughing and pulls me into his arms. "Personally, I love this look on you. Especially when I put it there." Then he places his lips on mine and kisses me soundly. "Let's head up there and get this place ready for occupancy."

He reaches for my hand and pulls me to the path. We make our way there, side by side, and I prepare to face the onslaught of questions and knowing looks.

* * *

Come Thursday, I take off to town to catch lunch with my sister. We try to meet up whenever we can, but with my schedule at the bed and breakfast, it doesn't happen nearly as often as we would like.

Today, I've grabbed sandwiches from the deli and am meeting her at her shop. Kiss Me Goodnight is located in the heart of Rockland Falls, right in the middle of the town square. There's a bank on one side, and a small empty building on the other that the owner refuses to sell. It's been vacant for more than a decade, yet the lady who owns the building holds on to it for some reason. On the other side of the empty storefront is a family owned hardware store that has been in the same location for two generations.

The bell sounds, notifying Harper and Free of my arrival. My sister runs her store, working the floor full time, and spending her evenings with the office side of the business. Her best friend Freedom (or Free as we tend to call her) helps a couple of days a week as her schedule allows. The business is booming, despite a little hesitancy in the beginning of a sexy lingerie store moving into our family-friendly town square.

"Lunch is served," I holler as I approach the counter where my sister and her friend are working.

"I'm starving," Free sighs dramatically, pushing aside whatever new product she was pricing.

"What's that?" I ask, setting the sandwiches on the counter and nodding toward the small bottles of what appears to be lotion.

"Coochie Cream!" Harper boasts proudly.

I can already feel the blush. "Coochie what?"

"Cream. It's a thick, specially formulated shaving gel that doesn't leave razor burn on your muff," Free adds, unwrapping her sandwich and attacking it with her mouth.

"Muff?" I gasp, trying not to laugh at her terminology.

"Makes the muff diving smoother," Free says with a mouth full of food.

"I found a company here in North Carolina that specializes in body products like lotions, shower gels, oils, and shampoos. I purchased my first order of Coochie Cream to see how it sells. I'd love to buy stock of most of their other products, but frankly, I'm just out of room," Harper says, looking around at the full shelves.

"Have you thought about expanding? I know we've talked about it before. Maybe it's time to look into another location. One that has more floor space for you," I offer, taking a small bite of my own sandwich. I know how much Harper loves this cozy space, but honestly, she's just outgrowing it. Between the intimate apparel and small amount of body products she has, there's just no more room to add new merchandise.

"Actually," Harper says, her voice a little hopeful, as she turns and glances at Free. "I heard that old Mrs. Morton is putting the building on the market. A bug was put in my ear about the possibility of a quiet, quick sale. I also heard Mrs. Morton was going to ask top dollar for the space, but I'm thinking it might be a solid investment for me."

"Oh my gosh, that's awesome! Then you can expand!" I'm so excited for my sister and what this could mean for her business.

"I'm trying not to get my hopes up, because I'm not sure what top dollar means yet. Business is going well now, but I still have my original loan that I'm paying on. I'm not sure if I can afford a second building loan."

"I'm sure you'll figure it out," I say, reaching over and touching her hand. "Maybe ask Samuel what he thinks," I offer. Samuel may be the driest human being on the planet, but he's great with numbers. Plus, Harper has the added bonus of getting him all worked up and uncomfortable when she starts talking about the lingerie.

"I was planning to this weekend."

"Oh, please let me be there when you do! I love how red Sammy's ears turn when I talk about the crotchless panties," Free boasts. She does everything she can to get under Samuel's collar, including calling him Sammy as often as possible.

"Oh my God, do you remember when you gave him the leather studded collar for Christmas last year? I thought he was going to stroke out right there next to the Christmas tree," Harper recalls, laughing at our oldest brother's expense.

"Hell yeah, I do, but my favorite was the boxer briefs I got him for his birthday that said 'Caution, Choking Hazard.' The look on his face when he tried to shove them back in the box before anyone could see them was priceless." Free doubles over laughing, as she recalls embarrassing him at his thirtieth birthday party a few years back. She made sure to loudly encourage him to show everyone his new skivvies.

"He hates you," I tease, joining in their laughter.

"I don't think he does. I think he secretly loves me and the way I torture him," Free proclaims proudly, going back to eating her sandwich.

"I'm not sure love is the word I'd use," Harper says as she polishes off her own lunch. "By the way, before you leave, I want to show you the new line I got in yesterday. They're practical with a touch of elegance and sexiness. I instantly thought of you."

I love how she says practical. I've never been a fan of barely-there underwear, and have always gravitated to the pieces that cover all my girly bits. Yes, I'm the completely opposite of my sister, who prefers the more risqué options with very little material. She can pull it off, though. Not only does she have a body for it, but the attitude too.

As soon as we're done eating, she leads me over to one of the small tables in the center of the store. There, we find simple, yet sexy satin panties with matching bras. A few small gems between the bra cups in a midnight blue color instantly draw my attention.

The line has very neutral, subtle colors including nude, white, ivory, and a light pink. But they all have the same dark blue gemstones in the shape of a heart between the cups, as well as a small heart in the front left side of the panties.

"These are gorgeous," I state quietly, picking up a bra and touching the delicate stones.

"They are. The lace overlay adds a beautiful touch, don't you think?" she asks, running her finger over the bra in my hand.

I instantly think of Rhenn and what his reaction would be if he were to find this beneath my clothes later tonight. We're down to our last three nights, and the thought just makes me want to either vomit or cry. Or both. Like many things that are blue, the stones remind me of his eyes. Even though this isn't the sex kitten outfit I'm sure he's used to seeing, I still think I'd get quite the rise out of him if he were to find me wearing it.

Rise. I snicker aloud.

"I'll take it," I say before I can give it a second thought.

Harper digs through the small stack and finds my size in both bra and panties and heads up to the counter. She rings me up, a total that is much less than the sum of two price tags, and places my new purchases in one of her signature turquoise and lavender bags with her store logo.

"I could pay full price, you know," I remind her, as she hands me back my credit card.

"I know you can, but I don't mind giving my favorite sister a discount if her purchase is going to help her get laid," Harper states boldly just as the bell jingles over the door. We all turn to the entry and find Mr. Douglas, the owner of the hardware shop down the street.

"Good afternoon, Mr. Douglas," Harper hollers, handing me the bag containing my newest pretties.

"Afternoon, sweet Harper. How is business today?" he asks, eyeing a black leather corset that adorns the midsection of a mannequin with a look that's a mixture of shock and interest.

"Very well, thank you. How's the hardware store?" Harper replies politely, coming around the counter to speak with the older man. Bud Douglas is the second generation of Douglas men to run town's only hardware store. His father, Ernest, opened the business in the fifties and it has been a staple in town from the beginning.

I wave at my sister and her friend, who are both now in deep conversation with their neighbor, and head out to my car. Needing to get back to the bed and breakfast, I opt to send Mom a quick message, letting her know I'm going to be just a little bit longer. Then, I head to my favorite nail salon and have a pedicure. Nothing makes you feel seductive like new panties and a bra, as well as pretty pink toes.

Three nights left with Rhenn.

I might as well make the most of it.

* * *

The rest of the days fly by.

Nights too.

For the last week, every morning, I've woken beside Rhenn, and go to sleep knowing that in the morning, we're one day closer to saying goodbye. It has become difficult to fall asleep, and by the time Friday night comes, I have to pretend to be asleep so that Rhenn will doze. I've found out over the last two weeks that he never falls asleep first, always waiting until I'm out.

Saturday morning, I feel him slip from my bed. He's an early riser, even when he keeps me up half the night with sex. A creature of habit, Rhenn slips on his shorts and running shoes to pound the sand on the beach. Since I don't have guests to feed, I've been able to sleep in a bit or, as I have more often than not, taken my cup of coffee to the beach and watched for his return.

Rhenn running up the beach, covered in sweat, is truly something to behold.

This morning, I don't find myself anxious to get up and meet him. After I hear the soft click of the door closing, I give in to the sadness and despair that's been threatening to overcome me since our dinner last night.

One more night.

That's all we have.

The tears start to fall, and I don't even try to stop them. I cry for the cruel hand fate has dealt me, and the fact that I'm not strong enough to follow the number one no-strings rule that I, myself, put in place.

Don't fall in love.

Well, jokes on me, isn't it, because not only did I go ahead and fall in love with him, but I fell hard. Harder than I've ever loved before. My heart soars and yet weeps at the exact same time. This time tomorrow, we'll be saying goodbye, and I'm not sure how I'm going to do it. But I will. I will because that's what the arrangement was. Sex. Two weeks. Nothing more.

And the tears fall harder.

* * *

By the time Rhenn returns from his run, I'm up and showered, opting to wash my face and scrub away any remnants of tears, and in the kitchen, cooking.

"Something smells good," he says, his wet T-shirt thrown over his shoulder as he approaches me and places a kiss on my cheek. "Good morning." His voice. Even though he's been up for more than thirty minutes, it's still deep and husky from sleep. I know I'll never forget the way he sounds first thing in the morning.

"Morning," I reply, clearing my throat and pushing down the emotion that seems lodged there.

Rhenn places his hands on the counter and rests his chest against my back. "Is that what I think it is?"

I smile through the pain, loving that this last breakfast makes him so happy. "It is."

He nuzzles my neck, inhaling my freshly showered skin and says, "I'm going to miss these pancakes."

And my heart cracks. It becomes hard to breathe. My knees threaten to buckle. I have to set down the knife I'm using so I don't chop off a finger.

"You okay?" he asks, placing his lips on my collarbone and sliding them along the sensitive flesh.

I nod, not trusting my voice, even though I'm slowly dying inside.

I'm not sure if he believes me or not, but I don't complain when he holds me against the counter for a few minutes longer. Breakfast doesn't matter at this point. Nothing really matters.

"I'm going to run through the shower and then I'll help you finish these," he adds, placing another kiss on my neck and turning away. I miss his presence immediately.

The door to the bathroom shuts and the sound of the water running fills the small house, yet it feels emptier than ever before. How am I going to get through this weekend? Pasting on a smile (albeit fake) and showing him how much I've enjoyed our time together, because this time tomorrow, I'll be alone.

He'll be gone.

Chapter Twenty-Four

Rhenn

She's not fooling me. In just a short period of time, I've learned so much about that woman, including when her smiles are real or fake. That one she gave me before I came into the bathroom? Fake as hell. And don't get me started on the slight red tint to her eyes and the fact that they were a bit swollen. She's been crying. Even me – a man who runs as far away as humanly possible from female tears – knows it.

That's why I had to step away. I don't want to see her hurt, and watching a tear fall down her beautiful face would certainly kill me.

When did I become *this* guy?

Yeah, we both know the answer to that one too.

I take a fast shower, anxious to get back out there. Not just because she's making me her famous lemon zest and blueberry pancakes, but because I don't want to waste one second with her. Soon, I'll be gone, and all I'll have are my memories to keep me warm at night. I might as well get to making more.

With fresh shorts and T-shirt, I step out of her small bathroom and drop the wet towel in the laundry. The process is familiar and comfortable at this point. All of my stuff is already washed, back on my boat, and ready for my trek back home. When I make my way back to the kitchen, I see she already has the pancakes made and in the middle of the table. The syrup is warming in the bowl of water, something I never in a million years would have thought to do before my working trip to Rockland Falls.

We're both quiet as we take our seats, fresh cups of coffee placed beside each plate. I sip my black coffee, watching her over the rim of my cup as she eats. Or pretends to eat. I think she's moving her pancakes around on her plate more than she's eating them.

"So, what's on the schedule for today?" I ask, drawing her eyes to mine. Those eyes. Those fucking beautiful eyes that are sure to haunt my dreams for the rest of my life.

Marissa clears her throat and paints on a smile. "I thought maybe we could go to the park for a bit. There's a walking path that Jensen takes a lot, and a clearing that's perfect for picnics."

"Sounds great," I answer. Honestly, it doesn't matter much what we do as long as I get to spend my last day here with her.

We chat lightly through breakfast, but there's a heavy air in the room that's filled with dread and finality. I hate it. Almost as much as I hate the thought of leaving tomorrow. Nothing about my old life is as appealing as it was before. Sure, I have a great job and a thriving dojo that I love, but what about the rest of it? It means nothing. All of it. Everyone who came before her.

Pushing away those gloomy thoughts, I polish off the best fucking pancakes I've ever had. I know what you're thinking. They're pancakes. What could make them so amazing for such a daring proclamation? They're light, fluffy, and a bold combination of flavors. Plus, there's the woman who makes them. They're as delicious as she is.

I help her clean up the mess, silently working side by side to tidy up her space. When the dishes are clean and drying and the floors swept, I reach for her hand and pull her against me. "I'm yours for the rest of the day. I don't care what we do. I just want to spend it with you." Just before my lips claim hers, I see the flash of pain in her eyes. This goodbye is going to be hard on her, I can tell. I hate that I'm causing her pain.

After kissing the hell out of her, I reluctantly pull away.

"Let me grab some tennis shoes and we can get ready to go," she says, heading off to her bedroom.

I go over to my overnight bag and grab a fresh pair of socks. Once my shoes are in place, she comes out of her room, her own feet covered in pink and gray walking shoes. "Ready?" I ask, extending my hand. She readily takes it, grabbing four water bottles from the fridge and placing them in the bag I didn't even notice she had packed.

"Ready."

Together, we head out the door and off to our first excursion of the day.

* * *

"This is beautiful," I state, taking a long pull from one of the water bottles and handing it back to her for another drink.

"I don't come through here much, but my brother does. It's a bit more rugged than I like," she says with a shoulder shrug.

The walking path from the park turned into a pretty hearty workout. We've snaked our way through the woods, walked up steep inclines, and wound our way along the river. We've actually found ourselves at the waterfall, but this time from the opposite side. The rocks are jagged and slippery as the water rushes past, making it too dangerous to be on the cliff, so we just stand there, both of us breathing heavy from the trek up, and watch the rushing waters.

"Let's sit and rest for a bit," I tell her, taking the backpack off and setting it on a flat rock. Marissa retrieves the food inside and hands me a Ziploc baggie. "What's this?" I ask opening the package and pulling out the sandwich. When I realize what it is, I can't help but laugh. "PB and J?"

"Only the best PB and J sandwich ever made! The jelly is fresh from a farm on the other side of town. We've been serving it at the bed and breakfast for years. You seem like the type who would appreciate blueberry rhubarb jelly."

My mouth waters as I take my first bite. "Holy shit, that's amazing," I say right before taking my second bite.

"Right? It's my favorite of all her jellies. Well, that and apple butter."

I moan in pleasure as I think about all the ways she could use apple butter for breakfast. "I love apple butter. My grandma used to make it when I was little."

"Sooo good," she moans as she takes her first bite.

"I'm completely turned on right now," I deadpan, watching her devour her PB and J sandwich.

"Of course you are. You're breathing," she teases, shoulder bumping me as I polish off my lunch.

"It's you. You have this reaction on me," I confess, though I assume she already knows. It's definitely no secret.

We're both quiet, as she pulls out a bag of potato chips and together we finish off the sour cream and onion flavored snack. The waters rage around us and off in the distance, we can see several couples and families enjoying the falls, walking back and forth down the flat path that we took last weekend.

"Can I ask you something?" I break the silence and stretch my legs forward, leaning back on my hands.

"Sure."

"Do you think you might come up to Jupiter Bay on the Fourth?" I've known that her family was planning to come up for the next holiday weekend, but it's the first time the topic has been broached between us.

Marissa toys with her hair, shoving it behind her ear, and dropping her eyes. "I don't think so. I have a lot to do here, and we'll have guests by then. I think it's best if I stay behind."

She doesn't look my way, but I nod anyway. There's something so wrong about her family coming up to spend the weekend with their family and her not coming too. Realization that I won't be seeing her in a few weeks doesn't sit well. "I had kinda hoped to see you again," I tell her.

Finally, Marissa looks up, sadness etched on her face. She gives me a smile, but it's not the kind that lights up her face. "I'm not really sure that's a good idea. I mean, when we made this arrangement, it was for two weeks. I think it's best to just end it tomorrow; you go your way, and I'll go mine."

My stomach drops to my shoes. The chances of me running into her again are pretty good, considering my best friend is married to her cousin, but I hadn't really thought far enough ahead to when that actually happens. Or the fact that she wouldn't want to see me again. Even if you take sex out of the equation, I consider her a friend now. I'll admit, that hurts.

Not wanting to show any reaction, I go with, "You're right." I clear my throat, nodding too much to be deemed normal, and start picking up our trash. Once it's put in the backpack, I stand up, hating the fact that she is right. This is exactly what we agreed upon, exactly what I wanted. No strings. Just sex. If we see each other again, great. It doesn't have to be weird or uncomfortable.

Then why does it feel like my heart was just kicked with a pair of steel-toed boots?

Not trusting my voice, I reach for her hand and, together, we start to make the winding trek back on the path. Our walk down is more leisurely than it was coming up, and we often find birds, cool rocks, and trees to stop and look at. We barely talk, but I feel like so much is being said. We're communicating with our body language, with our unspoken words, with our touch. I never in a million years thought I'd be so…sad at the prospect of leaving someone I'm sleeping with, but do you know what? This shit hurts. It sucks, and by the time tomorrow rolls around, I'm not sure how I'm going to walk away. I don't want to see sadness on her face – or worse, indifference with my leaving. That might actually kill me.

So I know what I have to do.

* * *

I refused to let her cook on my last night here. Instead, I took her to that little hole in the wall steakhouse that I took her to the first time. I've done everything I can to stay away from her place, since I know her family is there. Nick and Meghan drove over to help me get my boat back home, and with them, Emma and Orval. I'm just not in the mood to share Marissa right now. Not on my last night with her.

The good news is that they all went to Samuel's place for dinner, so when we return to the bed and breakfast, we're alone. I help her from my truck, and with her hand nestled in mine, guide her around the house and to her place. The lights are off, creating a dark, mysterious ambiance, so when we enter, I take the opportunity to pull her into my arms. My lips are on hers instantaneously, eager to taste her one more time.

One last time.

Marissa comes into my arms willingly, opening her mouth when my tongue glides along the seam of her lips. She tastes like heaven, that sexy combination of sultry and sweet. I'm not sure I'll ever forget her taste, nor will I find another pair of lips as amazing as hers. That fucking ball of dread tightens in my chest once more, so I do what I do best: push it aside and ignore it.

It has gotten me through life, thus far.

Slowly, I guide her backward to her bedroom. Her arms wrap around my neck as she presses her body tightly against mine. I'm already hard and aching for her, but I want to take this slow. I want to memorize every move, every sound, everything I feel when I'm with her.

I kick off my flip-flops as soon as we enter her room, and she does the same. My hand snakes under her light blue dress, sliding up her outer thigh and coming in contact with smooth satin. With my hand under her ass, I lift, her legs wrapping around my waist as I gently lie her down on the mattress. My lips continue a slow, seductive kiss, nipping at her plump lips and dragging down the delectable column of her neck.

"Rhenn," she whispers in the dark of night, my chest tightening and my heart pounding. The sound of my name on her lips will forever be ingrained in my memory.

"I'm right here, Angel," I answer as I push her dress up, exposing her wet panties. My hands keeps moving, tugging at the dress until it's over her head and thrown on the floor. Then, my eyes feast on the beauty before me, splayed out on the bed like the goddess she is. "This is new?" I ask, taking in the nude colored bra and panty set she's wearing, noticing the little blue gemstone hearts on both pieces.

"Yes."

"Did you buy them with me in mind?" I ask, gliding my hands up her waist and cupping her breasts.

She nods, not saying a word, as my hands continue to explore her body. When they begin to trek downward, her legs instantly fall open, an invitation I can't refuse. My palm moves over the panties and find them wet, which I already suspected. My Angel is always wet and ready for me.

"You look so beautiful in them, I don't really want to take them off," I whisper as I move my palm over her pussy, loving the way her hips buck against the pressure. "But I need to see you, Angel. I need to feel you." No truer words have ever been spoken.

I unclasp the bra and gently slip the panties down her legs. Even though the caveman in me wants to ruin them so no other man could ever see her this way, I don't want to be a dick. I know this shit is expensive. My eyes feast on her body as I toss the panties over my shoulder. Her legs fall open again, and my mouth starts to water. "I need to taste you." One last time. I don't say it, but I think it.

Needing something to focus on besides the end that's drawing near, I position myself between her legs. The first swipe of my tongue against her pussy is pure heaven, sending my blood pumping feverishly. Marissa writhes beneath me as I lick and suck, driving her closer and closer to her first release. When I add two fingers, I know she's there. She bucks against my hand, grinding and taking what she needs. The sweetest noises fill the room as she begins the climb, my name falling from her lips as she flies over the edge. It's beautiful to watch, and I don't take my eyes off her for one second.

When she relaxes on the bed, I use the opportunity to shed my own clothes. I reach for my wallet, but something stops me. We had sex on that tree last week without a rubber (my first time ever), but have used one ever since. Tonight, I don't want anything between us. I want to feel all of her for as long as I can. When I glance down at her, she seems to understand my thoughts. Instead of insisting I get one, both of us knowing I should be wearing one, she reaches for me.

And I'm too weak to resist.

I cover her body with my own, my lips devouring hers. I can still taste her on my lips, and it only fuels my desire further. I position myself between her legs, my cock hard and ready, falling to where it wants to be on its own. With her lips securely pressed against mine, I slide home.

Home.

Where I belong.

When I'm seated completely inside, I open my eyes and my breath catches. Her eyes shine brightly with emotion and unshed tears. My hand moves to her face, her beautiful, angelic face, and I catch a lone tear as it slips from her eye. My emotions are all over the place. I want to stay, but know that I can't. I want to be here – with her – for the rest of my life.

But. I. Fucking. Can't.

I'm not good for her. I'm not good for anyone. I'm not the staying kind, and even though my heart is telling me that's complete bullshit, I know it to be true. There are so many things I want to say, but know that I shouldn't – I can't. So instead, I say them with my body. I slowly pull out and gently glide back in. Our pace is unhurried but deliberate, as we move in perfect harmony together. More tears slips from her eyes, and it guts me. Like a steak knife to the sternum, I feel the pain reflecting in her eyes.

I make love to her. That's the only way to describe it. We're not hurried. There's no magical position I pull out to get us both off. We lie together, face-to-face, as I make love to the only woman I've ever loved.

It took me a mere glance to fall for her, but three weeks to finally admit it.

The orgasm I'm trying to hold off is barreling down on me. My spine is tingling and my balls tighten almost painfully. My lips drag lazily down her neck, expelling little gasps of delight and desire. Her pussy starts to tighten, grabbing my cock in a vise grip, basically ensuring that there's no way to slow this train down anymore. I make sure to keep my movements slow and deliberate as I pump into her, kissing her lips and touching every square inch of her body. She tilts her hips upward and I press forward once more, sending us both over the edge. Bright white lights filter through my vision as I come, pulsing inside her, and emptying myself of everything I have.

That includes my heart.

I will never be in possession of it again.

It is hers.

When the trembling finally subsides and our bodies start to relax, I turn to my side, taking her with me. I stay buried inside of her pussy, not wanting to feel the emptiness that is surely to come when I finally pull out. Instead, I continue to hold her tight, and she does the same. Her arms are snaked around my chest, her cheek nestled against my shoulder. We lie together like that, for how long, I'm not sure, holding each other and just…breathing.

And then I feel the tears against my skin.

I know that if I look at her now, I'll forever see this look on her face.

So I don't look. I can't.

I hold her so tight that I'm not sure she's able to breathe. I kiss her forehead and run my hands up and down her body. I memorize every piece of this moment, of her. Exhaustion starts to settle in and the tears finally stop. Her body begins to grow heavy, and I know she's finally drifting off to sleep. But me? I won't sleep. Not tonight, and probably not ever again, because when I close my eyes, I know who I'll see.

My cock finally slips from her body, but I make no move to grab something to clean us up with. I don't want to move. Not until I have to. I lie there for hours, holding her close and kissing her face. She mumbles a few times in her sleep before softly sighing and snuggling in closer. My name is that sigh.

When the clock finally reads five and I know the sun will be filtering through the windows soon, I start to pull away. I can't do the goodbye thing. I don't want to say it. So in a total dick move, I hug her tightly against me, kiss her pliant, soft lips, and say the one thing I told myself I'd never say again. "I love you."

Then, I extract my body from hers, instantly feeling the loss of her skin against mine, and climb out of bed as quietly as possible. My heart pounds furiously in my chest as I slip on my clothes, only taking my eyes off her sleeping form to pull the shirt over my head. When I'm completely dressed, I know there's only one last thing to do.

Leave.

Walk out that door one last time.

Needing one last touch, I run my hand over her face. She turns into the touch, another soft sigh spilling from her lips. When she settles again, I know I need to move. If I don't go now, I'll never go.

And I need to go.

With leaded feet, I grab my flip-flops and make my way to her door. I don't look back as I go through the doorway, grabbing my bag on the way. My heart cracks open and slowly starts to bleed as I gently open and close her front door. The early morning air is warm and inviting, yet I feel none of it. I feel nothing but pain. I make my way through the clearing and toward the dock. My boat sits there, mocking me with its bright white color and happy memories.

I may never be able to sail again.

On autopilot, I start up the trolling motor and make my way to my sailboat. I secure the small boat and climb aboard, throwing my bag down the stairs to the galley below. With heavy legs, I head to the helm and prepare to depart. When the boat is ready and the sun is peeking over the horizon, I shoot off a quick text message to my best friend to tell him to bring my truck home. With my phone placed back in my pocket, I fire up the engine. I make one last glance toward the shore, wishing she were standing on the dock one last time, and pull anchor.

I'm off.

Heading back to Jupiter Bay.

Away from Rockland Falls.

Away from Marissa.

Away from my heart.

Chapter Twenty-Five

Marissa

I know.

The moment I start to rouse from sleep, I can feel the difference. The room, the bed, my heart, it all feels…empty.

He's gone.

And he didn't even say goodbye.

Chapter Twenty-Six

Rhenn

The sail back home is anything but smooth. The seas are choppy and that once bright sunshine is now replaced with the gloom of an incoming storm. I guess it matches my mood, though. Throw in the fact I haven't slept, and I know this ride is going to be a miserable one.

But that's what I get.

What I deserve.

At the end of the day, I lied.

I promised I wouldn't fall in love with her and I did. Jokes on me, right? The man incapable of love falls head over heels for the shy bed and breakfast owner's daughter who lives three hours away.

And who doesn't want him in return.

It's for the best. She deserves to be loved wholly, and I'm not capable of that. She deserves everything. So while she moves on with her life, occasionally thinking about the amazing two weeks we shared, I'll be at home, miserable and wishing I were with her, and praying that emptiness doesn't last for the rest of my life.

But I know it will.

Because she's gone.

Chapter Twenty-Seven

Marissa

"You look like someone broke your favorite vibrator."

My head snaps up in shock as Emma gazes over at me from across the yard. Her eyes are all knowing, yet filled with kindness and understanding. "I'm not quite sure what you mean," I respond, wishing she'd just drop it and quit talking about vibrators. Why must my eighty-five-year-old aunt bring up one of those…things in front of everyone?

More importantly, why is she drawing attention toward me.

While talking about the vibrator.

"Of course you do. Your eyes are filled with sorrow." Emma's are gentle and speak volumes.

Before I can say anything, Meghan joins us. "He left without saying goodbye."

"He did? That sexy karate master took the pogo stick before you could take one final hop around the yard?" Emma declares, again drawing more attention.

"Wow, that's…graphic. There was no…yard hopping, Aunt Emma, and besides, we all knew he was leaving," I say, shrugging my shoulders casually, yet feeling anything but. As much as I love and enjoy my family, I really just wish they would all leave already so I can wallow in peace. This fake smile and pretending I'm fine is exhausting.

Harper snorts. "Maybe no yard hopping, but I heard there was something freaky going on in the timber. Rumor has it Rhenn had bark embedded in his T-shirt and Riss had one of those big dopey smiles and smelled like sex."

I gasp.

"Mom told me," Harper shrugs. "Plus, Rhenn returned without a shirt, 'claiming' that Riss got something on hers and needed a new one. I'm sorry I missed that part."

I stare wide-eyed at my not-so-innocent sister as she continues to tell all my secrets to my horny old aunt and my cousin.

"Spoog. It was definitely man juice on her shirt. When the volcano blows, that lava flies everywhere," Emma adds, completely ignoring my silent pleas for mercy.

"Don't say man juice," Meghan chastises.

"Spoog isn't much better," Harper mumbles.

"Nut butter? Anyway, all I'm saying is that it's messy. Just be glad you didn't get it in your eye, dear. That happened to me once when we were driving out to Brian and Trisha's house years ago. I couldn't see for an hour."

We all just stare at Emma, completely horrified at the very vivid picture she just painted. I'll have nightmares for days...

"We're ready," Nick hollers, heading over to Rhenn's truck. The truck that has been taunting me for the last several hours. It's almost noon, but instead of eating together, they've opted to make a stop along the way.

"I'm riding with Nick, my love," Uncle Orval says to Emma before placing a kiss on her cheek. "It was lovely to see you again, Marissa," he adds, pulling me into a big hug.

"You too."

"I'm sure you're coming up for the Fourth of July, right?" Emma asks, giving me one of those looks that tells me there's only one answer, and it isn't no.

"I'm not sure yet. We'll be open by then," I answer, not really giving them a definite.

Emma steps forward and pulls me into her tiny arms. "He's a man, honey, so let him have a bit of time to think about what he lost. They never catch on too quickly. Something tells me that if he's half as miserable as you pretend not to be, he'll be back. They always come back to the one they love."

I stand there, stunned, and try to come up with a response. "Love? That's not what this was."

Liar.

At least it was for me.

"You sure?" she asks, offering me a wink. "I'll see you on the Fourth."

She gives no room for argument. Nodding, I watch as they walk away, hand in hand. He leads her to Meghan's car and helps her inside before placing another kiss on her lips. I can't help but sigh at the exchange. It's comforting to know that some loves are forever, even if I have yet to find mine.

"They're disgusting most of the time, but their love is genuine," Meghan says beside me, watching her grandparents. Just then, Emma reaches out and grabs her husband's rear before giving it a little pat.

"Relationship goals," I state. "Well, maybe without the groping."

"It was good to see you again," Meghan says, pulling me into a hug. "He's an idiot." I don't have to ask who she's referring to.

I gaze up at her and shrug my shoulders. "His loss then, right?" I plaster on a smile, this one not as fake, and silently send a prayer to the man upstairs for sending us an extended family like this.

"That's right," she laughs, squeezing me one more time before walking toward her husband.

Nick helps her into the driver's seat and, following suit with Orval, kisses his pregnant wife soundly. It isn't until Emma in the seat beside her starts to hoot and holler that Nick finally pulls away, a wide smile on his face. Before he heads over to his best friend's truck, he comes over and says goodbye to all of us. When he reaches me, he pulls me into a friendly hug. "Thank you."

"For what?" I ask, completely stumped by his random statement.

Nick offers me a smile, and I can see exactly why his wife went all googly-eyed for her boss. "For changing him." Nick places a kiss on my forehead and grips my upper arms. "He'll be back." Then, he offers me a wink and heads to the truck.

I wave as my family heads home, but it's the sight of the truck that has my heart aching. It's the last time I'll see it in the driveway. The last time I'll watch it head down the lane. When it reaches the end, the brake lights shining brightly in the trees, my heart cracks open and the tears start to fall. It rounds the corner, turning onto the road, and drives out of sight.

For the last time.

* * *

After a small dinner, it feels like the walls are closing in on me. Everywhere I look, I see Rhenn. In just a short amount of time, he wormed his way into my heart, embedding himself in my life. My tiny couch he used to sit on, looking like a giant. The two-seater table we'd have our breakfast at most mornings and dinner at in the evenings. The mixing bowls I used to make pancakes for what could possibly be the last time. There's no way I'll ever be able to make them again without thinking of him.

My bed.

I don't even want to think about what it's going to feel like tonight when I go to bed.

Alone.

Needing out of the house, I grab a lightweight sweater and slip on a pair of sandals. For mid-June, the air is brisk from a recent rain shower, the sky as dull and gloomy as my mood. I walk down the path, anxious to get away from my cottage. Too many memories.

But then, I reach the clearing and stare at the ocean.

The ocean that no longer houses a sailboat two hundred yards offshore.

A dock that is empty.

I kick off the sandals and walk through the sand. I used to love the way it felt between my toes, but now, it almost holds no joy. There's no excitement, no newness. Only memories. I step onto the wooden dock and make my way to the end. Sitting on the edge, I let my feet dangle in the cool water, the chilly breeze whipping through my hair.

I can't help it. I glance out to the vacant spot where his boat was once anchored. Memories of the boat, of our time together filter through my mind in rapid-fire sequence, each one ending with the way his blue eyes shined down at me when he gave me a smile. Not the smirk (even though I still secretly love it), but that genuine, open smile that made me fall in love with the man he hides. Not playboy, cocky Rhenn, but the real him. The sweet and sensitive guy who guards his heart, yet loves and protects his family and friends fiercely.

A lone tear slips from my eye as I stare off at the vast, empty space of water. It doesn't take long before his friends follow and I'm crying for everything I've felt and lost. I want nothing more than to look back on our time together and smile, remembering fond memories of a wonderful experience, and do you know what? I will.

Just not yet. Right now, my heart hurts too much to see the bright side of our brief affair.

I hear footsteps on the dock, but don't turn to the sound. I already know who it is. Harper sits down beside me and doesn't say a word. Instead, she reaches for my hand and holds it. Her gesture makes me cry even harder, resulting in being pulled into her arms. I cry on my sister's shoulder, letting go of all the fun, the laughter, and the love I had felt, and letting the sadness take over. At least for a little while.

"I brought ice cream," she says, my head resting on her shoulder.

I laugh through my tears. "Chocolate mint?"

"Is there any other flavor?"

"No," I reply, sniffling and wiping away the remnants of tears. When I look at her, I see nothing but sadness and empathy in my sister's eyes.

"I'm sorry," Harper says.

"You should be."

"Me? Why are you mad at me?" she asks, placing her own feet in the water.

"Have no-strings sex, she said. It'll be fine, she said. Liar. You're a liar."

She's quiet for a few moments before she finally speaks again. "The key to no-strings sex is that you're not supposed to fall in love." She glances my way again. "But you did, right? You fell in love."

Her blue eyes shine back at me. Even though they're the spitting image of our father's, the deep color reminds me of another pair of blue eyes. "Yeah, I fell in love with him."

She pulls a face, this one filled with pity and anguish. "I'm sorry, Marissa." My sister pulls me into her arms once more. "He doesn't know what he lost."

Resting my head on her shoulder again, I stare off at the ocean. Our time together is over, but that's okay. I'm going to be okay. With time, I'm going to be able to think about him without wanting to cry, without feeling like a piece of my soul died when I realized he was gone. I'll be able to smile fondly when I picture him, much like the original plan.

Before I fell in love.

Before I knew what it truly felt like to have my heart broken.

Chapter Twenty-Eight

Rhenn

The steel door opens and slams shut, indicating I have a visitor. I know who it is. There's only one other person who has the key. I continue to pound my fist into the heavy bag, ignoring the sweat pouring from my brow and running into my eye. My muscles are tired, exhausted from such a strenuous workout, yet I keep beating. Pound, pound, pound. Fist meets hard bag. Heavy metal pumping through the speakers.

It's the only thing that has gotten me through this week.

A week from hell.

Nick doesn't say a word, just comes over and holds the heavy bag while I continue my assault. The harder I drive my fist into the bag, the worse the memories come flooding back. That only pisses me off even more. Punch, ignore, punch, ignore. But there's no ignoring her and the recollections she evokes.

When my body is too tired to go on, I drop my arms, panting hard and sweating even harder. "You look like shit," my asshole best friend says, pushing against the bag and hitting me in the chest.

"Thanks," I reply, sarcastically. Sarcasm has become my friend. Well, that and tequila. "I've been busy."

He stares at me from a few feet away, his arms crossed over his chest. Even though my friend is a few inches shorter than me, he's a scrappy little bastard, and there's no doubt in my mind that if he wanted to, he could kick my ass to Sunday right now. And do you know what? I'd welcome it. Maybe having my head pounded on would actually help me sleep at night.

"You're not returning my calls."

"Like I said, I've been busy." He continues to stare, and it's starting to piss me off. "If you have something to say, say it. You're interrupting my workout."

"Why'd you leave?" Okay, so he's coming out swinging right out of the gate.

"Because the job was done."

"Bullshit."

I glare down at him, my heart pounding in my chest and my breathing slightly erratic. "Come again?" I ask, taking a step toward him. The tension in the room is getting thick, but I'm not about to back down.

"You heard me. I call bullshit."

"Whatever," I mumble, turning and tossing the gloves onto the floor and heading over to the weight machine.

"Not happening, man. I'm not going to stand here and watch you kill yourself."

"What the fuck," I growl, turning and going nose to nose with my best friend.

"You're exhausted. Maybe instead of lifting weights, you should go home and sleep."

"I can't!" I bellow, angry at him for knowing me so well. Angry at him for calling me out. Angry at myself for not being strong enough to deal with this hurt I feel in my chest.

"So you're just going to keep going until you drop? Then what?"

"I don't know," I mumble, turning and heading toward the treadmill. If the bastard won't let me lift, I'll run. Even as dog tired as I am right now, I can still run circles around his sorry ass.

"No."

"What?" I ask, stopping and turning around once more.

"Go home. Get some rest."

"Fuck you," I yell, turning and continuing my trek to the treadmill.

I don't know he's coming until his shoulder is planted in my back and we're hurling to the mat. Instinct takes over and I roll to the side, grabbing at his leg and using my momentum to pin his arm. But he's too fast, too strong. Maybe I am a little tired. It should be easy for me to overcome my friend, but suddenly, I find myself on my back, him trying to hold down my arms. I get in a gut shot and find a little comfort in hearing him grunt. What I wasn't expecting was the solid right hook to my jaw, or the immediate left that meets my ribs.

"Bastard," I grunt, reveling in the pain that sweeps through my body. I use my legs and throw him off me, swinging around and pinning him to the mat. My fist lands a kidney shot, but it's short lived when his leg bucks back and takes out my knee.

We both lie there, side by side, grunting and panting. "What the fuck was that?" I ask, slowly rolling onto my hip and looking over at my friend.

The asshole is smiling. "That was you getting your ass kicked."

I snort. "What the fuck ever, dreamer."

He reaches over for the towel on the bench and throws it at my face. "You're bleeding."

Swiping at my nose, I find a slow stream of red staining the white towel. "When the fuck did you do that?"

"When you were crying about your ribs."

"Bastard," I grumble, tossing the towel to the side and lying back down on the mat. We're both quiet for several minutes as we regain control of our breathing.

"You want to talk about it?"

"No."

Again, he's quiet for a few long seconds. "She's miserable too."

My world tilts on its axis and my eyes close. All I can picture is her sweet smile and the way her eyes lit up with excitement when I would kiss her. Fuck, I miss her. "How do you know?" I find myself asking, even though I shouldn't. I shouldn't care, yet I do.

"Meghan talked to her last night."

I don't say anything. What the hell am I supposed to say? I'm sorry? Well, she's not the only one fucking miserable, okay? I'm dying a slow death without her, and I hate it. I fucking hate it so much I'm not sure how I'm going to make it through the night, let alone the rest of my life.

"You know, there comes a time in every man's life when he has to admit he was wrong. You, my friend, were wrong."

Rolling over to my side, I arch my eyebrow. "Please, oh wise one, elaborate on how I was so wrong." Honestly, I'm pretty sure I don't want to know the answer to this.

"You find yourself incapable of love, but you're wrong. You are the most giving, trusting man I've ever known, Rhenn. You just refuse to see it yourself."

Well, hell. Pull out the big guns, why don't ya?

I open my mouth to argue, but he stops me. "You love her, but you're scared. Afraid you'll do something to fuck it up, so you kept it light and easy, just like always. But do you know what? This time is different. *She's* different. I've never seen you sullen and pissy before and do you know why?" I arch another eyebrow. "Because you. Love. Her." He goes ahead and pauses between each word for emphasis.

Dick.

"And," he continues, "you haven't felt this way since Suzanne, who dicked you around and broke your heart. Do you know why?"

"Keep going," I tell him.

"Because she wasn't the one for you. Marissa is. Everything that has happened in your life has led you to this moment, to this woman. So what's it gonna be? You gonna walk away and go about your life like the lifeless dick you are, or are you gonna go back there and fight for the woman you love?"

I hate him.

Yet, I love him more.

Because he's right.

I love her. So much it hurts to be apart from her. But am I capable of giving her what she wants? What she needs?

I already know the answer to that question, because I'm not the same man I was before I met her. I *want* to be better – for her and for me.

"When did you get so smart?" I ask, smiling over at my friend, even though it hurts just a little – but I'm not about to show him that.

"I've always been this brilliant, you've just been too preoccupied to see it."

I laugh. "I guess you've got me there. So what do I do?"

Nick smiles at me, and I can practically see the light bulb click on above his head. "This is what you do…"

Chapter Twenty-Nine

Marissa

It's been nearly two weeks since Rhenn left, and I haven't heard a peep out of him. Not that I expected to, mind you. That was the arrangement, right? Yet, a part of me (the part that controls my heart) had hoped maybe, just maybe, he'd reach out to me. That maybe he'd find he is missing me as much as I miss him.

No such luck.

The first guests seem to be enjoying themselves. We're filled to capacity on our first official weekend back in business. I've been working like crazy in the kitchen, preparing some of my favorite comfort food meals, partially for them, but the other part for me. They're easy to make and require no brainpower. Considering I'm still not sleeping well, that's definitely a plus.

"Marissa, I'm cooking dinner tonight," Mom states as she enters the kitchen.

"What? Why? I've already started the prep for the chicken and noodles. The rolls are rising on the counter and the chocolate éclairs in the fridge. I don't mind," I tell her, cutting the last bit of homemade dough into strips.

"I can take it from here," she says breezily, coming over and practically taking the knife from my hand. "Why don't you enjoy a night off? You've been working crazy hours for the last several weeks. Everything is going well, so there's no reason for us both to work this evening."

She's right, everything *is* going well. Once the construction phase was complete, the building inspector found no issues with the house and granted us immediate occupancy. After the walls were freshly painted, new bedding and towels placed in all of the rooms, and the fridge and freezers restocked, we were ready to reopen the Grayson Bed and Breakfast. Our first guests arrived last night, and we have one more couple due in the morning.

"I don't mind, Mom. Why don't you take the night off? You were the one who finished painting the downstairs," I offer, reaching for the knife and heading to the dishwasher.

"I insist. Plus, I'm taking next weekend off to go visit the family in Jupiter Bay."

Ahh, yes. The Fourth of July weekend trip to meet the rest of the family. I'm not going, of course, even though Mom seems to think it'll be okay if I do. She's already arranged for Free and Mrs. Gillenwater to cover the B&B for the weekend, but I don't have the heart to tell her I just don't want to go. Seeing my family? Yes. Seeing Rhenn? Not yet.

"Mom," I start to argue, but she instantly cuts me off.

"Marissa," she says in a mocking tone.

"You're mean," I grumble, making her laugh.

"I'm not mean. I just care about the health of my daughter. She's been working herself to the bone lately, and I want her to relax. Don't think I haven't noticed how much you've been putting yourself into your work in hopes that you'll forget about him for just a little while." My eyes fly to hers. "I've been there, baby girl. I know all about working hard to escape memories." Her eyes flash with the hurt and sadness she experienced at the hands of our father.

"Anyway, enough of that. All I'm saying is I know what you're going through, and eventually, the pain starts to dull. The memories will start to fade and be replaced with new ones."

The thought of slowly forgetting about Rhenn makes the pain that much more intense. I couldn't imagine closing my eyes and not seeing his vivid smile.

"Tonight, you're off duty. I'll cover breakfast in the morning and lunch too. Hell, just take the weekend. See you Monday morning," Mom says, making a shooing motion with her hands.

My mouth drops open. "What? You want me to take the rest of today and all of tomorrow off? Are you mad? Did you hit your head? Do you have a fever?" I ask, reaching for her forehead. "I'm calling Samuel!"

"Knock it off," she insists, batting away my hand. "I'm fine. I just want you to relax. Is that so bad for a mother to want to take care of her daughter?" Then she bats those doe eyes and I know she's got me.

"No," I grumble.

"Great!" she rejoices, pushing me out of the way and continuing to work on the dinner I was preparing. "Go. Enjoy."

I slowly turn and walk to the door, glancing over my shoulder to see if aliens have taken over her brain. She's definitely acting weird, but it's not like I can argue with her further. I mean, I *can,* but something tells me it will be pointless.

"Oh, Marissa? Before you go, will you take the stack of towels in the laundry room to room five?"

"Room five? I thought that couple wasn't coming until morning?"

"Early arrival." She doesn't look up, just keeps cutting the few remaining noodles until the dough is all finished.

"Of course," I mumble, heading into the laundry room to grab the stack of dark blue towels waiting to be delivered to room five. Stupid blue towel. Why does it feel like this color is mocking me?

I head up the stairs and down the hall until I'm standing before the closed door. This one is my favorite room, with its breathtaking views of the ocean. Knocking, I hear a distant, hoarse response. "Come in."

"Fresh towels, sir," I say as I gently push open the door, careful not to disturb the couple within. No one appears to be in the room, but the bathroom light is on and I can hear movement. I head over to the massive bed and set the fresh linens down on the bedspread. Since our guest is in the bathroom, I'll leave them for the guests here. "Let us know if you need anything else," I holler as I make my way toward the door.

"What if what I need is finally standing right in front of me?"

That voice.

I'd know it anywhere.

I whip around and find Rhenn standing in the bathroom doorway, leaning against the doorjamb, with his hands stuffed in his pockets. He looks...nervous. And so amazing. Freshly showered with a pair of khaki shorts and a polo that molds perfectly to his arms and chest. His blue eyes are bright, and even though they look a bit tired, they shine vibrantly like sunlight on a sapphire. And his mouth. Oh, that sinful, smirky mouth that reminds me of late-night kisses and wicked wet dreams.

My eyes return to his, my heart trying to pound out of my chest. "What exactly is standing in front of you?" I ask, my voice all crackly and gravelly.

Rhenn pushes off the doorway and strides my way with long, purposeful steps. When he's right in front of me, I gaze up at him for the first time in nearly two weeks and a glimmer of hope bubbles to life in my chest. He smiles a soft, gentle smile and cups my cheek with his big hand. I almost tilt into his touch, but hold steady, needing to hear his words first.

And then he speaks.

"You. I need you."

The tears start to fall as I reach for his shirt, pulling myself into his chest. "I need you too."

His lips are urgent, hungry even, as they finally touch mine. I immediately open my mouth, his tongue diving inside, tasting and savoring. He smells the same, tastes the same, and the best part is – he's here. I grip the back of his shirt, holding on tightly for fear he might disappear. Rhenn's hands dive into my hair as he continues to kiss me as if I were the very oxygen he needs.

When we're both breathless, he finally pulls back, guiding his finger along my jaw. Goose bumps pepper my skin as I release a shaky breath. "You're here," I whisper, still trying to wrap my head around it.

"I am. I have something I needed to tell you." He stares down at me, so open and honest.

"What's that?"

"I came back for the pancakes." I look up at him, not really sure I heard him correctly. When he offers me a big smile and a burst of laughter falls from his lips, I find myself doing the same. The heaviness I've been carrying around with me just fades away.

"Is that all?" I ask, my smile mirroring his.

"No, that's not all," he says, pulling me flush against his body. His erection presses between us, hard and ready, and my own body instantly starts to react. Rhenn grazes his thumb over my bottom lip as he says, "I needed to tell you I love you."

Another tear slips from the corner of my eye, but this time, out of elation. Joy. Happiness. And love. It's followed up by a giggle. "That's good, because I love you too."

Rhenn grins widely before his lips claim mine one more time. I give in to his kiss, his love, and let it fill my heart. This man, this amazingly sweet, yet complicated man, just confessed that he loves me. Me. The quiet girl who works too much and would rather read than live the highlife. The girl who loves him with everything she has and wants to show him how much every day.

"I have other news," he says without moving his lips from mine.

"There's more? Don't keep me waiting," I answer, licking at his bottom lip.

He groans, tightens his hold on my body, and flexes his hips forward. "I talked to my boss, and it turns out, his brother is short-staffed here in North Carolina. They own a small apartment above the shop in Harriston, and as of this weekend, that's where I'll be staying."

"Harriston? Like thirty minutes away?" I ask, my eyes wide with surprise.

"That's the one, Angel. Do you think that you might be interested in, I don't know, seeing where this thing goes?"

"Which thing are we talking about?" I ask, wiggling against his hard-on. "I'm pretty sure I know exactly where it goes," I tease.

"Vixen," he growls, taking my face in his hands and kissing me hard on the lips. "I like where you're going with that, but believe it or not, that's not what I was referring to. I mean you and me. Us."

"Us?" I ask, already liking the sound of that.

"Yes, us. My hours might be a little crazy like yours, but I think we can make it work. Don't you?"

I want to scream my approval, and almost do, but somehow, I keep it composed. "Yes, yes I do. I want to see where this goes. Us."

He offers me a real smile, not that smirky one that makes me all crazy, but the real one that makes my heart sing. "Thank Christ," he says, releasing a huge sigh of relief. "I was prepared for much more groveling. I even had a speech prepared."

My eyebrows shoot heavenward. "You did?"

"I did, but since you've already agreed to be my girl, then we can skip to phase two," he says, reaching around, grabbing my rear, and pulling me up and into his chest. My legs immediately wrap around him.

"Phase two?"

"I'm going to show you where this thing goes," he declares with another hip flex. He walks me to the bed, lays his body down on mine, and kisses me with everything he has.

Rhenn proceeds to show me, not once, but three times exactly where his cock belongs.

Epilogue

Rhenn

Fourth of July Weekend

"I'd rather take you back to bed," I whisper in her ear as she scoops pasta salad onto her plate, dropping the spoon in the process.

"Knock it off," she gasps, elbowing me in the stomach.

"I can't help it, Angel. All I can think about is how wet your pussy was this morning when I was eating you out. I want to go back to my place and do it all over again."

She gazes up at me with wide, hungry eyes. "You're bad."

"I'm so fucking good, Angel. So good."

"Are you two about to have sex? I think Lexi and the stripper went up to the guest room under the guise of changing a diaper, yet didn't take the baby. Anyway, so that room's occupied. You can use our room," Emma says brightly, pretty much squashing my boner under her frail little hands.

Marissa gasps. "What? No! I'm not using your room for…that!"

"Why not? It was good enough for us just a little bit ago. Right, Emmy?" Orval adds behind us, grabbing a plate and throwing on a piece of chicken. "I just love the breast. So juicy and tender. Don't you agree, Rhenn?" he asks, stoic look on his face, but eyes full of mischief.

"I do, sir. Best part of the…chicken," I reply, trying to keep my smile at bay.

"Well, I don't know about that, son. Best part is the –"

"Anyway," Marissa interrupts loudly. "The food looks delicious."

"Oh, Levi makes the best fried chicken, dear. You are all in for a treat," Emma adds, throwing a little more food on her plate and heading off to one of the picnic tables under the shade of a tree.

We're at Brian and Cindy's house, and Marissa just met the rest of the Summer family for the first time. Of course, with six girls, all married, and with kids or kids on the way, it's a packed affair. Everyone is here, laughing and enjoying themselves. Hell, I even saw ol' Samuel crack a few smiles over the course of the afternoon.

I join my lovely girlfriend at the table, across from Meghan and Nick and right beside Harper. My girlfriend. I didn't think I'd ever use that term again, but do you know what? I'm more proud of my new title as boyfriend than I am of any of my other accomplishments to date.

"I have exciting news," Harper says to her sister.

"Do tell," she says, taking a bite of her chicken leg. I wouldn't mind taking a little bite out of her...leg...

"Remember the rumor I told you about Mrs. Morton? Well, I called my realtor, and she confirmed she's definitely selling! We're putting in an offer," she exclaims, bright smile on her face.

"Oh my gosh, Harper, that's amazing! I can't wait to see what you could do with that additional space," Marissa says, reaching out and squeezing her sister's hand.

"Well, I don't have it yet. I already called the bank and we've discussed how aggressive I can be with my bid."

"You'll get it. I know it," Marissa adds.

"I hope so. I already have two local vendors interested in selling product in the store," Harper says, before turning and telling Meghan all about her lingerie shop. Meghan immediately calls all of her sisters over to hear about it, the group vowing to make a trip to Rockland Falls soon for a little shopping.

After dinner, we all hang around the yard, playing games and visiting. A few of the guys are throwing bean bags, while I'm over with Nick, watching Sawyer play catch with Marissa's nephew, Max.

"How long you in town?" Nick asks, taking a drink from his beer.

"We're staying through tomorrow afternoon, and then heading back. Free has to be out of there by eight," I tell him.

Nick glances around before meeting my eyes. "What did you decide about the dojo?"

I smile when I think back to my earlier meeting. "I'm going to take a step away this year. Tyler is going to step up and teach my usual classes, and will help with the self-defense classes too." Nick teaches two classes at my place, and with Tyler's help, will continue to do so until his baby is born.

"It's pretty cool that one of your very first students is taking over in your absence," Nick adds.

"No one I trust more than him. Well, besides you. Plus, he's staying local, so if I decide to move to North Carolina, he wants first right of refusal to purchase the business."

Nick just smiles. "Look at you. All grown-up and shit."

I snort. "Who would have thought?"

"Can we catch breakfast? I know you're having lunch with the cousins again."

"Sounds good. You cooking?"

"Hell no. You want it edible, don't you?" Nick retorts, resulting in a hard laugh from me.

"No shit. Do you make your pregnant wife cook all the meals?" I tease, following Nick's line of sight and landing on is wife.

"I cook on Tuesday nights."

"Isn't that your late night?"

He laughs. "Yep. I order the food while she's getting her station ready for the next day. That's all the cooking she'll let me do anymore."

"Can't say I blame her. I've tried to eat whatever charred shit you pull off the grill."

"Asshole," he grumbles, finishing off his beer. "Do you want to meet at the diner?"

I glance at Marissa, whose eyes land on mine at the same time. Offering her a knowing, ornery smirk, I answer, "Come by my place. We'll make breakfast."

"You?"

"I can cook like Emeril."

"Who?"

"Never mind," I say, throwing my own drink in the garbage and heading toward my girl. As soon as she spots my movements, she excuses herself from her group and makes her way to me. We meet in the middle, her arms snaking around my neck as mine rest on her lower back. "Hi."

"Hello," she whispers just as my lips find hers. It doesn't take much to coax those plump lips open to slide my tongue inside. I'll never tire of the taste of her. "What was that for?" she asks when I finally pull away.

"Just letting everyone know who you belong to."

Her eyebrows pull together. "At a family function, where the only single men are my brothers?" she asks, rolling her eyes at my possessiveness.

"Fine, I just like kissing you. It had been too long. I was starting to forget what it felt like."

Again, she rolls her eyes. "Really? It has been a whole thirty minutes."

"Too long," I insist, wrapping my arm around her shoulder and pulling her into my side. Together, we turn and watch her family. "By the way, I'm sorry I broke my promise."

She looks at me with shock and concern. "What promise?"

"The one I made back in your cottage when we originally set the deal. The one where I don't fall in love with you."

Marissa smirks. "You did break that promise."

"I'm not sorry in the least. In fact, it was the best broken promise ever," I confess, sliding my lips across hers gently. "Oh, we're having Meghan and Nick over for breakfast in the morning."

"Sounds good. What are you making?"

"Coffee?"

She laughs. "Fine, what am I making?"

Waggling my eyebrows, I give her a wide smile. "Pancakes."

Marissa gazes up at me, a similar smile on her gorgeous face. "Pancakes."

The End

Meet me in Rockland Falls! Harper meets her match in Love and Lingerie, coming Spring 2019!

Acknowledgments

This book wouldn't be what it is without the amazing team I have in my corner!

Sara Eirew – For your wicked talent behind the lens.

Melissa Gill – For bringing to life this stunning cover.

Nazarea, Kelly, and the InkSlinger PR team – Thank you for your tireless promotion and work on each new reveal and release.

Cristina and Lucas – For bringing Rhenn and Marissa to life on this cover.

Kara Hildebrand – For taking my words and making them flow, and for falling in love with each hero before the word gets a chance.

Sandra Shipman – For being by my side with each new release and making sure each book is as good as it can be before it release.

Jo Thompson – For everything. Just everything. For brainstorming and not making fun of me too much when you find those silly spelling errors. I'm glad I'm usually good for a few laughs.

Kaitie Reister – Thank you for reading it early and helping find those pesky little errors.

Danielle Palumbo – For chatting with me about fire damage and cleanup. Your information was so very valuable.

Karen Hrdlicka – I'm short about one hundred words now, thanks to removing unnecessary that's, but it's better because of you! Thank you!

Brenda Wright of Formatting Done Wright – As always, the BEST formatter ever. Thank you!

Holly Collins – For always cheering me on and getting just as excited with each new release as I am!

Lacey's Ladies – Thank you for loving my books, my characters, and keeping me sane in this crazy business.

My husband and two kids – I love you. So much.

Every single blogger who helped with the cover reveal or shared the release – THANK YOU!

And last but not least, the readers - THANK YOU for purchasing this book! Thank you for putting your trust in me as we dive into another series.

About the Author

Lacey Black is a Midwestern girl with a passion for reading, writing, and shopping. She carries her e-reader with her everywhere she goes so she never misses an opportunity to read a few pages. Always looking for a happily ever after, Lacey is passionate about contemporary romance novels and enjoys it further when you mix in a little suspense. She resides in a small town in Illinois with her husband, two children, and a chocolate lab. Lacey loves watching NASCAR races, shooting guns, and should only consume one mixed drink because she's a lightweight.

Email: laceyblackwrites@gmail.com
https://www.facebook.com/authorlaceyblack
https://twitter.com/AuthLaceyBlack
https://laceyblack.wordpress.com